MONKEY TALES

and other
SHORT STORIES

MAHMOUD HIRJI

◆ FriesenPress

One Printers Way
Altona, MB R0G 0B0
Canada

www.friesenpress.com

ISBN
978-1-03-912964-1 (Hardcover)
978-1-03-912963-4 (Paperback)
978-1-03-912965-8 (eBook)

1. FICTION, SHORT STORIES (SINGLE AUTHOR)

Distributed to the trade by The Ingram Book Company

Table of Contents

―――

Author's Note:

Dear Reader,

Thank you! "Shukria!" "Merci!" "¡Muchas gracias!" "Asante!" for making the decision to read my book among all the other fine books out there!

Having travelled the world, lived and worked in many countries, I have finally put pen to paper to share my experiences in a collection of fourteen short stories for your reading pleasure.

I am sure that on many levels your own experiences will relate to my own encounters and anecdotes from locals and other world travellers— spiced up by our vivid imaginations and "Murchi Masala", mixing fact with fiction and hopefully, inspire you to share your own stories!

I have tried to be funny, mysterious, surprising, thrilling and, most of all, entertaining. I hope to keep you guessing as you read along, with a twist-in-the-tale occurring somewhere in the story!

Some of my stories hark back to my childhood memories of a distant past set in 1960's colonial and post-independence Africa and of the 1970's East African Asian immigration to Canada—capturing attitudes, biases and behaviours of the time. I have altered names and events wherever and whenever I could, to respect the privacy of others.

In my first story, "When the Sun comes Up," inspired by my favorite author Jeffrey Archer, I have challenged myself to write a story that is exactly two hundred words in length.

In my title story, "Monkey Tales," you will read about the daily conflicts between man and animal, among peoples and races, about greed and corruption, and sadly, about the way our world turns.

In "Quod Erat Demonstrandum" (also inspired by the writing style of Archer), I have provided three different story endings, leaving you to choose your preferred ending.

In "Churro," I have attempted to shock and entertain the reader at the same time, sprinkling it with macabre humour in the style of another great author, Stephen King.

And finally, in "La Colorada," my most ambitious and complex short story—a novella, really—I have written about a family's sad, poignant history, switching back and forth across almost two centuries, with threads of love, romance, terror, the supernatural, and the omnipresent greed and savagery of mankind running through it.

I truly hope you will enjoy reading my book as much as I have enjoyed writing it.

So, sit back, relax and have a joyous reading experience!

WHEN THE SUN COMES UP

———

This is an anecdote passed down between generations
of Masai herdsmen of northern Tanzania.

"The rising African sun ascends over the Ngorongoro Crater, slowly bathing the savannah and its microcosm of life in golden light. The gazelle wakes, instantly alert, looking over her calves, making sure they are safe.

Her fears allayed, she licks the early morning dew off the long grass stalks hiding them, ears pricked upward for warning sounds of a monkey's cry, a startled bird's flapping wings, of snapping twigs, the stealthy rustle of parting grass –signalling an approaching predator.

Each morning, when the sun comes up and the gazelle wakes, she knows they must outrun the fastest lion or be eaten…

Each morning, when the sun comes up, the lion also wakes. He too gazes at his sleeping lioness and cubs, thin and emaciated, their ribs and bones protruding against their skins.

He stealthily raises his head above the long veldt, eyes squinting to catch any imperceptible movement, ears pricked to catch any tell-tale sounds…

The lion also knows that today he must outrun the slowest gazelle or they must all starve to death.

In the end, it doesn't matter if you are a lion or a gazelle. What matters is, when the sun comes up, you better be running!"

MONKEY TALES

Michel Fleury winced at the ice-cold blast in his face as he strode purposefully into the site office trailer complex at the Nyani mine site. Although this was in welcome contrast to the insufferable hot humidity pervading the Central African country he now found himself in, Michel raged internally at the needless waste of energy and money that his employer Lyons Construction Ltee of France was having to foot the bill for.

Michel was a six-foot tall, powerful, good-looking man in his late thirties with a firm square jaw, chiselled features, and piercing blue eyes. But despite Michel's physical attributes, or perhaps because of it, he harboured an insufferable air of arrogance, especially towards non-French people and cultures. He was also a focused and impatient man who did not suffer fools on his projects. He had a reputation for getting projects executed in an efficient and professional manner, on time, and almost always on budget. After all, he came from a family of successful construction professionals and had grown up in a hard-working and disciplined home.

Michel stepped back from the icy blast in his face, pausing to reflect on his day ahead and on how and why he had arrived in Central Africa from his native France. Barely three months ago he had been summoned to head office in Lyons from the district office in Grenoble. At which time, Michel had met with his managing director who commended him on his excellent performance and loyalty to the company. The MD had matter-of-factly informed Michel of his promotion effective immediately and that he was being reassigned to Lyons' copper mining project in the Democratic Republic of Nyani, commonly referred to as Nyani. The project director at the Lyons site had been fired and Michel was to step in as his replacement, which was quite an accomplishment for a man of his age and years of experience.

Michel learned that the company was inexplicably losing money on their project to construct Phase 2 of the Chokozi Ore Leach plant located at a major mine site in Nyani. Michel was tasked to identify and neutralize the problem and to get the project profitable again— at any cost.

In short order, Lyons' team procured Michel a passport, overseas work permit, internal legal signing authority, and other required paperwork. Michel was also provided a short video presentation on Nyani. To be more precise, it was an update, since Michel had spent a few years of his childhood growing up in Nyani where his father had been a construction manager for Lyons.

He learned that the population was evenly divided between ten million Nyanans and an estimated ten million simians—or monkeys—of every type and breed! Formally a banana republic prior to French colonization, as an independent republic, it now also produced and exported cocoa, exotic nuts, animal skins, lumber, metals, and minerals. The latter two were now the main source of the country's wealth.

Nyani was governed by an elected president residing in the capital Nyani City. In addition, there was a small but influential team of regional commissioners governing each of the eight regions of the country. Chokozi, being the principal mining region, was by far the wealthiest. The local currency, the Hela, was no longer in wide circulation. The real currency of banking and commerce was the US dollar, which was pegged to a fixed exchange rate.

There were about a thousand foreign nationals, including expatriate staff and their families presently residing in Chokozi. There was a Lycée École and an American International School as well as several private clubs for the expats and their families. Being single, however, Michel had no use for any of these facilities. He well knew that he was not going there to live a proverbial colonial lifestyle, that is, sipping G&Ts and cracking the whip while watching the workers work! He was going there on a very specific mission, and failure was not an option!

Within a week of his promotion, Michel Fleury arrived at the local airport in Chokozi and was driven to his gated residence, located in the hills on the outskirts of town. They drove through broad, concrete boulevards flanked on both sides by bright purple and red flowering acacia trees, paid for with the proceeds of rich mining royalties, in stark contrast to the narrow dirt roads of his childhood which he dimly recalled.

The streets were crowded with brightly dressed locals milling about and chatting in *Shairi*, their sing-song language. Above them, the trees were teeming with monkeys playfully swinging through the branches, sometimes venturing down to steal a fruit or vegetable or brightly coloured object from the street hawkers' stalls or sweets from a small child.

There appeared to be monkeys of every sort and variety: small-faced childlike dash monkeys, cheeky grinning chimpanzees, brightly coloured male rhesus monkeys with distinctive blue faces and bright-red erect penises set above electric-blue scrotums. Michel also recognized colobus monkeys, wise-looking with knitted brows, long sideburns, and hairy faces.

They were soon driving up into the hills through a forested area when suddenly they were forced to stop. A troop of baboons were strung out across the road in a coordinated effort to form a roadblock.

The baboons reluctantly and sullenly moved aside as the loudly honking car pushed by them, and for a few moments Michel came face to face with a baboon peering through his side window. It was a large, king baboon with a long, ugly, vertical scar running along the right side of its face. It bared its curved, yellow fangs at Michel, dripping strings of spittle onto the window, while raising its nose up, sniffing loudly, and glaring at Michel with bloodshot pondering eyes that continued to follow him until the car was out of sight.

The driver apologized to Michel for the baboons, in particular the one with the scar. It was the troop leader and had a reputation for frightening people. He went on to say that recently some missing livestock had been attributed to this particular troop of baboons, although there was no proof. The driver, however, decided to omit mention of an episode from a few years ago when it was suspected that the scar-faced baboon might also have been responsible for two missing village children. Their crushed bones were found in an abandoned monkey den months later. But again, there was no proof it was Scarface and his troop of baboons. What is more, it was rumoured that for some strange reason, Scarface had the protection of the Police Commissioner, and that is why nobody dared to kill it.

Still a little disconcerted by the baboons, Michel soon arrived at the safety and security of the gated compound, which was surrounded by an electrified perimeter fence. As they drove through the guardhouse, the duty guard welcomed Michel with a big smile and smart salute. Michel soon forgot the baboon episode, despite a fleetingly familiar and nagging uneasiness he had felt upon encountering the king baboon.

Michel got to work immediately and within a relatively short time had fired a dozen staff members, both expats and locals. In order to stop the bleeding from his company's coffers, Michel was steadfast in his drive to eliminate laziness, inefficiency, waste, couldn't-care-less attitudes, and corruption.

Michel's first target was a French expat manager's expense claim. The expenses were actually incurred for personal family travel to the game parks. In addition, they included his almost daily "lunch" expenses with his local mistress accrued over the preceding six months. Since the expenses had already been paid out, Michel instructed the site accountant to deduct the costs with interest from the manager's paycheques and to close his expense-account privileges. The outraged manager was warned of public exposure and job loss if he should ever attempt anything like this again. It didn't matter to Michel that the manager was related to the MD back in Lyons—his job had to be carried out systematically and impartially.

Michel's second target was dealing with the numerous complaints of food poisoning from the 800-strong local workforce. His investigation revealed substandard food, improper food storage, and unhygienic food handling practices by the camp caterer. In the process, he uncovered kick-backs were being paid to the culprits, who he promptly fired. Michel estimated company losses would eventually have amounted to three million dollars for the expected six million meals expected to be served over the five-year project term, had he not intervened. Not to mention the lost days of work and lower productivity due to sickness - and their associated costs to Lyons.

He had discovered to his disgust, that monkey meat, ground-up monkey entrails, fur, bone, and tail ligaments, were being mixed into the daily special: goat stew. The monkey population in Chokozi had exploded in recent years and a government-sanctioned monkey cull had been in force, so this was a convenient and profitable way to dispose of monkey carcasses.

Third on his hit list was the local superintendent and two of his cronies in charge of the dump truck fleet. Michel summarily fired them for their scamming, which was to exact tolls from the trucking subcontractor for every truckload of excavated soil leaving the site. This would eventually have amounted to a half a million dollars in kickbacks at Lyons' eventual expense.

Next, he set his sights on the expat contracts manager and his local assistant who he fired for their corrupt practices. They had suppressed the low bidder's price offer to supply ready-mix concrete. Instead, the contract had been awarded to the "preferred" bidder whose eventual overcharges would have amounted to two million in additional cost to Lyons.

Michel was now navigating the difficult process of switching concrete suppliers to mitigate the issue, while being mindful of death threats to himself and threats of legal action against the company made by the terminated ready-mix concrete supplier.

Michel also terminated several large mining equipment supply contracts made with vendors from China and Romania at a premium cost of several millions of dollars. The contracts were brokered by his predecessor through the Police Commissioner's offices. It was rumoured that the Regional Commissioner was ultimately involved. This scam had been a particularly tough one to crack and the political repercussions were yet to be felt. Michel was the hitman with a job to do, and this was not his problem. Let the MD handle any political fallout, he decided.

Michel shook himself loose of his thoughts, stepping into the office corridor. Shivering in the blast of super cooled air, he spotted a short, wiry man and barked at him, "You! What do you do here?"

The man smiled obsequiously at Michel replying, "I am the new office manager, John Fungo, at *yo seywiss sah!*"

Michel had fired the previous office manager for diverting their office supplies to another company in town, but he had not yet met his replacement. Here he was. Fungo stood a good five foot nothing tall, had deep-set eyes, a small, upturned nose, and large perfect teeth. He walked with a springy gait, his longish arms dangling at his sides.

"Why is the air-conditioning turned on at full blast?" Michel demanded. Before the poor man could reply, Michel yelled, "And why haven't we provided passcodes for the photocopier to make people accountable for the amount of paper being needlessly printed?"

Fungo bowed his head and replied, "As to *yo fast question sah*, the National Mining Directorate staff who share our offices have requested we turn up the air-conditioning. As to *yo* second question, Mr. Fleury, we are still awaiting the service technician to come and program the passcodes. They have cited the delay to injury and sickness due to an unfortunate monkey bite and resulting infection suffered by one of their two technicians."

"*Sacrament!*" exploded Michel, "nothing but delays and excuses every day in this damn country! And you people think my company has unlimited money to pay for your each and every need! Turn the

A/C back down immediately, do you hear me?" he screamed as he angrily stalked off to his office.

An hour later, Michel's shirt collar felt damp and his armpits sweat stained. He unbuttoned another shirt button with clammy hands. The humidity was now intolerable and he felt a little sluggish in the oppressive heat. Finally, not able to stand it any longer, he jumped out of his chair, striding towards the cafeteria terrace. The terrace was surrounded by a grove of acacia trees, which provided a nice cooling breeze wafting through.

Entering the cafeteria, Michel spotted Fungo seated among his colleagues drinking coffee and laughing with them. Michel suddenly lost his cool, turned to the unfortunate man and yelled at him, "You stupid man. Why have you shut the air off completely? Don't you know how hot and humid it gets in this freaking monkey's country? You're all a bunch of monkeys, you especially! "

Michel's outburst was met with shocked gasps and consternation throughout the cafeteria. Everybody including a few European and Pakistani expats put their cups down and stared at him in horror and disgust. Michel abruptly strode outside to cool off on the terrace, after which he closeted himself in his office for the rest of the day. He was relieved that the "monkey" had turned the air-conditioning back on, at half strength this time.

Later, on his drive home, Michel rolled the windows down to catch a breeze, halting at the stop sign at the turn-off to his estate. He spotted a group of baboons grunting loudly and pointing at him from just inside the treeline on the side of the road. Michel sensed a strong malevolence in the air. Turning he saw Scarface the king baboon at his open window, sniffing and glaring evilly at him. Spooked, Michel quickly rolled up his window and sped off, not relaxing until he drove through the guarded and secured compound.

The next morning, Michel drove out the gate to bright glaring sunlight and to what promised to be yet another hot and humid day. He sped down the hill but something didn't seem quite right, although he wasn't able to put his finger on it. He shrugged it off and concentrated on the tough day ahead of him. For Michel had planned on another round of firings after uncovering another money draining scam. This time it involved the accounting department, including one of Lyon's French expats—yet another scam to grapple with.

Striding purposefully to his office, the air-conditioning felt just right and Michel had a twinge of remorse at his rough handling of Fungo the day before. He came to a full stop at his office door, balking at the two policemen waiting for him. Seated in Michel's chair was their commanding officer, wearing a stern look on his face.

He wore a crisp white uniform adorned with medals, topped off with a smart peaked cap on his greying head, all of which accentuated his authoritative bearing. The other two policemen standing by the doorway were large and beefy and had their truncheons drawn.

"Good morning, I am Police Commissioner Askari," he announced in perfect French. "Mr. Fleury, I will get to the point. I do not take kindly to foreign guests of my country speaking in an insulting and abusive manner to my people - or to my family for that matter. Did you or did you not publicly scream racist and offensive insults at my nephew, Mr. Fungo, yesterday?"

Michel's guilty expression confirmed the commissioner's query.

"Specifically, did you not liken my nephew and countrymen to monkeys?"

This time, Michel nodded slightly in shame. With a swift movement, the commissioner stood up, raised his metal-tipped hardwood cane, and whipped it down onto the glass-topped desk—cracking the glass with a loud gunshot sound. He continued to sweep all the papers, files, stationery, and photos off the desk, sending them crashing onto the floor. He walked around the desk nodding at his men who roughly grabbed Michel's arms and frog-marched him to the far wall.

The commissioner went on. "Behind the picture of our illustrious President Paka Jimmy that you so hypocritically display on your wall is your company's safe. No doubt, inside we will find important company documents, your passport, and undeclared cash. Money which you on behalf of your company intend to steal from our country! Open the safe now!" he barked, "Take out your passport and seven hundred dollars in cash—just enough to buy you an economy one-way ticket back to Paris."

He produced a sheaf of documents, which he thrust at Michel. "This is your deportation order issued for non-desirables in our country and it is signed by our High Court magistrate. He also happens to be my golfing partner," he murmured, allowing himself a little smile.

"You have six hours to leave Nyani. If you do not leave, you will be arrested and thrown into Kifaru prison. Kifaru is populated with the worst kind of criminal scum, and I promise you, once inside, you will never manage to walk out of there alive! It is now just past 9:00 a.m. and luckily for you there is a 2:00 p.m. flight departing for Paris."

Michel duly opened the safe, took his passport, and counted out seven hundred in cash. He glanced wistfully at the tens of thousands of dollars of Lyons' money left behind. He had no doubt the commissioner would find good use for it. He also wondered if he would still have a job when he got back home.

He left the policemen to the small fortune inside the safe, striding swiftly toward the exit, passing Fungo on his way out. The man's head was bowed and he had a crestfallen look on his face. *Not a bad sort after all*, thought Michel.

Michel called his shocked second-in-command, Remy, as he drove home to pack, instructing him to purchase a business class ticket for him and to meet him at the airport in a couple of hours. The cellphone tower in the hills servicing his subdivision had been down for a couple of days now, and he wondered if it was back up and working again. Rumour was that the antennae atop the tower had been mangled and ripped out by vandals.

Michel slowly drove across the beautifully landscaped boulevard for the last time. He took in the playful monkeys gamboling and the colourfully dressed locals going about their daily work and play. He felt a pang of sadness and regret about the corruption cleanup he had yet to achieve but would not do so now. He had been very successful to date in making his company profitable again and which would no doubt have boosted his career path had he stayed on. Now it was all up in the air.

Michel raced up the hill to his subdivision along the eerily quiet road and suddenly realized what it was that had bothered him on the way down less than an hour ago—it was the unnatural stillness and quietness. *Where were the tweeting birds, the chattering monkeys, and the loudly grunting baboon troop?* he wondered. He shrugged it off, deciding they were all probably on strike and smiled. It was not his problem anymore. His mind raced ahead to what he needed to pack away with him and what to leave behind. He'd give away any unwanted and unpackable clothes to the guards and his kitchenware, bedding, and linens to his maid.

He would allow himself no more than an hour to pack his things before leaving for the airport. Michel knew he must catch the 2:00 p.m. flight out of the country. The last thing he wanted was to end up in the infamous Kifaru prison, whose bloody and barbaric reputation he had heard of. *Perhaps I should ask Remy to bring their lawyer along in case the Police Commissioner tries anything funny at the airport,* he wondered. *Yes, I must call Remy from my landline phone.*

He turned into his subdivision entrance to find the electric gate open and the guardhouse unmanned. As Michel drove in, perplexed, he smelled burning plastic. Glancing up at the fence, he saw the burned out and still smoking transformer and blackened wires. *Yet more problems with this damn country,* he mused and was glad in a way that he was leaving. It was eerily quiet. There were no sounds other than the soft purr of his car and the crunching of gravel beneath his tires.

There were no children or nannies in the playground, nor any exercise classes going on for the mothers in the pavilion across the way. He had once spent a couple of days working from home and had found the subdivision to be a hive of activity. As he turned the corner to his townhouse, he caught a glimpse out of the corner of his eye at what appeared to be a pair of bare feet sticking out from beneath the bright purple acacia hedge grove. This type of thing didn't surprise him anymore, and he reminded himself again, *Whatever went on in this godforsaken country is no longer my problem... probably just the gardener asleep on the job.*

Michel parked in the shared driveway behind the car of his neighbour, Mr. Bartholomew, a retired local mining engineer. He had proudly recounted to Michel in perfect French of how as a young man he had obtained his advanced mining degree in Quebec, Canada. Following which he had obtained his professional engineering certification working in the hazardous asbestos mines of Northern Quebec.

Michel knocked on Mr. Bartholomew's door as a courtesy to let him know he was temporarily blocking him and also to say goodbye, but there was no answer. He knocked a little louder. Michel thought he glimpsed a shadowy figure through the gauze curtains quickly dart across the room, but the door remained unanswered.

Very strange. A little tense now, the hairs on the nape of his neck beginning to rise, he took the exterior stairs two at a time to his unit above.

Michel stopped in shock at the top landing. There appeared to be what looked like a pool of blood dripping off the landing into the bushes below. He stepped gingerly around the bloody, sticky pool and looked down. And there in the bushes quite unmistakeably, was a human arm! It had been ripped right off its socket, displaying torn ligaments and a bloody stump. He noticed the engineer's iron ring on the right hand. *It must be Mr. Bartholomew's arm*, he realized with mounting horror.

What the hell was going on? Should he run back downstairs to the safety of his car and hightail it to the airport? After all, he had his passport and the seven hundred in cash, plus another hundred dollars or so in his wallet. That's all he would need to get out of the country…

To hell with his new custom-made suits, his semi-important paperwork, his personal laptop and iPad, about five hundred dollars in emergency money, and other personal effects. Plus the .45 Colt revolver issued to him by company security, which was safely locked up in his bedside table. He could always have Remy pack and ship his personal effects to him later.

But then there was that fast-moving shadow behind Mr. Bartholomew's curtains, which might come after him if he went downstairs again. Better to dash into his unit and call for help from his house phone, he decided. How ironic, he thought, that he wanted to call the police to rescue him when they were the ones throwing him out of the country! He chuckled aloud as much in irony as in fear. He swiftly let himself into his unit and double-bolted the door behind him.

Michel dashed to the phone on the wall next to the kitchen only to find the cord had been ripped off the wall! Michel froze. From where he stood, he could see into the kitchen and the back window. To his mounting horror, the window was shattered, shards of jagged glass ringing the window frame.

Suddenly, a small furry object shot out of the kitchen, headed directly at Michel. It jumped onto a chair, somersaulted onto the table, and leaped onto his shoulder. Michel felt a mind-numbing pain as the furry object bit off the top part of his right ear, prompting him to let out a blood-curdling scream. The object quickly retreated leaping onto the nearest windowsill and sat there hunched over, happily munching on a piece of Michel's severed ear.

Michel immediately ripped off his white shirt and balled it against his bloody and throbbing ear stump to stem the bleeding. The object appeared to be a small brown monkey, the playful mischievous kind you see everywhere, which people think of as kind of cute—much like the proverbial organ grinder's monkey. Except without a tasseled fez, red vest, and steel chain shackled to its leg. Michel hurriedly scanned the room, searching for a weapon to fight it off with and kill the bastard, should it attack again. A large knife or heavy blunt instrument would be perfect, if only he could find one.

Michel slowly backed up to the credenza still pressing his balled-up shirt against his bleeding ear, his eyes fixed on the monkey who ignored him, immersed in eating his fresh tidbit. With left hand searching behind his back, Michel found a heavy cut-glass vase just as the monkey decided to renew its attack! Michel's timing was perfect as he swung at the flying monkey, hitting it squarely in the chest, but not before it attacked his left hand and arm with its filthy finger nails, leaving blood-streaked scratches.

Thank God for the tetanus shot amongst other shots I had to get before coming to Nyani, thought Michel.

The felled monkey dropped to the floor. Michel kicked it with his steel-toed work boot, sending the monkey flying into the glass cabinet, which shattered, cutting the monkey in a dozen places. Michel was swiftly upon it. In a frenzy, he continued his massacre, stomping on the animal with his size 13 steel-toed work boots.

The monkey eventually stopped struggling. But it still had life in it, whimpering as Michel gingerly hauled it up by its tail, hurling the mass of blood and fur into the kitchen sink. With a pair of wooden salad spoons, he stuffed the still struggling and shrieking creature into the drain hole and turned on the garburator. He didn't flip the off switch until the metallic grinding and crunching sounds ground to a halt. The steel blades of the garburator were now firmly embedded in the animal's skeleton, having mangled the monkey into a slurry of blood, guts, and crushed bone.

Michel knew he had to act fast now. He had lost a lot of blood, which was soaking his entire right side. Grabbing the flint gas lighter, he balled and clamped a kitchen towel between his teeth to bite on and kneeled on the floor in front of the reflecting glass panel of the microwave oven. He slowly and methodically cauterized the top of his ear with the lighter's flame. The pain was indescribable and the smell of his burning flesh and skin overpowering, but he knew it had to be done or else he would soon pass out and die from loss of blood. Michel followed through by wiping the blood off the long scratches on his left hand and then liberally splashing whiskey onto it, wincing at the stinging sensation.

Finally, with a mixture of shock and triumph, Michel staggered back into the living room, his ear still smouldering. Collapsing into his favourite armchair, Michel took a swig of whiskey out of the bottle, savouring his victory. Then he heard something! Michel sat up in alarm at the sound of his bed creaking behind the shut bedroom door, as if somebody heavy were just getting up. This was followed by a loud belch and a long, disgusting staccato fart.

The bedroom door flew open and Michel rose to his feet in terror coming face to face with Scarface the king baboon! Instead of attacking, Scarface knelt down on the floor, emitting a high-pitched shriek of fear, his eyes pleading for mercy with arms raised in supplication. Scarface's posture and demeanour, added to the smell of his own smouldering flesh still in his nostrils, suddenly made it all come flooding back to Michel…

The sun was setting fast as it always does in the tropics, and Michel's face burned with the scorching heat from the ring of flames in the forest clearing. Michel was about six years old; his father had picked him up after work, telling his mother that there was a treat in store for Michel. His father's men had somehow corralled a troop of baboons into the forest clearing and then set off the fire ringing it, leaving just one small opening as an escape route. As the baboons frantically squeezed through the flaming gap one at a time, Michel's father and his men smashed in their skulls with sledgehammers and axes, laughing savagely at their massacre. Little Michel was terrified and didn't want to look, but his father made him, telling him he had to be a man!

A mother baboon clutching her cub leaped through the flaming gap and the men were immediately upon her, cudgelling her to death. The terrified baboon cub was yanked up by its tail and held upside down while Michel's father doused it in gasoline from a jerrycan, setting it alight! The men laughed with glee as the cub pirouetted upside down in the air, shrieking pitifully. Amid its high-pitched squeals as it burned, the father baboon with another cub on his back leaped through the flames. The cub lost its grip and fell to the ground. Raised sledgehammers were poised to pound the cub to a pulp, but the father was too quick and fell protectively upon his cub while they clubbed and beat him to death. The little cub blindly darted out in between the men's legs towards Michel. It reached the child, fell to its knees shrieking in terror, beseeching the little boy with its eyes and raised arms to please save it.

Now, each man has his own particular scent, which baboons are able to distinguish, much like a unique fingerprint. The baboon cub smelled a similar smell to the man cub, except much stronger and coming fast from behind. The cub heard the swish of the machete slicing the air, wielded by Michel's father, on its wicked trajectory to decapitate it. But the resourceful cub twisted out from under the machete, the tip striking the side of his face just a centimetre off the right eye, cutting through skin, flesh, and bone down the length of his tiny face.

Somehow, the cub managed to twist away again and escape the massacre into the growing darkness. He took away with him that night the smells of the man-cub and the man who butchered his family which he vowed never to forget … until now. Meanwhile, little Michel had urinated himself in fear and terror while he was forced to watch the massacre continue until every baboon was brutally killed.

Now once again, more than thirty years later, Michel felt a gush of hot urine escape down his legs. Scarface stood up slowly, grinning evilly, no longer feigning fear. He approached Michel slowly with long arms loosely hanging at his sides, his grotesque torso and despicably savage face smeared with caked blood. His yellow fangs were bloodied, thin strips of pink flesh and black skin dangling in between his teeth.

With desperation lending him superhuman speed and strength, Michel ducked behind the large heavy armchair, picking it up and hurling it in one swift motion at the charging baboon. Michel sprinted to the front door, turned the latch, pulled the door open a crack, springing onto the landing outside before yanking it shut just as the recovering baboon charged again! The baboon screamed in frustration as it tried vainly to open the latched door from the inside. Michel heard it scampering away and the tinkle of broken glass as it leaped out the shattered kitchen window. With shaking hands, Michel quickly got his key out, unlocked the door and let himself back in, slamming it shut and dashing into his bedroom.

As Michel ran around the bed to the dresser, he saw a thick pile of stinking baboon shit smeared across his bedspread. Gagging he managed to unlock the dresser drawer, fumbling inside for his revolver. Thankfully, it was loaded and he whipped around with renewed courage and determination to shoot the monster. He ran into the living room, but Scarface had not yet reappeared through the kitchen window. Michel waited on trembling legs until they gave out from under him, dropping him to his knees in numbing pain, shock, and exhaustion

The minutes ticked away until it dawned on Michel that the cunning baboon was waiting him out—a classic hunter's gambit— allow the injured prey to weaken with loss of blood and exhaustion before coming back in to finish him off. Either that or wait for Michel to go back downstairs to his car and then finish him off, knowing that he had no way to call for help. It also dawned on Michel it must have been the baboon who had climbed up the cellphone tower to vandalize and disable it! But Scarface obviously didn't know about the gun, Michel's trump card!

Michel stepped back into the kitchen, gingerly looking out through the broken window. He could see nothing unusual happening around his parked car. He wondered for a moment if the baboon had given up and run away, but he knew that was just wishful thinking. Scarface was full of hate and revenge and was lying in wait somewhere; he was sure of that. *Why he might even be on the landing outside his front door, waiting in ambush!* Michel opened the fridge door, taking out a can of local lager, swigging on it to cool down while he thought of his next move.

Michel devised a plan in no time, being the resourceful man of action that he was! Stuffing the gun in his waistband behind his back, he draped a triple-folded towel over the glass shards on the window sill. Michel then pulled on a pair of oven mitts, and gripping the top of the jagged window frame, with one smooth athletic motion, vaulted out the window—baboon-style—onto the thick springy grass below.

Michel picked himself up and dashed towards his car as fast as he possibly could… twenty seconds… ten seconds… and then skidded to a halt. The car's rear window had been smashed in "Oh no not again!" he gasped.

Then suddenly, two baboons sprang out of his car, two or three more jumped down from the trees, and more appeared from the surrounding bushes. Another baboon, a huge bastard, this one, flung open Mr. Bartholomew's front door and slowly approached. Bingo; the large shadow he had seen behind the gauze curtains in what now seemed ages ago.

The baboons quickly formed a ring around Michel, some ten of them in all, grunting loudly, dancing, and clapping their hands above their heads. Michel pulled out his gun, snarling and waving it at them, knowing that he only had six bullets. B*ut did they know?* he wondered.

They were waiting for something, it seemed. Then Scarface the king baboon sauntered down the stairs from Michel's landing, swaggering like a big boss, as though he lived there himself. *What a cheeky bastard,* thought Michel!

Michel pointed and fired at Scarface, but the huge baboon, Mr. Bartholomew's killer, jumped in front of Scarface, taking the bullet for him! It all went fast from there. Several baboons in the circle charged at Michel from different directions. Michel spun around firing around the circle until dull clicks of the empty chambers told him it was over. Three more baboons lay on the ground, either dead or dying.

Before Michel could react, Scarface was upon him, his long arms encircling Michel in a crushing hug. Michel felt the air escape his crushed lungs as his ribs snapped one by one against the baboon's barrel chest.

The last two things Michel remembered were the sickening thud of his father's machete striking the little baboon's face and the stench of Scarface's vile breath laced with human flesh, blood and rancid bacteria.

Scarface's curved yellow fangs punctured Michel's neck, sinking into his jugular as Michel mercifully blacked out.

THE THREE JONESES

The village of Cwm-bran was a sleepy little hamlet in Monmouthshire, Wales, before later amalgamating with surrounding villages into the township of Cwmbran in the early 1950s. The villagers numbering just a few hundred good souls knew each other well and looked after one another like extended family. In fact, many of the residents were indeed related to one another, with the quintessential Welsh name "Jones" being the most common denominator.

Cwm-bran likely had a quarter of its population named Jones. Three of the Joneses knew each other rather well, having been in the same class together through kindergarten, primary, and middle schools. In order to differentiate between people with same last names, it was common practice among the villagers to hyphenate occupations with last names. Unless they were immediate family, in those days it was considered forward and improper to address people by their Christian names.

Accordingly, Jones, the local postman was known as Postie-Jones. He was a kind, soft spoken friendly Welshman, full of concern for his fellow villagers.

Jones the Railway signalman whose only two tasks were to lower and raise the traffic barrier at the village's single level crossing six times a day, and to manually switch tracks and trains once a day, was known as Level-Jones. In stark contrast to the postman, Level-Jones was a large, brutish, hot-tempered man, feared for his quick flare-ups at anyone who displeased him.

And last but not least, there was Jones the local milkman who, not surprisingly, was called Milky-Jones. He was in fact a very sallow milky toned man, a little slow-witted and prone to clumsiness. He was known for regularly dropping and breaking milk bottles on his delivery rounds. But he was quite harmless and well-liked in the village.

One fateful day, Milky-Jones was pedalling across the bumpy level crossing in his three-wheeler milk cart. He must not have been paying proper attention to skirting around the protruding railway wood ties and iron switches within the railway ballast. This despite his tricycle cart being inherently unstable.

Milky-Jones hit a bump, wedging one of the rear wheels in the switch's splayed ironwork and overturned, spilling and breaking most of the village's daily supply of milk. This resulted in spraying shattered glass and milk onto the level crossing, into the hard-to-clean spike pockets, and into the freshly cleaned and polished open signal booth. The unfortunate Level-Jones was also sprayed with milk and broken glass.

Well, the signal man was not amused! He rushed out, puffed-up, and bellowing at the top of his lungs, picked up the shaken Milky-Jones by the throat with one massive paw and with the other began raining blows onto his head, face and neck in an uncontrollable rage!

He only ceased his pummelling upon hearing a loud tearing, cracking, sound from his victim's neck. Level-Jones released the unfortunate Milky-Jones, dropping his limp body onto the tracks, horror slowly registering onto his face. By now passers-by had gathered around, having witnessed the entire incident.

The local constabulary soon arrived on the scene and Level-Jones quietly and tearfully allowed himself to be handcuffed and led away. He was duly remanded in custody pending his trial. Over the next month, Cwm-bran and surrounding villages were abuzz with gossip of this horrific killing amid them, and of the probable consequences for the killer.

The topic dominated evening debates in Cwm-bran's only two pubs. Most folks agreed that the killer was by and large a decent person but well-known for his sudden explosive tempers. Therefore, the killing was not premeditated nor committed with intent to kill.

The death sentence which was in force in the 1950s, was at stake for Level-Jones if the verdict meted out was to be murder in the first degree.

The entire village was on tenterhooks as the court trial date came up, and the village residents resolved to each send at least one family member to witness the trial. As hard luck would have it for Postie-Jones on the afternoon of the trial, he was required to ride his bike over to the next main town to pick up an urgent medical package for the local dispensary in Cwm-bran.

Being a bachelor and having no family member to send to the trial in his stead, and should Postie-Jones now not make it to the trial at all, Gwillum, his neighbour, promised to apprise him of the verdict as soon as it was pronounced. After a hot sweaty afternoon cycling twenty miles round trip and after having delivered his package to the dispensary, Postie-Jones realized it would be too late for him to be admitted into the courtroom and resignedly went home.

Still hot and sweaty from his bicycling trip, he jumped into the tin bathtub and was relaxing in the warm, soothing bathwater when he heard a loud rapping and urgent yelling at his front door.

Knowing it must be Gwillum, his neighbour, bearing the verdict, he leaped out of the bathtub, streaked naked down the stairs, eagerly throwing open the front door to hear the news. Gwillum, a little taken aback at the naked display, looked him up and down, and announced,

"They're not hanging level, Jones."

CHURRO!

———

"Churro, churro, churro... Churro, churro, churro..." called a shrill voice, trilling the Rs, as the man approached the Khan residence veranda. He repeated the shrill calls and Mrs. Razia Khan opened her front door beckoning him over.

She glanced up beyond him at the cumulus cloud cover hiding Mt Kilimanjaro, vainly hoping to catch a glimpse of Kibo peak's snow-capped majesty. No luck today; it remained hidden. Kibo usually showed herself just twice a day at dawn and dusk, when cloud cover was absent. They lived in Moshi, Tanganyika (a British mandated territory before 1961), a gateway town of about 10,000 souls[1] located at the foot of Mt. Kilimanjaro. And on rare occasions, Kibo was also visible for short interludes during the day.

It is said that Moshi, meaning smoke in Swahili, got it's name from the smoke that used to be visible from the dormant volcanic crater of Kibo, at 19,340 ft, the highest peak in Africa.

Three-year-old Aziz peered out from behind his mother's skirts at the shadowy figure walking up to the veranda. The harsh mid-morning sun beat down on the man's dark, creased face, bathing him in light as he shuffled sideways crab-like onto the veranda. He wore a stained khaki uniform, clutching a long-handled metal ladle and stiff wire brush in one hand. He also held a tall rectangular heavily stained and rusted biscuit tin in his other hand.

The crab-like figure looked up from beneath his crumpled khaki hat and smiled ingratiatingly at Mrs. Khan, baring his yellow-brown stained teeth.

Mrs. Khan tried hard not to pinch her nostrils shut nor to gag. All she could do was hold her breath for as long as she could.

The stench of feces exuding from him was overpowering. Aziz ran back inside to escape the smell as Mrs. Khan handed the outhouse key to their weekly toilet cleaner or "churro" as he was called. The word originated from the Swahili word "chura"[2] or frog. Mrs. Khan

---

1   60-years later Moshi's 2021 population is estimated at 201,000 - a twenty-fold increase.

2   Origin of the word "churro." It was common to see wild frogs - "chura" in the Swahili language - jumping in and out of open latrines, caked in feces. And in the Indian Gujerati language, "o" and "i" endings to nouns and names differentiate between genders, hence the masculine word "churro." No wonder feces-caked frogs wore happy smiles all the time, revelling after their spa mud bath!

took great care not to touch his hand while handing him the key. She turned back inside and gasped, lungs bursting, inhaling deeply. She smiled to herself, marvelling at his punctuality.

The churro arrived at exactly 10:30 every Friday morning and left exactly at 10:55 with a tin full of feces scooped out of the Asian-style open latrine. This was basically a hole in the cement floor of the wood shack or outhouse. Mrs. Khan shuddered at the thought of her hated chore upon his departure, which was to hose down the outhouse wood footboards and then vigorously wipe down the floor, water jug, paper wire holder, pull chain, door, and latch with Dettol disinfectant.

It was exactly 10:54 when she heard a tapping on the front door and the trills, "Churro, churro, churro," except this time in a softer tone. She opened the door and Aziz ran to the back of the house again. The churro's teeth looked even browner under the shade of his wide-brimmed hat, the deep dark creases in his face looking almost fluid and alive.

The churro moved sluggishly, his stiff wide khaki shorts and shirt sleeves accentuating his skinny legs and arms. In contrast, the bulge around his middle stretching his shirt to the limit gave him a grotesque and comical appearance

Mrs. Khan gingerly took the key back from the churro, holding it by its tip, placing in return a shiny silver shilling[3] in his open palm. He snapped his fingers tightly shut over the shiny coin. She saw with mounting revulsion the dark brown fillings beneath his long, curved fingernails. Inhaling deeply, she shut the door on him, gathering her mops, cloths, and disinfectants, turning her thoughts to the visitors arriving the next day.

---

3   One hundred cents to a shilling and seven shillings to a Canadian dollar, fixed exchange rate in the 1960s. Today, it is around two thousand shillings to a Canadian dollar, a devaluation of almost three thousand per cent!

"Churro, churro, churro," he called shrilly once again, as Mrs Khan opened the door beckoning him over.

The Khan family of Moshi had been busy the last week, hosting their visitors from Tanga, a port city on the Indian Ocean, about a six-hour bus ride away. Mrs. Khan senior, Razia Khan's mother-in-law, Gulzar, her sister-in-law, husband Ahmed, and their three kids aged eleven to six were visiting for a couple of weeks.

There was an air of merriment and pandemonium in their small three-bedroom house bursting with people, nine to be exact, and one outhouse between them all! As the churro shuffled off with the outhouse key, Mrs. Khan wondered if his metal biscuit tin would suffice for three times the regular volume of sewage. She deduced he'd have to make a couple of trips at least to the public works department treatment plant, which would likely cost her an extra shilling. This was fair, after all.

Mrs. Khan turned on the kerosene burner to heat the oil in the deep cauldron, as her niece Mumtaz finished rolling the *puris,* small round savoury dough balls rolled into flat discs which would fluff up lightly when properly fried. The puris soon billowed out, hot oil spitting, delicious spicy smells wafting in the air. The potato curry was also on the stove, filling the kitchen with spicy aromas of turmeric and cumin and the freshness of freshly chopped coriander leaves.

It was already 11:45 a.m. and the churro hadn't yet returned. *He ought to have completed his second trip to the treatment plant by now,* she thought fretfully. Her husband Tariq and brother-in-law Ahmed would soon be home for lunch, and she still had to clean and disinfect the outhouse.

A few minutes past noon, the two men burst through the front door, laughing jovially. The women were just finishing up the cooking, the potato curry and sweet milky cardamom-infused chai already simmering. Razia called out to Tariq as he hugged his mother in the living room

"Tariq please go pay the churro and get rid of him. We don't want him interrupting us during lunch. Oh, and you'll need to pay him two shillings this time. He's probably sunning himself on top of the low stone wall by the outhouse, too sluggish to move as he always is after a big cleaning."

Tariq's mother shrieked, "*Arre,* woman! Why do you pay him two shillings? We only pay our churro 75 cents?" Mrs. Khan groaned inwardly but held her tongue - what was the use explaining for the umpteenth time that house cleaning rates were higher than apartment rates, and besides she was now paying for two families' waste removal!

"Do not worry, dear. I will take care of it," Tariq interjected hastily. Come on, kids, everybody; let's go find the churro!" They all trooped out laughing merrily, mother-in-law included, to find the churro and poke fun at him, leaving Razia alone to finish up in the kitchen and lay the table.

The churro was nowhere to be seen. He was not at the stone wall as predicted, nor was he in the outhouse. The door was propped open by the biscuit tin, which was filled to the brim, spilling over with feces and remnants of sodden toilet paper. They puzzled over the churro's whereabouts until they heard a strange gurgling, snuffling sound from within the outhouse, and gingerly approached it.

Suddenly and without warning, a shaved head popped out of the hole in the cement floor, shaking itself like a wet dog, streaking long tendrils of wet brown sludge through the air, splattering them all! The deep creases in the churro's face ran with liquid feces, his teeth heavily stained and coated with dark brown goo dripping from his insanely grinning mouth. The whites of his eyes were stained brown to match his pupils, giving him a terrifying visage of blanked-out eye sockets!

The churro looked just like the frogs, or *churas*, revelling in his spa feces bath!

Exclaiming, "*Ya Allah!*" ("Oh, dear God") Tariq's mother fell in a faint and both men managed to catch her before she hit the ground.

Meanwhile, Mrs. Razia Khan was just setting out the hot, dripping puris, delicious steaming potato curry, and cups of steaming sweet-smelling masala chai onto the dining table. She was lost in happy thoughts about how nice it was to have the family over and all the kids together (yes, even her complaining but well-meaning mother-in-law), when her reverie was shattered by the kids' terrified screams and her sister-in-law's wild blood-curling shrieks.

MR B., I PRESUME?

———

Aziz just made it aboard the Boeing 737 as the doors were closing.

Thankfully, he didn't have far to walk to his business-class aisle seat, 2B. He sank back into the soft wide leather seat, stretching out his long legs, taking full advantage of the ample legroom. He breathed a sigh of relief at having beat Friday afternoon traffic to JFK from his Manhattan office. He found it always helped to motivate cabbies[4] with a nice bonus to get to the airport in record time.

On the spur of the moment, Aziz had decided on a weekend flight home to Toronto as a preferred alternative to another boring, empty, hot weekend alone at his bedsitter in New York. Having no luggage to check-in for his weekend trip, he was able to breeze through security with no more than a flash of his Ontario Driver's licence, a smile, and a wave. The flight attendant actually re-opened the aircraft door upon hearing his shouts as he ran through the boarding bridge. (It was the innocent 1980's when airport security personnel were relaxed and friendly and one could actually laugh and joke with them – this of course, well before the horrendous 9/11 catastrophe and the 2020's COVID lockdown, when the world twice changed forever).

Aziz was looking forward to surprising his girlfriend Zena who he'd call from a payphone as soon as they landed at Pearson airport in Toronto. (No cellphones in existence yet)

Upon takeoff, he turned to look out the window and set eyes on his neighbour for the first time, a tall, handsome and distinguished looking Indian man, striking in dress and appearance.

The man flashed Aziz a charming smile and with eyes twinkling shook hands, introducing himself by first name only. He raised his eyebrows at Aziz, who mumbled his name in reply. Aziz who had

---

4   See "Taxi in Prague" about a hair-raising taxi ride, in my next book of short stories, coming soon. -Author

just got through a brutal week at work, was in no mood for affable conversation or chit-chat with a stranger. He politely turned away, resting his head back, hoping to get some shut eye on the short eighty-minute flight.

Aziz's thoughts turned to Zena, who he felt was aptly named considering her striking resemblance to Xena, the Warrior Princess. With long black flowing hair cascading over her shoulders, she was just as pretty and statuesque. Her flashing eyes and fitted blouse over her generous chest made her look like she wore pointed armoured breastplates, ready to do battle. Aziz was very much looking forward to getting reacquainted with them, er, her, that weekend.

"Would you like something to drink sir?" intoned a soft female voice, jolting Aziz awake just as he was nodding off. He jerked awake, glancing up at a pretty smiling stewardess holding a tray laden with orange juice, Perrier and champagne. He helped himself to a Perrier, thanking her as his neighbour reached over for a flute of champagne, eyes twinkling, smiling broadly at them both.

The Indian man asked Aziz about himself and what he did for a living. Aziz spent a good ten minutes with his answer and then asked the same of his friendly neighbour. He smiled, waving dismissively, saying.

"Oh I'm only an entertainer, we just performed in New York and are performing in Toronto at a musical show tonight and tomorrow night. My entire group is on this flight as well, actually, seated in the section behind us. All our instruments, props, and costumes are also in the cargo hold beneath us. We all work, live, and travel together!" he laughed.

The Indian man had a copy of the *New York Times* and they spent a pleasant hour discussing the news of the day, American and Canadian politics, the upcoming elections, cricket, soccer results, and predictions for the British soccer leagues.

As the plane touched down, he turned again to Aziz, thanking him for the pleasant conversation and wishing him luck with his interesting job in construction and with his girlfriend that weekend. He then produced two VIP tickets from his inside jacket pocket, proffering them to Aziz. "In case you'd like to bring your girlfriend to my show tomorrow night. It's at the Exhibition Place downtown," he smiled.

"What kind of a musical show is it, exactly?" asked Aziz.

"Oh, it's a bunch of Bollywood types singing and dancing and making jokes for a predominantly South Indian audience. It'll be good fun and a break for you, I dare say, even though it's evident you're not into Bollywood and Indian stuff, but your girlfriend might enjoy it," he said, still smiling affably.

"Thanks, old chap, but I don't think we can manage the time. I have my mom and sister to spend time with tonight, then perform household repairs and chores all day tomorrow while Zena will be working – she's an events organizer. I'll only get to be alone with her tomorrow evening, because we have our large family picnic on Sunday. And I'm not yet ready to introduce her to my huge 'tribe.' So I'll pass on it this time, if you don't mind. But wonderful to have met you, and I'm sure your show will be a great success. All the best to you!" Aziz shook hands with him.

As they deplaned, Aziz turned back to the distinguished gentle-man and asked him for his name again, having already forgotten it. The man mouthed his first and last name this time, still smiling at Aziz and the attentive stewardess. She fluttered her eyelids, arched her trim figure, and smiled coyly at the tall handsome Indian gentle-man as he departed.

Aziz was unable to reach Zena at work from an airport payphone and eventually reached her later that night.

"Aziz you should have told me you were coming home this weekend!" she pouted. "I just snagged tickets for two of my girl-friends and myself to a Bollywood musical event at the Ex for tomor-row night! Damn, I do wish you'd told me you were coming, Aziz. I would have gotten you a ticket too, and they're all sold out now! "

"That's funny you say that, because I was sitting next to an Indian gentleman on the plane today who said he was performing in a Bollywood show at the Ex tonight and tomorrow night," Aziz replied.

"He was sitting next to you in *business* class?" she asked, raising her voice slightly.

"Yes, he was in charge, it seemed; the rest of the performers were sitting at *the back of the bus*," Aziz replied.

"What was his name?" she asked, a little breathlessly now.

"Oh he told me his name twice but I can't remember now, some-thing very Indian... He was actually quite nice, even offered me a pair of VIP tickets for tomorrow's show. But I turned them down, thinking you and I could go for a nice dinner, some slow dancing, and you know... sweetheart."

Ignoring his suggestive offer, she asked plaintively, "But can't you at least *try* to remember his name?"

"Well... it was something like Amrit-something I think," he answered a little peevishly.

"Amitabh! Was it Amitabh Bachchan?" she screamed

"Yes, that's it! He was a very tall, handsome, well-spoken and cul-tured man. Do you know him?" Aziz asked incredulously.

"Do I know Amitabh Bachchan?" screamed Zena. "Do I know him? Do birds fly? Do fish swim? Do bears have fur?" she continued hysterically. "Apart from being a fantastic dancer and entertainer, he is only the star of the show tomorrow night and one of the most famous Indian actors of all time!" she screamed again, more shrilly this time.

Zena paused to catch her breath while trying hard not to choke. "And you turned down VIP tickets as Amitabh Bachchan's guest and a chance of meeting him and his Bollywood stars in the dressing room after the show? You chump. You total goofball. What the hell am I doing going out with a loser like you? You happily live in your bubble in New York and know sweet FA about famous people! And then you randomly visit home and expect me to drop everything without warning and just run into your arms?" she ranted on at poor Aziz.

* * *

Some years after the Amitabh Bachchan fallout with Zena, Aziz was now happily married to his lovely bride Serena and back working and living in Toronto. Serena too was very pretty but without the flamboyance and explosiveness of Zena and Xena.

While on a short vacation to Morocco, Aziz and Serena had many interesting encounters, and where Mr. Bachchan resurfaced once again.

The morning after their arrival in Casablanca and following a crazy evening, Aziz and Serena decided to visit the leather market near their hotel, which from all indications promised to be a shopper's paradise.

They stood out immediately as foreigners, despite being Canadian Muslims in a Muslim country.

Serena, being a stylish lady of the times, sported an afro-style hair perm, no doubt popularized for non-African people by Hollywood stars such as Cher and Barbara Streisand.

The market vendors were quite nosy and curious as to the couple's heritage. Naturally, with her afro hairdo and light-brown skin they suspected Serena of having mixed African and Arab heritage.

And oddly, Aziz appeared too tall to be Moroccan, despite his fair brown skin and aquiline nose. And as Aziz and Serena didn't speak Arabic, the locals deduced they were both southern Spanish of mixed heritage!

Back in the '80s, it seemed that most Moroccan men encountered were rather short, much shorter than Canadian men or North Indian or North Pakistani men, for instance.

After much pointing and laughing at Aziz's height, accentuated by his lankiness, the vendors demanded to know Aziz and Serena's ethnic origin, if not Spanish. When they explained that they were born and raised in East Africa, of Indian heritage, then lived in England and were now living in Canada, it caused quite a stir. Even more so when they explained that they spoke Swahili, Gujerati, English and French, but no Arabic or Spanish!

The Moroccans were however, delighted to learn of the Indian heritage revelation, because it turned out they adored watching Bollywood movies – which were apparently one of the twin national pastimes, the other being soccer. Their absolute Bollywood favourites were two classic movies from the '60s.

The first, *Dosti*, a movie about the deep friendship and mutual dependency between two homeless and exploited street boys, one blind and the other lame. And the second, *Waqt*, a movie about a family torn apart by an earthquake and then reunited years later in a courtroom drama at the end.

And of course, the current swashbuckling Bollywood movies starring the inimitable Amitabh Bachchan, who the Moroccans couldn't stop raving about!

After a good morning's haggling and shopping for leather jackets, hats, gloves, and curios including a studded wood and leather air bellows for their fireplace, the happy couple returned to their hotel.

The next day enroute to another shoppers' delight, Aziz and Serena passed by the same leather market, but on the opposite side of the busy street. Suddenly, somebody screamed and pointed at them. Then kids ran out from behind tables laden with fruit and leather goods, from in between spice and food baskets, and up to the edge of the bustling road. They waved frantically, yelling gleefully at Aziz, "Amitabh Bachchan! Amitabh Bachchan! Amitabh Bachchan!"

Aziz and Serena stopped in amazement and Serena couldn't stop laughing, which seemed to encourage the others because the merchants suddenly abandoned their stalls, also running out to the curb edge, laughing and waving and yelling, "Amitabh Bachchan! Amitabh Bachchan!" They waved the couple over to them, happily chanting, "Amitabh, Amitabh, Amitabh!"

Then, cupping their hands to their mouths, the crowd began ululating loudly, beckoning them over.

More people came running out of the market, pouring out of nearby buildings and running over from adjacent streets to see what all the excitement was about!

Serena got into the mood of the crowd and grabbing his arm, coaxed Aziz to cross over to the crowd. The busy traffic incredibly stopped to let them cross, despite Aziz's protests that the vendors only wanted the Canadians to spend more dollars at the market.

They entered the market, met by people with hands pressed together in supplication, followed by big joyous hugs as though Aziz were really the great Mr. Bachchan, who'd come to visit the people of Casablanca!

A man with shiny gold teeth garlanded Aziz with a wreath of roses, a woman bent down with hand to breast and momentarily touched Aziz's feet with her finger tips. A young girl ran up to him, jumped onto an upended wood crate. Then, dipping her finger into some hastily prepared red paste held by her mother, she pressed it onto Aziz's forehead, leaving a big red dot. All of these actions were signs of love and respect in Indian culture for elders, dignitaries and newly married couples and much popularized in Bollywood movies. Somebody brought over cups of mint tea and a platter of dates, enveloping the proclaimed "Mr. Bachchan" and his wife with love and laughter and dancing and merriment...

GERMAN SAUNA

Frankfurt was a long way from what one might call home. Originally hailing from Moshi, Tanzania, Maximus Mendoza was the son of a Goan police officer, his parents having emigrated to Africa from Goa, India, in their youth. Maximus had received the best possible education available in Moshi during the 1960s. His policeman father had been a slave driver and disciplinarian, insisting on the very best performance in whatever activity his only child partook in—or else. Sports was unfortunately not an option due to Maximus' slight and diminutive figure, mirroring that of his father's, and in this regard, his father had to acquiesce.

Luckily, Maximus was endowed with a high level of curiosity and intellect and applied himself diligently to his lessons at the Moshi Primary School. Captain Mendoza would drop Maximus off to school at exactly five minutes to eight each morning (the timing was not negotiable). This allowed him ample time to march over to the assembly field, heavy satchel slung over his slight shoulders, to be the first boy in line before the assembly bell rang at 8:00 AM.

He would be picked up at exactly 4:05 PM, no dawdling with schoolmates allowed. After school, his classmates played sports or goofed around and the majority Muslims among them went to mosque each evening. Maximus however, studied at home each night for three hours after supper, and most Sundays after church, under the watchful eye of his stern father.

It was no wonder that Maximus always placed first in class out of the thirty-five pupils. Exams were held three times a year, every year for seven years. Placing less than first was not an option, although nobody realized the parental pressure he was under until the unthinkable happened in the Grade Seven primary school finals. A fellow student, Najibullah Jamaludin, came in first, narrowly beating Maximus by half a percentage point! Maximus' unblemished seven-year coming-in-first record had been shattered. He was now just 20 for 21!

Shock waves went through Maximus' classroom and the Teachers staffroom when the results were announced. Eleven year old Maximus was observed silently crying in a corner, before hanging his head, and dragging his feet to his impatiently waiting father's car.

Maximus was subsequently absent from school for the remainder of the week. Just as the headmaster steeled himself to call Captain Mendoza, Maximus returned to school, a changed and strangely subdued boy. Even stranger, he wore long pants and long shirt, which was a punishable deviation from the mandatory school uniform of khaki shorts and white short-sleeved shirt for boys. But the teachers overlooked it, sensing it was a private matter.

At week's end on the last day of school, Maximus confided in a friend that he had been thoroughly flogged by his father for coming in second! He showed his friend the black whip marks and red welts on his back, buttocks, arms and the back of legs.

As things go among children, the news soon spread to all the classmates and to some teachers too, but since it was a festive last day of school, nothing more was said. And besides, Maximus' father was a strict police captain and nobody wanted to mess with him.

During the summer holidays, Maximus' father was transferred to another town. Then to various other towns and cities, and Maximus attended schools wherever his father's police work took them.

Eventually, Maximus found himself emigrating with his parents to Toronto, Canada, in the late 1970s. He received his higher education at a community college and later at a university in Ontario.

Now he worked as a sales executive with an international industrial tool company, based in Toronto.

Maximus Mendoza closed his notebook slowly, reluctantly gathering his pens, handout papers, and text books, precisely arranging them into his new brown leather briefcase, purchased specially for this occasion. He neatly tied the buckles of the briefcase and was the last to leave the boardroom-cum-classroom at the Eine Kleine Nacht hotel situated near Frankfurt International Airport.

The other students, all males, upon waking with stifled yawns abandoned their paperwork on this their last night in Frankfurt, but not before one of the students presented their lecturer Herr Dieter Klein with their company calendar. Typical of the industry in the 1980's, most industrial sales staff and their buyers were male and the calendar proudly featured scantily clad female models, suggestively holding on to rock hammers, power drills, and concrete vibrators.

Their employer was hosting their annual week-long training course-cum-junket for their top salesmen. Maximus of course, had placed first among them all. These junkets were held in rotating locations around the globe wherever the company had a national headquarters. This year it was in Frankfurt, West Germany. New York and Rome had hosted training in the previous two years, so Maximus had been told.

Most of the attendees however weren't serious about learning, just interested in having fun. Somebody yelled, "Everybody make sure to be downstairs in the lobby by 6:00 p.m. and ready for our last night of never ending fun. Yahoo!"

Of the dozen lucky course attendees selected this year from company offices around the globe, just the two married men and Maximus, still young, single and eligible, had stayed back in the hotel each evening.

The other nine single wild bucks would race into the city's hotspots each evening. The bucks usually departed between 6:00 and 6:30 p.m. after getting "slicked up" for a night of never-ending frothy beer, loud thumping music, dancing and yes, debauchery.

They began their schmoozing in the *Alt Sachsenhausen* district downtown, some ending in the seedier *Bahnhofsvierttel* district with the express intent of bedding down briefly with someone. This meant getting back to their own beds wasted, well after midnight. Hence the need to catnap during day classes. That is, of course, if Herr Klein weren't boring enough.

However, to their credit, the entire group had planned a cultural visit at the end of their stay to fly to Berlin, to visit the Berlin Wall before flying back home later that evening. Maximus was very much looking forward to this, the highlight of his trip.

The week passed quickly and Maximus had learned much, taking notes, asking questions, studying, and doing his homework for the next day's class, working in his room each night before retiring to bed.

Mind you, it wasn't all work for Maximus. He took time each evening to relax as well. He was a creature of discipline and habit, being quick to establish a fastidious daily routine for himself at the hotel.

Each day after classes at 5:00 p.m., Maximus would head to his room, strip to his underclothes, put his feet up, read the paper, and relax over a couple of cups of hot tea. At exactly 6:00 p.m. he would turn on the TV to watch BBC World Service. He'd then pee, change into his swim trunks, and don the hotel dressing gown in quick succession. At exactly 6:30 p.m., he'd slip into a pair of hotel slippers and head downstairs to the indoor pool that was usually emptied out of other swimmers by then, mostly vacationing families with kids.

He sometimes ran into a couple of stragglers from class on their way out who always invited Maximus to join them for a rollicking fun time downtown, but he politely declined, citing some excuse or the other.

After a half hour swimming laps, Maximus would return to his room, shower, blow dry his hair, liberally splash Old Spice aftershave onto his face and neck, and dress in neatly ironed slacks and golf shirt. At exactly 7:30 p.m., he would head downstairs for dinner.

Maximus was always first to enter the hotel restaurant, snagging one of two corner tables providing a panoramic commanding view of the restaurant. He also overlooked the glass walled pool area, which was colourfully lit up at night, and the glowing downtown high rises in the distance. One or both of his married colleagues would arrive shortly thereafter to join him. Not quite finishing his bland airport hotel meal, Maximus would bid his colleague(s) a goodnight and retire to his room at around 8:15 p.m.

On just one occasion, he deigned to join his colleagues at the bar for drinks after dinner, sitting there until 9:00 p.m. All the while doing his best to ignore the two heavily lipsticked women in short tight skirts and revealing blouses sitting at the far end of the bar. They smiled at the men with sly, hopeful looks. Maximus deeply regretted going to the bar with his colleagues as it disrupted his carefully planned schedule.

Returning to his schedule post-dinner and back in his room by 8:20, Maximus would change into his pyjamas, brush his teeth, and complete his ablutions. He would then dutifully call his parents in Toronto for a ten-minute chat to let them know he was alive and well, as was expected of him. Following the call, he would sit at his desk to study and review the day's work for an hour and a bit until 10:00 p.m. before packing up his briefcase and neatly laying out clothes for the next day. He would then kneel by his bed and pray to a photo of the Lord (which he always carried with him) for fifteen to twenty minutes and turn in at exactly 10:30 p.m.

However, this being the final day of classes in addition to being a Friday, the students were let off an hour early, at 4:00 p.m. Earlier on, during their lunch break, the young bucks had managed to talk Maximus and the married men into joining them for dinner and drinks downtown for their last night in Frankfurt. They were to depart on a rented bus at 6:00 p.m. After all, there was no homework and study time required that night, so Maximus had reluctantly agreed to be flexible and deviate from his beloved schedule.

There was still time however to get in a swim before departing for downtown, so Maximus decided to forego his newspaper and TV ritual and go to the pool instead. After a quick change and arriving at the pool by 4:15, to his delight he found it had already emptied out. Maximus enjoyed swimming alone for about twenty minutes.

As the week had been intense and long, Maximus decided to relax in the sauna for the first and last time. The sauna was accessible via a long narrow corridor from the men's change room. He entered the empty sauna, noting it was also long and narrow, mirroring the geometry of the corridor he had come through. Predictably, the sauna had long, narrow bench seats along one side of it's length and Maximus sat at the very end of the sauna, where the benches formed an L-shape. Fifteen minutes later as he was about to leave, the door at the other end swung open to admit a young blonde woman in a scanty bikini.

She appeared not to notice Maximus at the far end, deftly slipping off first the top, then the bottom of her bikini, sitting down on the bench nearest to the door! Maximus was suitably shocked and didn't know what to make of it when the door opened again and in came two more young women in bikinis, merrily chatting together. They greeted the naked woman in a guttural tongue, and then to Maximus' horror, they too removed their bikinis and sat themselves down stark naked.

Maximus realized what must had happened. He had somehow walked into the Ladies sauna, not having understood the signage in German! He was petrified, because they would surely at any moment notice him cowering at the other end. He presumed the dim lighting and dark stained wood made it quite dark in the sauna, and because he was relatively dark skinned with a mop of black hair, that somehow they hadn't noticed him in the corner!

Would the women scream when they eventually spotted him? he wondered desperately. *Would they call security who would call the police who would charge him with being a voyeur and a sexual offender? Caught molesting multiple naked women at the same time, would that be a world record? How would his boss in Toronto react to this? Would he be fired? What would his fastidious father and his church think of him?* Maximus pondered miserably.

Then the door swung open yet again, and five or six more young women entered the sauna. By this time, they were all talking and laughing in loud guttural voices. The new arrivals also stripped bare and sat on the benches, getting closer and closer to Maximus now.

How on earth hadn't anybody spotted him yet?

Maximus couldn't believe it was possible! He cringed, bracing for the sharp cry of discovery followed by shrill screams at any moment now…

Minutes went by as Maximus tried to remain perfectly still, too scared to move a muscle, keeping his eyes hooded and his mouth shut, lest they spot the glint in the whites of his eyes or his white teeth gleaming in his dark face.

Inevitably the laws of nature were beginning to take over. Maximus felt an involuntary stirring in his groin area and knew they would surely notice him now… He couldn't help himself he reasoned, because after all he was actually living a young red-blooded male's wildest erotic dream come true: to be sandwiched in a hot, confined space with so many beautiful, naked, nubile young women! This was great in a dream, but in reality it was too much to bear! *Now they would also charge him with making lewd and threatening gestures!*

To his horror, the door opened yet again and more young women piled in. The only bench space left was next to him now, within touching distance anyway. He watched with hooded eyes as they came toward him, causally slipping out of their bikini bottoms, and shaking off their bikini tops, their ripe unrestrained breasts jiggling inches from his face.

Then the woman—girl really—closest to him turned, smiled and greeted him, *"Hallo hoe gaat het?"*

Maximus mumbled a response, not looking her in the eye. A couple more ladies turned to smilingly greet him.

So! They knew he was there! Perhaps they realized he was a foreigner who didn't speak German and was in the Ladies sauna by mistake. Yes, that's it! They were too polite to embarrass him or to make a stink over it. How civilized and kind the Germans are, he marvelled.

Well, he was now well and truly busted! No point in prolonging his agony, he decided. *He should leave quietly, but getting to the door meant walking past the gauntlet of a dozen nubile, naked, young women. How could he walk straight in his now rapidly tented swimming trunks?*

As though the girl who had first greeted him could read his thoughts, she glanced down his torso, raised her eyebrows, pursed her lips, clucked and handed him her towel, smiling sweetly.

Maximus thanked her, gratefully using the pool towel as a shield over his middle, and half bent over like an injured crab, sidled out of the packed sauna, nodding and smiling at his involuntary tormentors as he exited.

Maximus breathed a large sigh of relief as he re-entered the men's change room. *Boy what a close call and what a mind blowing experience that was,* he began to congratulate himself.

Just then, two young guys ran up to him "Did you just come from the sauna?" they asked in unison.

Maximus nodded.

"Were there a whole bunch of girls in bikinis that just walked in there?" they asked again

"Yes," Maximus answered. "I can't read German and I guess I went into the Ladies sauna by mistake! And they all removed their bikinis in front of me, not realizing there was a man in there with them!"

The guys threw their heads back laughing, pulled off their swim trunks and pushing past Maximus, whooped loudly, their penises swinging in the air.

"Hey what's going on? You guys can't go into the Ladies sauna, just because I went in by mistake!"

"No mate, this is Continental Europe, and they have co-ed saunas here—men and women share the same saunas—and they're *au natural* in Europe. They're not shy to be naked in front of each other, including whole families!" they laughed again.

"But… but… who are those girls and why have you removed your trunks?" Maximus called after them as they raced down the corridor.

They yelled back while still running. "The European Junior Water Polo championship is underway in Frankfurt this weekend. The girls in the sauna are the Dutch Junior Ladies team, and we're with the British Junior Men's team!"

"Wanga banga bunga!" Shouting in unison, the lads stormed into the sauna, their wildly swinging penises now fully erect and ready!

Maximus ignored the female shrieks, glancing at his watch. *Time to go back upstairs and get dressed for dinner… Thirty minutes to shower and dress, 15-minutes to watch the news, then go down at 5:50 in good time to catch the 6:00 pm bus departure. Make sure I have enough cash for dinner, one drink and return cab fare tonight – wouldn't want to carry too much money and risk getting mugged… then back to the hotel by 9:00 pm latest – in time for the nine o'clock news on BBC. Then follow my routine - call mum and dad, say my prayers and to bed by 10:30 and up early to pack. Breakfast down-stairs, then leave for Berlin, a short 70-minute flight away for our tour of the Berlin Wall!*

It never even occurred to Maximus, so well tutored and set in his ways by his disciplined father was he, to alert his mates about the nudes in the sauna. He could potentially have saved some of them a lot of effort and money in going out on the town that evening... Nor did it remotely occur to Maximus to re-enter the sauna himself, naked and boldly showing off his manhood, to try to snag a willing companion for the evening... or even... to have a quick fling in the steamy sauna right there and then - which is probably what the British lads were doing at that very moment...

FIVE MISTER WILSONS

1. Faux British Mr. Wilson, Moshi, Tanzania, 1970

The buzz of excitement was palpable in the staff common room that morning. Two new teachers would be arriving any minute. The first was a South African: Mr. Khuzwayo, to teach history. It would be refreshing to have an African from another country coming to teach at the government school in Moshi, Tanzania. Not least because he would bring a fresh perspective, not having been indoctrinated in the teachings of the government's Tanzania African National Union's (TANU) socialist view on life.

The second was an English teacher from none other than England. He was a recent Cambridge graduate and would make a nice addition to the school's international team comprising of expats and Peace Corps workers. The school already had a complement of teachers from Canada, the US, Denmark, Norway, Japan, India, Ireland, France, and Sri Lanka, as well as locals both of African and Indian origin. It had been quite a number of years since a Briton had taught at the school, despite the fact that the school was originally commissioned by the British during its colonial rule in what was then Tanganyika Mandated Territory.

Considering he was to be the new English Department head, his name— Mr. Shakespeare Wilson—was most appropriate. His resume was very impressive. He was a summa cum laude graduate, recipient of several medals, and had been on the Dean's list at Trinity College. Mr. K. K Shah, the school's Indian headmaster, wore a satisfied smile on his usually stern thin face, satisfied he had chosen well.

Mr. Kaleb Jutta, the assistant headmaster, breezed into the common room with a tall handsome Zulu striding alongside. He was dressed in a bright patterned *kitenge* print shirt and smart slacks.

"Teachers, this is Mr. Nelson Khuzwayo, our new history master," he announced. "He comes all the way from Cape Town in South Africa and is our Zulu brother!"

The assembled teachers greeted him with smiles and cheers, some of them shaking his hand as he was introduced around. However, he was the secondary act, as everybody was really waiting for the new English teacher to present himself. The minutes ticked by and no Mr. Wilson...

Just as the staff break was ending, the headmaster's secretary popped her head in and motioned for him to come outside. She whispered to him and Mr. Shah beamed at them through the doorway. " I shan't be long," he said in an excited voice. "He's here!"

There was a hubbub of excitement as the teachers eagerly awaited Mr. Wilson.

Mr. O'Toole, the sports teacher, spoke up in his soft Irish lilt. "Anyone want to place bets, then, as to what part of Blighty he hails from? I'll bet he's from the North country, just across the strait from Eire- begorra. He's probably my cousin!" He had no bet takers unfortunately, just eager co-workers awaiting the big moment.

Recess was long over now and the students would be back in class sans teachers. Miss Pundit, one of the English teachers, speaking with a sideways nod and a sing-song Indian accent intoned, "I must go; you never know what mischief the pupils will get up to in an empty classroom!"

Mr. Ram Jain the chemistry teacher lisped back, "Yaar, she's right. I have a chemistry lab to conduct and these pupils can go crazy in an empty laboratory! Why, just the other day a pupil named Hassani opened the burner gas tap, put his nose to it, and inhaled the sweet-smelling gas for a minute or two. The gas of course affected him making him jump up, let out a blood-curdling scream, and run out of the lab screaming like a banshee all the way down the corridor! This caused a panic among the pupils in the lab as well as in other classrooms lining the corridor and they all ran out of the building stampeding after Hassani, thinking that there was another earth-quake in progress!"

This brought a ripple of laughter as the teachers dutifully gathered their belongings to go and do battle with their pupils.

Just then, they heard voices approaching and in walked the head-master followed by a short slim man dressed in green army fatigues, jack boots, and red beret. He was also very black and certainly not an Englishman! With an ashen face, Mr. Shah made the introductions.

"Staff, please say hello to Mr. Shakespeare Wilson, the new English Department head. He is originally from Dodoma region and has just completed a term of voluntary national service in the Tanzanian People's Defence Forces!"

He clapped and some teachers dutifully followed suit. The staff greeted Mr. Wilson with limp handshakes and lack of enthusiasm hurrying out to classes leaving Mr. Shah and Mr. Jutta to show the new teachers around.

The headmaster had been so blinded by Mr. Shakespeare Wilson's poetic Anglo-Saxon name, Cambridge qualifications, and his desire to hire an Englishman that he had failed to conduct basic checks on Mr. Wilson's earlier schooling and post-Cambridge activities.

Needless to say, Mr. Wilson's army stint turned out to be an inspiration for discipline and fitness to his male students. Fascinated by his national service training to effortlessly do fifty push-ups in the classroom, twenty of which were with one hand behind his back, motivated the students to work hard to try and emulate his workout regime.

2. Police Chief Mr. Wilson, Entebbe, Uganda, 1971

The captain's voice crackled over the intercom on the British Airways flight from London that had just begun its descent into Entebbe airport. "This is Captain Mallory speaking. Please return to your seats, fasten your seatbelts, and extinguish all cigarettes as we have begun our descent into Entebbe. It is a bright sunny afternoon in Entebbe and the temperature is 78°F. Our ETA is 1:42 p.m., which is exactly twenty minutes from now. We wish to thank all passengers..."

I looked out the window, craning my neck trying to see through the dreamy white clouds to catch a glimpse of land, but was only blinded in return by the glare of the sun reflecting off the cloud cover. I was returning home after my first year at boarding school in England. Well, almost home. My home was actually in neighbouring Tanzania, however I would not be going there for now, and instead I'd be staying in Kampala, Uganda, as a guest of my mother's family.

My mother and sister were already there waiting to receive me. Because of recent socialist government upheavals, my parents deemed it unsafe for me to return to Tanzania just yet. The last thing they wanted was to have my passport confiscated upon re-entry which would prevent me from going back to school in England. Or worse, the secret police could arrest and intern me without trial, in a concentration camp for political enemies, labelling me a traitor for committing the crime of studying abroad. The airplane finally broke through the clouds and I saw my African homeland again. The intensely red earth, burnt brown vegetation, and muddy waters of bilharzia-laced and crocodile-infested Lake Victoria somehow reassured me.

The airplane glided in, touching down effortlessly and we taxied down the runway, brakes screeching. Turning back toward the terminal building, I saw the meeters and greeters standing on the rooftop deck, expectantly waiting for their loved ones. We deplaned directly onto the hot, steaming asphaltic concrete apron and walked into the terminal building to join a single long queue for customs and immigration.

The earthy raw animal smell of Africa filled my nostrils, making me heady with anticipation and expectation for what was to come. This was a welcome change from drab, dreary, and damp England. I thought I spied my mother and family frantically waving from the densely packed roof deck but could have been mistaken.

I got to the wicket in due course, wearing a big smile on my face, and greeted the officer in Swahili "*Habari ndugu!*" meaning, "Greetings, brother!"

He looked at me disdainfully, not returning my greeting. He rifled through my passport pages back and forth, looking a little perplexed. Without a word, he got up and walked into a back office with my passport.

Now, I looked a little perplexed wondering what was going on. He returned with a police captain, also accompanied by two armed policemen wielding rifles. The captain was young and handsome, smartly dressed in a crisp khaki uniform and wore his cap at a rakish angle. He introduced himself as Mr. Wilson, the commanding officer and chief of security at Entebbe International Airport.

Mr. Wilson thrust my passport at me saying, "You are Tanzanian, so why are you here?"

" I am a student, sir, and am here to meet my family and would like to stay for my summer holidays," I replied.

He didn't seem to hear me. "Step aside and come behind the counter" he commanded, opening a gate marked "Private." As we went through, he stopped and turned to face me. I winced and stood to rigid attention, tightly contracting all my muscles thinking he was about to hit me. Instead, he tapped my chest in several places, as though inspecting a soldier on parade and said, "I don't think you are speaking the truth. I think you are a Tanzanian soldier and are here on nefarious business."

I looked at him incredulously, not knowing how to respond. I mean I was just fifteen years old, albeit lanky and almost six feet tall. But child soldiers were not yet commonplace in Africa in the early-seventies.

Trying not to show my fear, I replied, "But I'm only fifteen years old, and I am a student. I swear I'm not a soldier!

"Then why is your chest so hard and why are you wearing your army jacket?"

"*Damn*," I thought, "*why did I have to be stupid enough to tense my muscles and to wear the latest British fashion—camouflage army clothing?*" (I had bought the camouflage jacket from an army surplus store in Croydon for two pound fifty just before leaving England and now fervently wished that I hadn't. It also didn't help my case that there had been recent border skirmishes between Tanzania and Uganda[5]

Mr. Wilson went on, saying, "We will have to send you back to England on the next flight out this evening, I'm afraid."

I was horrified at this and stammered "But... but... but... my mother and sister have come all the way from Tanzania to see me."

"Are they here at the airport?" he asked.

I nodded in the affirmative.

"Well, I am sorry about that, but we have to send you back."

"May I go upstairs at least to meet them before I leave?" I asked fearfully.

"No, you cannot leave the secure area," he said, "but you can go outside onto the tarmac and wave at them on the roof deck," he magnanimously offered.

I looked around desperately and an idea hit me. "The passengers are exiting by going up those stairs, so would it be possible for you to bring my mother, sister, uncle and aunt to the top of the stairs where I can wave at them from down here?" I asked, thinking we could then be a lot closer instead of looking up at them on a roof deck.

"Where does your uncle live?" he asked, now sounding interested.

"Here in Kampala," I replied.

"What part of Kampala?"

---

5   The ragtag army of the Ugandan dictator Idi Amin had tried to annex Tanzanian land along the border as I recall, but were quickly repelled by a tank division and infantry of the well trained and disciplined army of the Tanzanian People's Defence Forces (TPDF). Thanks to Tanzania's political and economic alliance with its communist comrades of the People's Republic of China, the Chinese "technicians" had done a crackerjack job of training the TPDF.

"In Kololo," I said. He looked quite interested now, Kololo being an upscale neighbourhood.

"Hmm. What does your uncle do?"

"He is a businessman."

"What business does he do?"

"Oh, he has many businesses. I'm not sure exactly," I replied causally.

"Okay, come with me. We will try to look at them from the bottom of the stairs," he conceded.

I couldn't believe my ears. *Thank God!*

We peered up the enclosed stairwell among the exiting mass of passengers and into another mass of meeters and greeters at the top, until I saw them—my uncle with a look of grave concern and the ladies with fearful expressions, as they had rightly deduced that something was wrong as I appeared to be in the custody of a police officer, not to mention the terrified look on my face!

Mr. Wilson bade me call my uncle downstairs, so I frantically motioned to him to join us below as I could never hope to be heard above the sounds of the crowd. My uncle came down a few steps hesitantly, not knowing if it was a trap and if he might be arrested or shot for entering a secure area.

As he reached us, I hugged him saying, "Uncle Alam, Mr. Wilson wants to talk to you about my Tanzanian passport."

Ever the itinerant salesman, Uncle Alam gave Mr. Wilson a confident disarming smile, introducing himself. "Alam Allidina at your service, Mr. Wilson. Is there a problem with my nephew's passport, and is there anything I can do about it?"

"Follow me." Mr. Wilson returned smiling for the first time as he led us into his office, shutting the door as we sat down.

After some small talk, Uncle Alam smilingly reassured Mr. Wilson that I was just a crazy young student, carried away with the latest British fashion and that I was in fact no soldier or secret agent at all. Encouraged by Mr. Wilson's altered demeanour he went on. "I am very grateful to you, Mr. Wilson, for understanding my nephew's situation, and if there is anything I can do for you at any time please feel free to call on me," he said while at the same time handing over his business card.

Mr. Wilson fastidiously studied the card as though searching for a divine revelation.

After a long silence, Uncle Alam repeated with a knowing look, "If there is anything at all I can do for you, Mr. Wilson, please allow me to help you."

I was mortified at the implication of this statement spoken so boldly and openly, albeit on my behalf, but of course I held my tongue.

Then to my utter amazement, Mr. Wilson stood up smiling, and with a satisfied look led us to the immigration kiosk. Ignoring the long lines from another flight that had just come in, he strode right up to the kiosk desk and stamped my passport with a ninety-day visitor's visa.

We then marched to the baggage carousel, where he asked me to identify the only baggage remaining on the conveyor belt and barked at a loitering porter to offload them.

Then in an even more bizarre turn of events, as he led us to the officers' private exit, asking my uncle where he was parked, he relieved me of my two suitcases.

And then Mr. Wilson—police captain, commander and chief of airport security at Entebbe International Airport—carried my bags himself like a common porter to my uncle's car!

As we arrived at the car, Mr. Wilson carefully placed the bags in the boot, shaking hands with my uncle, completely ignoring me. I spied a one-hundred-shilling bill being slipped into Mr. Wilson's palm as they shook hands. This generous "facility payment" elicited a big smile from Mr. Wilson and Uncle Alam pressed home his advantage.

"Mr. Wilson, my nephew's father will be flying in from Tanzania next Tuesday and I wonder if you would kindly also assist him with airport clearances?

"I would be honoured to help," Mr. Wilson replied. "Please send me his name and flight details and I will look after it myself!"

Uncle Alam and I returned to Entebbe airport the following Tuesday, and were led to the waiting and hospitable Mr. Wilson. Asking me to point out my father at the back of the fifty- to sixty-person strong line-up at the single immigration kiosk, we marched up to my father.

As we embraced, Mr. Wilson greeted my father warmly, took his passport, pulled him out of line and led him to the kiosk. There, Mr. Wilson stamped my father's passport, picked up his single bag, and led us all outside.

The passengers in line stared at us open mouthed, first in fear as they assumed my father was getting arrested, then in wonderment as to who this VIP might be to receive such preferential treatment.

Opening the boot of his car, my uncle pulled out a case of Tusker beer, exchanging it with Mr. Wilson for my father's bag. This time, Uncle Alam also handed Mr. Wilson fifty shillings in their handshake.

Mr. Wilson bowed and retreated, reminding my uncle that he was always at his service.

As we got into the car, I overheard my uncle say to my father, "The beer should make Mr. Wilson and his pals happy tonight." Then lowering his voice, he murmured, "and the money should pay for their entertainment tonight..."

3. Black & White Mr. Wilson, Vancouver, Canada, 1977

We were an excited herd of young bucks getting to know each other and our way around in the Department of Civil and Structural Engineering at the BC Institute of Technology located near Vancouver, BC. Of the thirty-odd students in our group, like many groups, we harboured a couple of real oddballs.

Ours were a Mr. Wilson and a Mr. Tillson. They were like two peas in a pod, like Bill and Ben the flowerpot men.

Their names rhymed, they drove to school together in their Chevy Corvair, wore similar clothing complete with red baseball caps, sat together in class, answered for each other, did their school home-work together at home, had coffee and lunch together, and even went to the washroom together! They were inseparable and also had the same twin passions—their girlfriends, a pair of sisters who they spoke about often—and baseball.

Tillson was the quieter of the two and rarely spoke about himself. Wilson, on the other hand, was the ebullient one, very sure of himself bordering on arrogance.

You know the annoying habit diehard golfers have where they are constantly holding an imaginary club, taking aim at an imaginary ball and swinging the imaginary club indoors? Well, Wilson's annoy-ing habit was to simulate an aggressive, crouching batting stance and taking a hard swing with an imaginary baseball bat. He followed this up with sprinting and panting, bowing, and smiling as he imagined the crowds wildly cheering him on.

The first time I saw Wilson do this, I asked him in genuine puzzle-ment as to what he was doing.

He replied, "I'm swinging a baseball bat. Do you know that with an expert flick of my wrists without even moving my body I could smash your face in if I had a bat in my hand? "

Nice guy, I thought as I slowly backed away from his grinning face.

He went on. "Have you ever played baseball?"

"No."

He muttered under his breath, "I didn't think so. They don't play baseball where you come from do they?"

I nodded and smiled back, not knowing how to respond to what seemed like a slur… I held my tongue as I didn't want to make enemies in my first week of college.

In our second week, a new prof walked into class one morning, introducing himself as Hamish MacKinnon.

"Let me start by telling you a little about myself and then you can tell me about yourselves," he smiled cheerfully.

"As you can probably guess from my name and accent, I hail originally from Scotland, Glasgow to be precise. I've lived and worked in Canada most of my professional life with short stints of work abroad in the summer. I work as a volunteer for *Engineers without Borders* where we engineer small aid projects for remote villages in developing countries. It is very rewarding work and lots of fun too! And of course I've been teaching at BCIT for some years now."

"Now, beginning at the back row, from left to right, tell me about yourselves in one minute or less—your one minute of fame so to speak," he said with a jolly laugh.

Hamish went through us all, quickly and efficiently, making mental notes about each student, sometimes saying something funny, followed by a loud guffaw.

After Wilson had finished his spiel but not before he glanced over a couple of times at Tillson for his silent consent, Hamish remarked, "I was just in Uganda this summer working on a project to provide clean drinking water and basic sanitation to a village near a place called Entebbe. We were afforded a police escort wherever we went and the police captain in charge who I became good friends with was a Mr. Wilson," he smiled. "You remind me of him. You have the same name and you even look like him, except you have a white face and he had a black face!" Hamish erupted into another loud guffaw.

Wilson's face went a deep red with discomfort and embarrassment as he writhed in his chair and wrung his hands under the table.

"What's the matter, lad? You don't look so happy?" said Hamish cheerfully.

Wilson smiled back weakly.

"Do you mind being compared to my black Mr. Wilson?" Hamish chuckled.

Wilson reddened some more, realizing he had been publicly caught out, looked over at his pal Tillson for support, but got none this time. He tried looking a little contrite.

It was good to see Wilson taken down a peg! I was also delighted to see my newfound pals Richard, George, Tim and Marshall—Canadians of Polish, British, Irish and German extraction, respectively—shake their heads in disgust and glance over at me in solidarity. You see, back in those days, local folk were often embarrassed or offended to be associated with or compared in any way to a black person…perhaps that still exists to some extent today, half a century later.

4. Rattlesnake Mr. Wilson, Penticton, Canada, 1987

Aziz parked his massive FWD Ford F250 ¾ ton pick-up truck, or "Doukhobor Convertible," as it was affectionally known as, in the shade of a rocky outcropping. He dismounted to inspect the work happening off to the side of the steep dirt road. The contractor was constructing tower footings for a 137- kilometre-long power trans-mission line that was to pass through this godforsaken location outside Penticton, BC. It was a very hot and dusty July day, really hot at 105°F in this part-rocky desert, part-forested landscape.

Aziz was really excited about the summer job he had just landed as an inspector for the Hydro authority, despite being cautioned about the terrible heat wave that year and resultant rise in the rattle-snake population along the semi-arid right of way. He wiped away the sweat running into his eyes, trying vainly to wet his cracked lips with his tongue as he approached the work crews. Plastic or stainless steel water bottles had not yet been invented, and he hadn't had time to shop for a thermos or army canteen to carry ice water in, as his colleagues were doing.

After casting concrete test cylinders to take back for compression testing at the lab and after measuring the formwork to check for conformity with the drawings, Aziz hung around for a bit to chit-chat with the work crews. They were glad of the distraction and were happy to shoot the breeze. To get a better sight line of footings already constructed prior to Aziz's arrival on the project, they told him he'd have a great view if he went up the rocky outcropping immediately above his truck.

As he began scrambling up, Aziz reached his right hand into a gap between the rocks to get a better grip and balance. The foreman yelled out to Aziz, "Keep your freaking hands to yourself, kiddo. Don't ever reach into gaps between the rocks! And keep your eyes peeled at all times for rattlers!"

Aziz hastily pulled his hand away, and managed to keep climbing by tightly gripping the visible exposed rock face. *What a fantastic view, well worth the climb,* he thought upon reaching the top. He had a clear unobstructed view of the straight line of tower foundations spaced a few hundred feet apart, going back as far as the eye could see!

After scrambling back down in a cloud of dust, the foreman explained to Aziz, "Last year we had a young surveyor working on the T-line, and like you he grabbed beneath a rock to keep his balance. Unfortunately, there was a rattlesnake coiled up in the shade beneath, trying to stay cool in this heat. Well, it struck and bit his hand, which immediately swelled up with the venom. He was alone but managed to stagger back to his truck and call for help on one of the three radios you guys have in your trucks.

Aziz indeed did have three radios. The first was the internal Hydro channel, the second was for local CB enthusiasts, and the third was for logging trucks. They barrelling around corners at top speeds, and the truckers regularly announced their approach at a bend to warn motorists to keep out of their way!

"So, what happened to the surveyor?" Aziz asked.

"They sent out a helicopter and a medic in short order and flew him to the nearest trauma hospital in Kelowna. They had to pump all his blood out and filter it—three times, apparently—until they got most but not all of the venom out, which had by this time circulated throughout his body. He remained in hospital recovering for a couple of months and was off work for a full year after. Don't know if he ever fully recovered from the damage the venom caused to his central nervous system."

Since that unfortunate incident, Inspectors had been issued with primitive snake bite kits and told to wear high work boots (purchased at own cost) going at least three to four inches above the ankle. The rationale was that oftentimes the snakes blended in with the dead grey tree branches littering the landscape, and it was easy to step on a rattler without seeing it. The snake's immediate reaction when stepped on was to snap it's head up and bite, hence the high boots. The crude snake bite kit comprised of a green rubber suction cup and a sterilized blade in a wrapper. The idea was that if you were ever bit, to calmly make a cross cut on the bite itself (unbelievably painful, I'm sure!), and then use the suction cup to suck out the blood and most of the venom before it had a chance to spread throughout the body.

Later that night, back in the motel room, Aziz woke to go to the bathroom. As he walked across the room in a half-asleep state, he caught myself instinctively scanning the floor ahead in the darkness, keeping a look out for rattlesnakes!

Early the next morning, Aziz went in to the project office in downtown Penticton to drop off the previous day's inspection report and to get instructions on his inspection area for that day. The base manager, Brian McPherson, asked Aziz to follow him into his office, shutting the door.

"Aziz, I'm glad that you're diligently filling in your inspection reports but I've received disturbing feedback from head office in Vancouver, in that they've made comparisons to the other inspectors' reports. They've said that the others need to fill in a lot more information than a single page. Because you're filling in three pages and giving them too much information, now they want everybody to do that! So, I think you should cut down on the length and detailed scope of your reports. I suggest you ask Ralph Potter (or "Potty" as he was called) to show you his reports before leaving the office to find out how you should be filling them in."

This was really bizarre, Aziz thought. Instead of a commendation for a job well done, he was being told to be less thorough and not to do his job so well! Aziz's face must have mirrored his thoughts, because Brian said, "You've got to understand that both Potty and Peter Martin are older guys and don't have a formal education like us, but instead they have years of hands-on experience in the field. They can't be expected to reference engineering terms such as you do, for example."

He read aloud from the report Aziz had just handed in.

"For the mini-retaining wall on the upward slope of the footing, I instructed the contractor to remove and reinstall the rebars correctly on the tension side of the wall as the rebars are supposed to act in tension and not in compression."

He squinted at me. "Or how about this?"

"The inside corners at the top exposed surfaces of the footing were missing chamfers, and the contractor was instructed to halt pouring concrete until the chamfers could be installed. The contractor did not have any chamfers on hand, and I accordingly got the foreman to cut rough chamfers out of the corners of a 2 x 4 for this purpose and further instructed him that by the following day I expected to see a bundle of chamfers delivered onsite."

He stopped reading and looked at me. "Just go with the flow," son, he said. "Don't sweat it, okay? So, the exposed knife edges of the footing will get chipped over time, but who really cares in the bush? And we'll all be long gone anyway!" he laughed.

"Right then. Stop dilly dallying and get your ass in gear. You've got a long drive to kilometre 25!" Brian smiled disarmingly.

Aziz walked over to Potty in the outer office, who sat waiting for him.

"Here you are. See how it's to be done," he said gruffly, thrusting a couple of his reports at Aziz.

Aziz read through them in fifteen seconds each, and realized these were just pieces of crap. There was nothing substantial and nothing to be gleaned regarding the actual work or quality assurance. It was just a roll call of the number of men working in particular locations, without any details of work performed or of any corrective work action required, probably because Potty hadn't bothered to properly inspect the work. Scary!

Aziz thought back to his first day on the job and of Potty showing him around the site. The contractor's rod busters were hurrying to finish up tying the rebar cages, while the ready-mix concrete truck stood by waiting to pour concrete. But Potty hadn't cared to inspect the work to ensure the rebar was installed correctly. He had stood nonchalantly resting his butt against his truck while lovingly unwrapping and eating a ham sandwich, not once glancing in the direction of the work frantically underway.

On his second day, Aziz drove with the other inspector, Peter Martin, who halted his truck to speak with a dishevelled looking man on the side of the road. Aziz later asked Peter about the man, who laughed. "That's Wilson, our mechanic. He roams the length of the site to fix mechanical issues with our roadworks equipment, cranes etc. He was asking if we'd seen any rattlesnakes along the way." In reply to Aziz's quizzical look, he said, "He collects rattlers; don't ask me why!"

Thanking Potty for his "help," Aziz left the office driving to his assigned site area at kilometre 25 wondering if it was even worth it, now that he was supposed to be just a payroll verification service to prove the contractor was actually at work, and nothing more.

As Aziz approached a heavily treed area, he chanced upon the same unkempt man seen earlier with Peter. The man signalled Aziz down.

"Howdy, how ya doin'?" he asked.

"I'm good, thanks. Mr. Wilson, isn't it?" Aziz noticed his glittering snake-like eyes, which made him a tad uncomfortable.

"Yup that's me, where you headed today?" He approached the window wearing a gummy smile, sans upper teeth, showing his large pink upper gum.

Aziz replied and Wilson said to give him a call on the radio if he happened to see any rattlers "up that a-way." Intrigued, Aziz asked him why he was so interested in rattlers.

Giving him a wide gummy smile, Wilson said, "Many reasons. First, they are a source of extra income. I cut off their heads and rattles and slit them lengthwise down the belly. Then I throw 'em on top of an anthill. I go back a week or two later by which time the ants have picked the snake clean. So, all I have to do then is to pull the snakeskin off the skeleton, and tan it on my clothesline, and then its ready to make belts and wallets, and larger pieces to sell to custom shoe manufacturers, depending on the size of the snake.

"And with the snake heads, I remove the venom sac and bottle the venom for sale for the Far East market. I then boil the heads, skin 'em and throw 'em in a lemony soup. Delicious—tastes better than chicken soup! I still gotta figure a way to can it and sell my Mr. Wilson's snakes' head soup.

"And the rattles I give to my kids to play with. They love the rattling sounds they make!"

What a charming, cultured man, Aziz thought to himself. "And what are your many other reasons?" he asked

"Oh, that don't concern you, young fella. You'd best be off now."

"Okay, I'll be sure to call you if I come across any snakes, Mr. Wilson," Aziz promised as he drove off.

A few days later, driving on his way home at the end of a long hot dusty shift, Aziz passed through Mr. Wilson's copse of trees and spied another green Hydro truck winding its way up a sideroad. Thinking this was likely a shortcut back into town, he decided to follow it. The vehicles continued to climb through the trees for about two kilometres when the green Hydro truck pulled off onto a bumpy path, which was almost invisible in the thick foliage. Now Aziz was cautious and following it at a safe distance.

Aziz backed his truck into the bush, turning it around trampling over brush and saplings, ready to make a quick getaway if he had to. The green Hydro truck was parked on the road about a hundred feet ahead. Aziz approached it gingerly, but it was empty. He spied more trucks parked ahead of it—an older Hydro truck and a rusty beat-up '50s vintage Chevy truck.

The area was littered with pieces of machinery amid thick, oily patches. The land ahead dropped off and beneath the road he could see the rooftop of a ramshackle building. Aziz turned away, realizing this was private property and that he had no right to be there. But then he heard what appeared to be voices chanting and turned toward it, finding himself drawn to the mesmerizing chants… he stealthily approached the house.

Aziz peered down at a ramshackle house and messy front yard well hidden in the trees, and was greeted with a shocking sight! There were four or five adults and three kids standing in a circle facing each other. In the centre of the circle stood Mr. Wilson, quite naked and expertly holding on to a rattlesnake by its head, waving it in the air, as it writhed trying vainly to coil its sinuous body over his arm and torso, which were well-oiled and gleaming in the fading sunlight. The children were naked too, and the other adults were stripped down to the waist, including two women, all chanting in an unintelligible tongue. Aziz recognized a tubby man—it was Potty!

Mr. Wilson drew a long hunting knife and with one expert movement plunged it through the snake's head, crouching down onto his knees and impaling the snake's head into the hardpack ground. The snake's frantic writhing abruptly ceased as it drew its last breath. Withdrawing the knife, he sliced off its head. Mr. Wilson stood up, rubbing the bleeding snake's head onto his toothless upper gum, smacking his lips as he did do. Then anointing his groin with the snake's blood, put his arms around the two half-naked women, and led them inside to the high-pitched chanting of the group.

Aziz tried to get in a little closer in the fading light to see what Potty was doing, crouched down by the dead snake. He cut off the rattles with his knife and handed it to the little girl. She couldn't have been more than three or four years old. She gleefully shook it listening for the rattles, then putting the freshly cut snake's rattles into her mouth, ran away with the other kids chasing after her.

Just then, an errant squirrel jumped down right in front of Aziz, causing him to rear back crashing into a tree, knocking over a resting shovel with a loud clatter onto the rocky ground. This unfortunate chain of events created a cacophony of sounds and Aziz immediately took off for his truck. Potty and the other men shouted, giving chase but Aziz had a good head start. Thankful for his foresight, he jumped into his well-positioned truck, accelerating away in a cloud of dust into the dusk. But smart as he was, Aziz didn't notice the sticky black oil stuck in between his tire treads to his mudguards and splashes of muddy oil over his truck's side panels.

Aziz handed in his full inspection report the next morning, having decided he wasn't going to shortchange Hydro, his employer, with just a workers attendance report. He wrote a good account of the day's work on site, including a warning he'd issued to the contractor for flagrantly disobeying safe work practices, putting his workers in danger. Of course, he kept mum about Mr. Wilson's and Potty's private practices after work, as this had no direct impact on the project—so far, anyway. Walking outside, Potty and Peter were standing next to Aziz's pickup truck. They looked away, then gave him hard looks as he drove off on his day's route.

The day was uneventful, except it was hotter and dustier if that were possible.

Aziz had an early dinner that night, hitting his pillow by 8 p.m. He slept soundly but woke earlier than usual. The sun was just rising as he walked out onto his second-floor balcony with a cup of instant coffee. His pickup truck was across the parking lot, parked alongside Peter's and Potty's trucks. Aziz sensed rather than saw a movement beneath his truck, and leaned forward on the balcony railing to squint at it, thinking it might be a racoon. Suddenly, a short squat figure jumped out from beneath his truck, appeared to tuck something inside his jacket, and raced away around the corner of the parking lot. The man wore a red cap, similar to Potty's cap Aziz thought, but why would Potty be lying beneath his truck? And why did he jump up and dash off like that? It just didn't make sense.

After showering and breakfasting in the restaurant downstairs, Aziz gave a cursory look beneath his truck on his way out, but seeing nothing he decided it must have been his imagination as he had not been fully awake. It wasn't surprising that his mind was playing tricks on him, considering the bizarre and weird Mr. Wilson and Potty scene he'd witnessed just a couple of nights before. Aziz was still trying to make sense of it.

Oddly, nobody was in the office that morning as he went in to drop off his report and pick up his daily schedule. Aziz headed to kilometre 13, which was an older part of the site that he thought had been completed prior to his arrival on the project. Nevertheless, that's what his schedule demanded of him.

Taking the turn-off from the main logging road towards the signposted kilometre 13, Aziz found himself on an extremely steep slope driving on the edge of an escarpment with a sharp drop-off on one side. The gravel surface was loose and slippery and had not yet been compacted he noted as he passed a working D8 excavator at the top. He stopped, pulled the hand-brake hard, and walked outside to turn the hubs on his rear wheels to engage four-wheel drive. Aziz continued driving slowly down with his heart in his mouth. Halfway down, he wondered if his truck would be able to climb back up on his return trip, when suddenly he heard a loud metallic snapping sound and he lost control of the steering wheel as the truck careened down the slippery slope.

As luck would have it, and with his foot hard on the brake, he was able to half steer the truck into a parallel earth berm just a hundred feet or so further down. As he ploughed alongside the berm, Aziz simultaneously switched off the engine and engaged the handbrake, until his truck ground to a halt in an explosion of loose earth. Aziz stepped outside the truck, thankfully planting his feet onto solid ground, but he was shaken to the core from his narrow escape with injury or death.

He radioed for help and they soon sent out a vehicle to pick him up at the top of the slope. He walked back up to the D8 excavator, which was able to winch his damaged truck back up.

Aziz spent the rest of the day in the office working at a desk, examining the project drawings, while his truck was towed into town to the local gas station and garage run by a pleasant man named Izzy.

By mid-afternoon Aziz, learned that the drive shaft had snapped in two. According to the base manager, Brian, it could only have snapped in that manner because it likely hit a rock or series of rocks due to inexpert and rough handling by Aziz.

Aziz couldn't believe the accusation levelled at him and strode over to speak to Izzy, who he knew to be a fair and decent man. Izzy looked uncomfortable, not looking Aziz in the eye, mirroring Brian's analysis of why the shaft had snapped. Aziz asked him point blank if the drive shaft might have been halfway sawn through and therefore snapped at the most inopportune moment.

Izzy looked even more uncomfortable and avoided eye contact, mumbling that he hadn't noticed any saw-marks on the metal shaft. Unfortunately, Aziz couldn't see the shaft for himself as it had already been tossed into the scrap metal bin.

Aziz briefly contemplated going to the police to file a complaint and to demand they investigate and retrieve and examine the shaft for saw marks or other signs of tampering. Aziz was now pretty sure that's what Potty had been doing beneath his truck. However, he wisely decided he couldn't go up against Hydro, against the unions, against his boss and co-workers and most importantly against the close-knit local townsfolk of Penticton, to whom he was an alien.

Aziz was sent home on the next flight the following morning. Exiting the cab at the airport terminal, he had an uncomfortable feeling of being watched, and glancing over at an older green Hydro truck parked across from the entrance, spied Potty and Mr. Wilson grimly staring at him through the windshield. Mr. Wilson rolled down his window and stuck his head out, snake-eyes glittering, smiling toothlessly. He shook his snake rattle at Aziz.

5. Security Guard Mr. Wilson, Cumbaya, Ecuador, 2007

All expatriate Canadians working on the project in Quito, Ecuador, were housed by our Canadian employer in gated communities in the affluent suburb of Cumbaya. I lived in a really cool building, which had just eleven stylish and expansive low-rise apartments arranged in a U-shape. The building, which was named *Alquimia*, meaning "alchemy" was an architectural masterpiece blending modern Miami architecture with a Spanish adobe style. The Ecuadorean architect and builder of this property was as nouveau stylish, sophisticated, and beautiful as her architectural masterpiece. She also happened to live in one of the two 4,500 square-foot penthouses on the property. The building was set farthest from the entrance gate in the enclave of three low-rise stylish apartment buildings. In stark contrast, the property had a tiny, cramped guardhouse the size of a telephone booth by the front door.

The one and only Guard was a triple seven, meaning he was on duty from 7 p.m. to 7 a.m. seven days a week. His name was, of course Señor Wilson (pronounced *Willysawn*)! He was around fifty-five years of age and had only twelve children! One or two of his many daughters usually came by at night with his dinner to sit with him while he supped before leaving with the empties. Sometimes late at night if I was still up and felt like it, I would take him a cup of coffee and cookies to keep him going through the night. We would chat then for a few moments in my broken Spanish, and I'd be lucky to understand a third of what he was saying. He was an Indigenous person of the Quechua Nation and his Spanish was very different and difficult to understand, especially with my beginner level Castilian Spanish!

Following one of my trips home to Toronto, I presented Wilson with a Wilson-branded tennis cap emblazoned with a large green and yellow Wilson logo. He was delighted and eternally grateful, having never heard of the Wilson tennis brand, let alone tennis.

One night when returning home, I saw that Wilson's guard house was missing! I immediately went looking for him and spied him patrolling at the far end of the property. I figured that it had been damaged and he was to get a new guard house, thinking nothing further of it. When I got a chance to ask him about it another night, he replied in a sad voice that management had taken it away from him without explanation.

Concerned, I approached a condo board member and was told that Wilson had gotten too lazy and complacent and usually fell sleep at night. In order to remedy this, they decided to take away the guard house and have him patrol all three properties all night long, *as this is what we are paying him for, after all!* Although I felt sorry for Wilson, there was nothing I could realistically do about it.

One weekend several weeks later, I noticed that Wilson was nowhere to be seen. I met Wilson a few days later and he said he had been told he was costing the property too much money and from now on there was no more weekend work. He appeared very concerned that he would not be able to continue to support his large family.

Inquiring with the board member again, I was told not to worry about it. They were looking to replace Wilson with a younger man to work seven days a week, since Wilson's work of late was unsatisfactory. It was time for the old guard to hit the road. Again, there was nothing I could do, and frankly it was none of my business.

Well, they say bad things come to people in threes, and Wilson was no exception, except this last one was a real doozy! Some nights later, I heard a frantic knocking on my door. Opening it, I was confronted by Wilson. He appeared very agitated and teary eyed, speaking rapidly in his Spanish patois. I led him to my Ecuadorean neighbour Alex's door, knocking on it and asking for help with translation.

Wilson thrust some forms at Alex while he explained his case at the end of which Alex looked quite shaken.

Alex's translation: "As you know, Wilson has a large family. His eldest daughter and her husband and two more of his daughters were travelling on a motorcycle yesterday. While they were taking a roundabout rather fast, his youngest daughter, aged five, lost her grip on her sister and flew off the motorbike! Her tiny body rolled beneath a truck and unfortunately the wheels ran over her foot! They were able to scoop her up and rush her to the hospital which was nearby. When the emergency doctor examined her there was no foot to be seen—just a crushed stump where it had been! An ambulance rushed over to the scene of the accident and luckily they were able to retrieve her severed foot. But the doctors determined that the foot was crushed beyond repair and that she would require a prosthetic foot."

They were able to attach a temporary foot until a permanent prosthetic could be specially constructed for her. The cost for the prosthetic foot would be several hundred dollars, which Wilson did not have. In addition, they would need to replace her prosthetic every two years or so as she continued to grow to adulthood. Wilson was accordingly asking around, reaching out to everybody he knew to chip in with donations. Of course, we both donated whatever we could, however Wilson worried about the years ahead and how he would manage to pay for a new prosthetic every two years.

What a tragedy that in one unfortunate accident, Mr. Wilson's little girl's life had been ruined forever! It was also questionable if she could survive long term and if so, how she could ever live a normal life in the times and society she was condemned to by birth.

FATHER AND SON REUNION

I found myself inexplicably walking westbound on Marine Drive. My surroundings looked foreign yet vaguely familiar. You see, I had previously lived on the North Shore during what seemed like a life-time away before moving to Toronto in 1985, some thirty five years ago. It had begun to drizzle lightly as I glanced north at the majestic, snow-covered twin peaks of the Lions, which were now hazing over with gathering rain clouds. I now realized I was in West Vancouver, BC, headed towards my uncle's boutique, "Bespoke Gentleman."

How weird is this? I thought to myself. *Why wasn't I at home in Toronto*, some 4,000 kilometres away? Crossing 18th Avenue, I heard a familiar voice call out my name. I turned and saw Uncle Alam walking briskly towards me with a concerned look on his kind face. He was smartly dressed as usual in the garb of a British gentleman, wearing a pair of spiffy Marks & Spencer brown slacks with precisely ironed creases, an M&S short-sleeved blue-striped dress shirt and brown leather brogues with tassels.

"Aziz, what are you doing here? You'd better hurry up and get to the Legion Hall!" he said urgently.

"Why? What's happening there?" I asked innocently.

"Haven't you heard?" he replied incredulously, his eyebrows shooting up with surprise.

I stared at him blankly.

Uncle Alam leaned forward placing his hand on my shoulder saying, "My boy, your dad has returned for a short time and has asked everyone to meet him at the Legion Hall, just up the road from here!"

"But… but…" I stammered, my head spinning, "Papa died in 1972. What are you talking about?"

"No, he isn't dead!" he exclaimed, a look of pure bliss on his face. "We all *thought* he was dead, but he actually went away on a long journey and didn't want anybody to know. But that was a long time ago, so now it's okay to let people know that he is alive. Your dad happened to be passing through town and has asked to meet everybody! Your mum, your sister, your aunty and your cousin Romana are already there. I just met your dad myself, and they're all waiting for you—so you better hurry before he has to leave again!"

Wow, I thought. *So that's why I'm here. How could I possibly not have known that Papa was here to meet us?* I thanked my uncle and hurried up the road just as the perennial West Coast drizzle intensified. I was confused, nervous, and excited all at once.

Arriving at the Legion Hall, Romana and Aunty were just leaving. They smiled warmly at me and urged me to hurry inside. I stumbled into the darkly lit hall, my eyes adjusting as they scanned the assembled crowd. I pushed through a sea of people and came face to face with my old friend Diamond Almasi. He had flown out from Toronto specifically to meet my dad, as had many others from our hometown of Moshi, Tanzania! Diamond smiled at me with moist, teary eyes.

I continued on and Sammy Castro appeared in my path, grabbing my hand and pumping it vigorously, throwing his head back and laughing happily, propelling me on. The dense crowd gently parted for me, then closed in behind, smiling and cheering me on.

It seemed like the entire town of Moshi had descended here! Why, here was Shiri Bunga, Mrs. Mansoor, Jimmy and Jenny Juma—old friends of my parents. Mr. and Mrs. Bamiyan and Musa Master, distant relatives, were also here. And some of my dad's associates were here too: Nilam Varnio, Babu Bakkar, Timmy Tea Room, Hasmook Medical, Nizar Pepsi. Don't know why, but even Gulio Gaparo, Fanteli, Kari Farida, Dhori Farida, Sadru Gop, and Papu Pop were here too. And most surprisingly of all, Caleb Mushi, Magan Chaggan, Chris Kumaran, Baldev Bicharo, Johnny Mangare and Lalubhai Patel, who all still lived in Moshi, had come all this way to meet Papa! But how could they all have known and incredibly I hadn't a clue…?

Wow. And here were Papa's two best friends, Ali Nasiruddin and Rumi Ram Dass, smiling triumphantly at me. *But hang on a minute, something wasn't right… Weren't most of these folks already dead?* It was truly surreal, but I wasn't going to argue.

Aah… Then I saw him!

My heart skipped a beat and I gasped audibly. Tall and handsome, a wavy puff of silken black hair over his forehead, his signature shy smile and white dress shirt, standing head and shoulders above the crowd, and barely six metres away from me. He had not changed at all in almost fifty years! I had a panic attack. Would Papa even recognize me after all these years? For I had certainly changed since I was a kid!

As I approached closer, I saw mum standing beside him, gazing up at Papa adoringly. My sister Lubna had her arm tightly linked into his, clinging on to him, too afraid to let go. I've never seen her look so happy. Papa's favourite sister Leila and my cousin Nilu were holding on to his other arm as the crowd pushed and shoved around them. Bapaji was also there, beaming proudly at his younger brother and close friend.

In slow motion, Papa turned and looked directly at me—our eyes met! Looking into his soft, kind brown eyes felt like looking into a reflecting mirror. I saw instant recognition in his eyes! I was giddy, weak at the knees but exuberant at the same time.

Papa gave me a big welcoming smile, my heart beat faster and faster. I wanted to shout, "Papa, dearest Papa!" but my throat was constricted and my mouth dry. No words could form. In slow motion, I strode triumphantly toward my incredulous and momen-tous "Father and Son Reunion," fifty years in the making. I yearned to give my Papa a kiss on his rugged stubbled cheek and the biggest bear hug ever! My arms eagerly reached out to him…

Suddenly, I woke with a start and a shudder! I looked around me with a knowing, sinking feeling in my stomach, reluctantly observing the shafts of early morning light dancing playfully through the curtains onto my bedroom walls at home in Toronto.

I came to the sad realization that I had only been dreaming…

I shuddered again as hot, heart wrenching tears coursed down my face onto my pillow.

QUOD ERAT
DEMONSTRANDUM

———

Aziz Khan stepped off the Edmonds bus onto Adanac Street and instead of waiting an indeterminate period for his connecting bus, he decided to walk downhill to the New West College campus. He didn't know how far the walk might be on this his first day at college, but he didn't mind; he had lots of time. Besides, he was young with boundless energy and opportunity!

Aziz had recently arrived in Canada from high school in England, with his mother and sister. He had always excelled in the sciences and was excited at the prospect of beginning his post-secondary education in Canada!

He had enrolled in the three core science subjects of math, physics and chemistry, plus two electives. He had chosen geology and expository writing, an English course that was a first-year mandatory requirement. Apparently in the mid-1970s, the provincial education board had determined the standard of written English in post-secondary schools in British Columbia was quite appalling.

Luckily, Aziz had an excellent command of English, both written and spoken, having been born and raised under the British schooling system in the former colony of Tanganyika. This was followed by high school education at a private boarding school in England, where the standard of English was hopefully a little better than in this westernmost British bastion in the former dominion of Canada.

Just then, a passing car, a 1970 Chevy Nova, honked and stopped for Aziz. An athletic, bespectacled, kind-looking man with greying sideburns, about twice Aziz's age, was at the wheel. Seated next to him was a young and pretty blonde lady, also very athletic looking. They both smiled pleasantly at him and the man asked if he was headed down to New West College, judging by his satchel and his youthful exuberance, which he said were a dead giveaway.

Aziz nodded and the man said, "Well, hop in then, we'll give you a ride; we're going there too!" He held out a New West College Staff ID card as he opened the back door for Aziz. It turned out that Bruce Smith was a zoology prof and Hannah seated next to him was one of his students. During the short drive there after ascertaining Aziz's field of study, he urged him to try one of his zoology courses if he found after the first class or two that geology was not to his liking. Aziz was tempted to be sure, especially since Hannah appeared to be in this class too.

After being dropped off at the registrar's office, exchanging cheery goodbyes, and receiving a beautiful smile from Hannah, Aziz thought to himself, *What a pretty girl. I wonder if I'll see her again and if I'll have the courage to ask her out!*

It wasn't until a month later when Aziz was attuned to campus buzz that he found out Hannah who was nineteen, a year older than him, was the divorced Professor Smith's girlfriend. She was shacked up with him, the kind, soft-spoken teacher, who was forty-years plus. Wow!

A few days into college, Aziz took a seat at the back of his first English class.

She entered the room, striding authoritatively to the teacher's table in front of the blackboard. She was tall, hefty, and bespectacled with short brown hair worn in a mannish cut. She wore a severely cut heavy wool suit.

"Good morning, class. I am Ms. Proven, and I will be teaching you how to write," she announced in a steely voice.

Picking up a piece of white chalk, she wrote "Expository Writing" on the blackboard, simultaneously voicing the words. "This is a writing style commonly used to convey ideas and to structure essays. It has an opening statement, a central body, and a summary paragraph, i.e., there are three distinct sections to the writing or essay and they all have to tie in together."

She continued discussing the writing style and rules a little longer before saying, "Let's go around the class now and introduce ourselves. I'd also like each of you to tell me why you are interested in taking my course."

Beginning with the front row of students, she worked to the back of the class. When it was Aziz's turn to speak, she looked at him suspiciously over the top of her half-moon glasses. She inquired how long had he studied in England. She seemed unconvinced and snorted when he replied, "The last four years, madam, from 1972 to 1976."

After the intros were over, she announced that she first wanted to know how well "everybody writes" and to "pick an essay topic from the three topics," she was writing on the board. Aziz picked "My drive through the Countryside" as his essay topic, thinking this held a wide spectrum of subjects to write about and had room for creativity.

Miss Proven informed the class they could begin writing "now" and to continue writing at home if needed as the essays were not due until the following week. "No more than five pages, mind you," she said. "You may, on the other hand, leave now if you wish!"

Of course, the entire class including Aziz emptied out right away! English being an easy subject for Aziz, he left the assignment to the very end, concentrating instead on his favourite subjects and on a geology field trip report. He finally got down to writing the essay the night before the class, working on it at home on the kitchen table after supper, polishing it up until well past midnight.

Aziz handed in his essay the next morning and thought nothing more of it. Ms. Proven said she'd mark and return the essays at the following week's class.

Aziz slept in a little the morning of the next English class and managed to cadge a ride to college with a classmate and her father, who lived close by. It was an Indian summer that September of 1976, and he revelled in the breeze of her dad's Mustang convertible as they drove listening to the radio belting out summer hits by Chilliwack,

Chicago, Tony Orlando… Life in Canada couldn't be any better, he decided.

Miss Proven handed back the essays that morning, calling out each student's name and announcing the grade received. A few As, mostly Bs, and a few Cs. The very last name she called out was, "Aziz Khan!"

She looked him over sternly and said, "I'm not sure I should accept your essay! It was obviously not written by you. I'm sure you have had help in writing it, haven't you?" she barked at him.

"Nooo," stammered Aziz. "I wrote it myself, Miss Proven."

"You are lying to me," she spat out, although the flying spittle didn't quite reach him at the back of class, "There is no way you could have written it on your own. You must have had an older university student or adult friend help you with it, come on, be honest with me, eh?"

"No, Miss," he said again. "I stayed up almost all night the day before it was due and wrote the essay on my own. I promise!"

She continued staring at him disbelievingly. "Look, what do you take me for?" she finally said in a more conciliatory tone. "There is no way somebody like you, where English is not your first language, could produce such a well-written essay with a vocabulary and command of English that is not possible with you people…"

Aziz's ears were bright red by now, and all the students had turned around to stare at him, some of whom didn't seem to believe him either, judging by their expressions. Thankfully, just then the bell rang and the classroom cleared out fast.

She said to Aziz, "I will hold on to your essay, all term if necessary, until you own up and tell me who wrote it for you." With that, she left the classroom.

Another student still seated in the room, smiled and introduced himself, "John, John Williams." He had a troubled look on his white face and said to Aziz, "Man, she really insulted you. You shouldn't let her get away with it. She's an effing racist and has no right to doubt your work! If I were you, I'd complain to the principal, and I'll back you up! I saw and heard it all, and I believe you one hundred percent!"

Aziz felt even more deflated now, and didn't know what to say, swallowing a lump in his throat. "What's the use. She just won't believe me, no matter what, and I don't want to cause trouble for her or myself!"

His thoughts wandered back to his former private English boarding school—Kent College in Canterbury, Kent. One year, he had won the "Methodist Recorder Prize," which was awarded annually to the most promising English student. He had beaten the upper-class English boys at their own language and was very proud of that!

Somebody in a fit of envy, smiling meanly, referred to it as the "Wog Prize," only given to "wogs" each year, while he and his mates sniggered at Aziz. The following year, the prize was won by Mark Ventress, a freckled, ruddy cheeked, blue-eyed boy with blond wavy hair. But he probably wished he hadn't won- because all the boys mercilessly teased him, chiding, "Wog Ventress!"

There was no use telling Miss Proven about his English prize to demonstrate his fluency and to try and prove his innocence. It just wasn't worth it! She had made up her mind about him based on her narrow-minded prejudices and that was it!

Over supper that night, Aziz relayed this unfortunate event to his mother and sister. His sister shed some tears at hearing how Aziz had been wronged (she had, in fact, made him a thermos of coffee to help him stay up that night to write the essay!). In contrast, his mother flared up in feisty defiance, saying that he should have told the woman: "You're right. I confess it wasn't me that wrote it; it was my seventy-five-year-old Indian grandmother who wrote the essay for me!"

The matter lay dormant over the course of the semester and after the tenth and final class Miss Proven handed out the final grades. She gave Aziz a "Fail" grade on his controversial essay and an overall "C" grade for the course.

She explained her reasons, saying, "I am sorry you never came clean about the ghost writer of your first essay. I would have given you an "A" grade for the essay had you written it yourself, and probably an "A" grade too for the entire course, but I will not tolerate plagiarism in my class! Let that be a lesson to you never to cheat again!"

It was abundantly clear to Aziz, that according to Miss Proven's prejudiced, narrow-minded thinking, the onus of proof for her baseless accusation was on him and a sad play on the words he just coined:

"What has to be proved has been Proven!" In Latin, *"Quod Erat Demonstrandum."*

Not that she'd understand Latin. She obviously wasn't educated at a British private school, Aziz consoled himself.

Author's note: Now, dear reader, you may have some empathy for Aziz and perhaps are a little disappointed with the ending describing the triumph of racial prejudice by educators in our colleges. So I offer you a choice of two alternative endings. Do read on and decide for yourself which ending you prefer.

QUOD ERAT DEMONSTRANDUM: FIRST ALTERNATIVE ENDING

"John… John Williams." He had a troubled look on his white face and said to Aziz, "Man, she really insulted you. I saw and heard it all, and I believe you one hundred percent!"

Aziz felt vindicated and rejuvenated by his fellow student's support. Yes, he would take this to the next level and beyond. Justice would be served! Aziz and John put their heads together in the empty classroom and planned out how to go about their quest for redress and justice.

On his third attempt at a meeting with Dr. McBride, the college principal, Aziz was granted an audience. He arrived promptly at the appointed time and after a short wait was ushered in.

Dr. McBride was a ruddy red-faced Scotsman with long sideburns and a thick Scottish accent. He listened politely to Aziz's grievances about Miss Proven. Aziz then handed over three documents to the good doctor.

1. A copy of his certificate for the Methodist Recorder Prize.
2. A letter from a Mr. Alfred Slater, BA, MA (Cantab), the head of the English Department at Kent College, his former British private boarding school, attesting to the authenticity of the certificate.
3. His GCE Examination O-level (Grade 12 equivalent) certificate showing his A grade in English.

Dr. McBride didn't say much, nor did he offer any assurances, except to say he would look into it. And at that, the meeting was disappointingly over!

Nothing further happened for two weeks after which Aziz decided to follow up with the principal's office, to no avail. Finally, in class one day, Miss Proven asked Aziz to stay behind, whereupon she let him have it, no holds barred!

"I am appalled at your cheating, lying, and plagiarism so far, and at your whining to the principal to make it look like I might be the culprit here!" she said sharply, glaring at him. "If it were up to me, I'd have you booted out, not only from this class but from the college. We don't need your kind around here!"

Sadly, she had made this into a crusade to punish the infidel until he was well and truly crushed.

But Aziz had anticipated such a response and was inured to her dastardly ways, so was ready for her this time.

"May I please speak in my defence, Miss Proven?"

She was a little taken aback at this, and grudgingly acceded to his request.

"You must have a lot of essays to mark, Ma'am, so how about I sit in the same room as you while you work, and I will write an essay in front of you, without any co-conspirator in the room? Please provide me with a choice of three topics to write on, and I will produce you a prize-winning essay in about two hours' time. How about it? And if I fail to write a satisfactory essay on the spot, I will voluntarily drop out of your class. So how about accepting my friendly challenge then, Miss?"

Miss Proven squinted at him, trying to imagine what sort of trap he was setting. Eventually she said she'd let him know, turned, and quickly walked away. A week later after class had emptied out, she actually smiled at Aziz saying, "I accept your challenge Mr. Khan. Why don't you meet me in the staff common room tomorrow afternoon where I'll be marking essays?"

Aziz was elated! His challenge was on. Hooray!

A little nervous as he entered the staff common room, Ariz scanned a typed sheet Miss Proven had handed him. The instructions on it read:

Challenge Essay: Pick one of the following three essay topics and write a 550- to 750-word essay in your own writing style. Take as much time as needed, however you cannot leave the room for any reason until your essay is handed in.

Aziz was prepared for the challenge and had figured out that he wrote about two hundred words to a page, so that meant approximately three to four written pages were required. *Quite short,* he thought. He'd have to be very concise yet make every word count. Licking the tip of his pencil, he got down to it in earnest.

Two hours later, Miss Proven glanced up from her desk at Aziz sitting across the room, and asked if he was nearly done. He replied that he needed another half hour or so, and she nodded assent.

Exactly two hours and twenty-five minutes after starting, Aziz put down his pencil, collected his stuff, and handed in his ten-page essay, turning it over as he placed it in her tray. Then thanking her, Aziz hastily walked away before she had a chance to pick up the essay and look through it.

A couple of days later, just as his physics class was ending, Aziz received a note to report to the principal's office immediately. Dr. McBride and Miss Proven looked at him sharply as he knocked and entered.

Dr. McBride wasted no time saying curtly, "You have broken the clearly stated examination rules, laddie, and frankly, I find your behaviour to be quite condescending and insolent." And he handed back the essay paper to Aziz, adorned with a large F in a circle penned in red ink!

Aziz stared at his own handwriting on the cover sheet where he had written beneath the instructions "Pick any one of the following three essay topics and write a 550- to 750-word essay"- *"Pick any one of the three following essays and mark it, if you please".*

You see, as the essays were to be quite short, Aziz had decided to write on all three topics with the intention to pick the best one at the end for submission. But once he was done and had re-read them all, he discovered that he liked them all equally. So he left the choice of picking his challenge essay to Miss Proven! Perhaps a little daring, perhaps even cheeky, but Aziz wouldn't have called it insolent!

Aziz walked away, shoulders slumped, thoroughly beaten and deflated. And he wasn't at all surprised at end of term when he received a C grade for the Expository Writing Course, his grade having been pre-ordained based on his race. Sadly, that's the way it was in 1970's Canada!

QUOD ERAT DEMONSTRANDUM: SECOND ALTERNATIVE ENDING

Aziz received a note to report to the principal's office immediately!

They looked up as he knocked and entered. Dr. McBride beamed at Aziz and Miss Proven looked a little crestfallen. Getting up, Dr. McBride walked around his desk, clasped Aziz's right hand and placing his other hand on Aziz's shoulder, guided him to a seat at the table.

"Young man, you have handily vindicated yourself and proved to us without a doubt that you are a very talented writer. Congratulations! Miss Proven?" he motioned to her to continue…

"Aziz, I agree you are indeed a good writer and with proper coaching you can become very good! I apologize for ever doubting you," she said contritely. "And I do hope that you can forgive my error in judgment."

Aziz smiled back and assured them both that there were no more hard feelings.

She went on, "I marked all three of your essays Aziz and I must tell you that I gave you an 'A' for each essay! I also gave you an 'A' for the original essay that you wrote in our first class. I guess you might say "*Quod erat demonstrandum,*" she smiled, raising her eyebrows.

Aziz followed through seamlessly, saying, "Yes, how appropriate Miss Proven: What has to be proved has been proven!"

Dr. McBride interjected, adding icing to the cake. "Aziz, we would like to make you an offer as follows: Should you decide at the end of this college year that you'd rather study for an English major instead of your sciences major, and provided you have kept up your grades in English, we would like to offer you a full scholarship to further your writing career!"

PIZZA PIZZERIA

Aziz stared into his almost full glass of lager, bought for him by his new friend Harjit sitting across him, sipping on his almost empty glass. The Legion Hall in New Westminster, BC was not busy at this time on a Monday afternoon, there were only two or three other men there—old timer veterans—sitting alone at far flung tables in the barroom staring listlessly, nursing their beers.

Harjit, a fellow student at McBride College, had quickly befriended Aziz. He had come to Canada much earlier from the Punjab at a very young age with his parents and had grown up Canadian. He certainly looked the part, speaking in Canadian colloquialisms and broadening his vowels, and not shy with inserting "eh" at the ends of sentences. He drove a fairly newish red Pontiac Firebird, dressed in check-patterned shirts and polyester pants, and always had spending money on him. He'd brought Aziz to the Legion to show him where he could buy affordable beer for forty cents a glass, not first checking if Aziz drank alcohol. Aziz did not want to insult his new friend and so took occasional sips of the horrible bitter-tasting stuff.

Harjit had a part-time weekend job during school, and full-time during school holidays, at an uncle's sawmill, in nearby Surrey. The pay at $4.50 per hour was almost double the minimum wage of $2.50 per hour. Hence the fancy sports car and never-ending supply of cash.

"You've got to look for a part-time job during school that can turn into a summer job," he counselled Aziz. "That's the way it is here in Canada."

Aziz nodded in agreement. He had been thinking just that. Some of his friends from East Africa also had part-time jobs to help pay their way through school.

Aziz with his mother and sister had spent their first couple of months in Canada at the brand-new Casa Loma Motel on Kingsway in Burnaby, BC. He had lucked in one weekend recently when on a Friday evening George the motel manager, offered him a weekend job labouring and cleaning up a messy construction site next door. Aziz had jumped at the chance to earn some cash to work on the three-storey wood-frame apartment building project, which he'd been keenly observing going up next door.

A weekend of hard labour later, Aziz received eighty dollars for his sixteen hours of back breaking work soon after he'd started at McBride College. With half the money, he'd bought a new-fangled invention called a hand calculator, a bulky rubber padded rectangular object which in addition to the four basic functions: add, subtract, multiply and divide, also had a memory bank to store numbers.

Aziz had handed over the remaining forty dollars to his mother to help pay for groceries. She'd still not found a job, despite her British education and superior English language skills, which far surpassed the average Canadian's English skills. It didn't count that she'd formerly been a director of two very large businesses in the old country. The age-old excuse provided to new immigrants of "No Canadian experience equals no Canadian job" applied equally to her as to most other new immigrants, especially if they were not of British or Western European stock.

A month later, Aziz responded to a job advertisement in the local paper: Wanted—weekend help at Pizza Pizzeria. No experience necessary; will train. Minimum wage. Call manager for appointment. Tel: 421-1234.

Aziz called the number and a Mr. Ryan told him to come to the Pizza Pizzeria located off Edmonds Street in New Westminster for a try-out that coming Friday at 2:00 p.m.

Aziz joined a mob of excited teenagers who were all asked to take a seat in the back part of the pizzeria cordoned off to customers, to fill out an application form. Terry, the assistant manager introduced himself, telling the thirty-two applicants that it was only fair to give everybody a chance at the one available job, so he had invited all callers to come down for a try-out. Each person would be given a slice of pizza and a pop for less than an hour of their time. Terry divided them into five groups of six to seven people, each group being assigned rotating tasks while everybody would be observed and graded by the three staff there: Mr. Ryan, the manager, Jimbo, the bartender, and Terry.

Aziz's group's first task was to sanitize and wash their hands and arms vigorously before chopping vegetables in the large kitchen, and after about five minutes, they rotated with another group to rolling pizza dough into exact uniformly round flat discs. Next, they learned to spread tomato paste in just the right consistency and add the right amount of vegetables and pepperoni onto the pizza.

Then they were shown how to expertly lift the pizza with large flat wooden spatulas into the 450°F oven, bake it for so many minutes, check that it was fully cooked, then remove and cut the pizza into equal slices.

In between the baking, they had to demonstrate their prowess with wet mopping the floors, washing up dishes, and bagging and taking out the garbage. Then finally they were made to serve phantom customers in the restaurant. Aziz was so busy working and enjoying himself that he hadn't noticed several applicants being thanked and asked to leave the restaurant.

Terry clapped his hands about forty-five minutes later, calling for everybody to stop what they were doing. Aziz looked around and realized there were only eighteen of them left. Fourteen had already been sent home. Terry smilingly pointed to several more people. "You, you, you, you, and you in the red T-shirt… yes, you too miss, and you and you with the green baseball cap!"

All eight of them brightened at being selected. "I'm afraid you won't be required to come back for this evening's session," Terry said. "Please see Jimbo on your way out and he'll give you a slice and a pop each. On behalf of Pizza Pizzeria, thank you very much for your interest and for your help in the kitchen today."

After they sheepishly departed, Terry turned to the remaining others. "Congratulations to all ten of you for passing our test.

However, we only have one position open at the moment, and we will make the selection this evening. We'd like all of you that are able, to return today at 6:00 p.m. for a final try-out with real customers to serve. We will also need you to tend bar and serve alcoholic drinks, so anybody under eighteen unfortunately won't be able to work here. Those under eighteen, please put up your hands." Fortunately for Aziz he had just turned eighteen!

One girl and one boy put up their hands.

"I'm so sorry; you won't be able to return," said Terry sadly. "Jimbo will give you a couple of slices and a pop each on your way out. Thank you and congratulations again on your passing the first test!"

It didn't occur to anybody to ask why Pizzeria's management had invited applicants under eighteen to the try-outs to begin with, only to unfairly axe them after they had proved their competence.

The eight finalists left after consuming their pizza and pop, promising to return at 6:00 p.m. It was now a little after 3:00 p.m., and Aziz didn't really have eighty cents to spend a second time on another round bus trip to Pizza Pizzeria. Instead, he opted to walk over to the nearby McDonalds to wait there until almost 6:00 p.m.

While at McDonalds, Aziz decided he deserved to treat himself for making it to the final eight, from the original thirty-two applicants. He went for their TV advertised special, which showcased young white teenagers sitting together and white parents with small blonde kids eating McDonalds' delicious cuisine indoors/outdoors, smiling and laughing happily, thoroughly enjoying their gourmet dining experience.

Then, a smiling blonde girl in navy blue work uniform beckoned the viewers over, speaking above the sounds of the happy customers, "Come on in to McDonalds, where you can get a burger, fries, and Coke and change from your dollar!"

This was really true! Thirty cents for a small burger, thirty cents for a small Coke, and thirty-five cents for a small fries, totalling ninety-five cents! However, if one opted for a cheeseburger instead, it cost an extra five cents for a total of one dollar plus five per cent BC Provincial Sales Tax (PST) for a total of $1.05. (PST was exempt for food purchases under a dollar.) The trick to getting a cheeseburger and avoiding the tax was to stand in line twice and buy them separately, thus avoiding the five cent tax!

At the appointed hour, Aziz and his cohorts returned to Pizza Pizzeria and were asked to wait until all eight lucky participants showed up. After a ten-minute wait, they got started. Just six of the eight people had returned. One latecomer arrived at 6:20 p.m. and was turned away for being tardy. They were told they'd be watched for an hour while they worked and served real customers. Although Aziz had never tended bar before, let alone knowing how to mix an alcoholic drink, he managed it quite well under clear instructions by Jimbo.

Within a half hour, the three bosses went into a huddle, and Mr. Ryan and Terry called the group together and announced, "Thank you, everybody. You may all go home, with the exception of Aziz!"

"You will each receive $2.50 from Jimbo, as well as a small pizza and pop for take-out. Please go into the kitchen and make the pizzas for yourselves under Jimbo's supervision."

As they filed in to the kitchen, all smiles for the cash and free food, Mr. Ryan said, "Aziz you can tend bar while Jimbo is in the kitchen, and after you can continue to work with him at the bar and in the kitchen as needed. Your pay will be $2.75 an hour to start, as you deserve slightly more than minimum wage. After three months, if your work is exemplary and acceptable to Terry and Jimbo, you will get another bump to $3.00 an hour! And you get free soft drinks and unlimited Pizza and beer at half price whenever you work a shift!

Aziz was ecstatic and worked hard and well all weekend long, enjoying the camaraderie with Jimbo, who was a kind and generous mentor. He was asked to report back the following Thursday evening, which was Jimbo's night off.

Returning on Thursday evening, Aziz was met by a squat, heavyset swarthy man called Balbinder, tending bar. Terry introduced them and left soon after. Balbinder sneered at Aziz all night long, making sure to give him all the hard and dirty tasks, while withholding any helpful advice. It was obvious to Aziz that Balbinder resented him for some unknown reason. The following two weekend nights were worked with Jimbo by Aziz's side, who apologetically explained that Balbinder was the oldest serving employee and had a special connection with Mr. Ryan. Balbinder had just cut back his shifts to four days, Monday to Thursday, hence the need to hire Aziz. Jimbo assured Aziz not to worry, that "Bal" as he was known, would come around eventually.

A few weeks went by, with Aziz working three nights every Thursday to Saturday, requiring him to team up with Balbinder on Thursdays. He continued to be unrelenting, insisting on giving Aziz all the dirty work and he continued to sneer at Aziz. Then one Wednesday evening, as Harjit was giving Aziz a ride home from college, they drove by Pizza Pizzeria, prompting Aziz to ask him to turn into the parking lot.

"Let me introduce you to my co-workers, especially Jimbo, who I have already told you about. And I'm pretty sure he will let us both buy pizza and beer at fifty per cent off—on me of course!" he laughed. They parked across from a long row of motorbikes, which Aziz had never seen before during his shifts.

Going inside, Aziz was momentarily disoriented! The place looked so different. Heavy blue smoke hung in the still air above several tables that were occupied by tough-looking bikers, eating, drinking, smoking, talking, and laughing loudly. The floor was littered with spilled food and drink and was slippery to walk on.

"Hey, Bal! What's happening, man?" Aziz greeted him brightly.

Bal sneered back, "What the freak are you doing here? You're not working till tomorrow!"

Taken aback, Aziz managed to say, "Oh I was just passing by with my buddy Harjit and thought we'd stop by to say hello to you all at work. Are Jimbo and Terry around?

"No," sneered Bal, "your pals are not in today."

Of course, he'd forgotten that Jimbo was off on Wednesdays too! And Terry never seemed to hang around too long on the night shift, returning sometimes later on at night to help close up shop. All the while, Bal completely ignored Harjit, who was of the same ethnicity and religion as him, which was quite unusual.

"So, I've met your buddy. Now scoot, unless you have business here today."

Harjit interjected. "Hold your horses, fat boy! I'm a paying customer and demand to be served, so mosey on over to my table in the opposite corner to your thuggish friends, and take our order—pronto, eh!"

Bal's stunned expression was priceless, and the two friends walked to their table! Of course, soft and pudgy Bal who sat around behind the bar all night while his assistant did all the hard work, was no physical match for a hardened sawmill worker, and he knew it!

They were digging into their hot delicious mushroom pizza, when the front doors flung open, and in walked a hard looking group of men, wearing long coats and hats. They stopped at the bar and ordered drinks. While they drank, their leader carefully scoped out each and every person in the room. Satisfied, he nodded at Bal. Bal reached under the bar, bringing out a small package wrapped in brown oilskin. While the men shielded their leader from prying eyes, he inserted the tip of a flick knife, which had suddenly appeared in his hand, into the package. Withdrawing the tip, he tasted the white powder on it, then nodded at one of his men. The man produced a package wrapped in newspaper and tied with rubber bands, pushing it across at Bal, who quickly stowed it beneath the bar.

Then the men downed their drinks, looked over at the bikers who were watching them intently, and left the restaurant.

Aziz and Harjit kept on eating their pizza dutifully, pretending nothing had happened. About five minutes later, a couple of bikers slouched on over to the bar, walking behind it while Bal stepped back out of their way. They crouched down out of sight and after a few minutes straightened up and walked out the doorway, the lead man holding a satchel. The remaining bikers followed them out, nodding at Bal who stopped the last man, an evil-looking dude with snake eyes.

Bal urgently whispered something to him. Snake Eyes continued on his way out, and just as he reached the doors, turned and fixed Aziz and Harjit with a withering stare, before exiting.

Too scared to speak about what they'd just witnessed, they gulped down their pizza in silence. Harjit threw a tenner onto the table, and they headed for the exit.

"Y'all come back now," called Bal after them. "See ya tomorrow, fucker" he added.

Walking to the car, Harjit remarked, "Did you notice that nobody, neither the long coats nor the bikers, paid for their food and drink?"

Aziz merely nodded, too stunned by the drug deal he'd just witnessed to say anything. They stopped suddenly, for there were three long-base motorcycles surrounding Harjit's Firebird, with two mean looking men sitting astride their bikes. The first, a bald flat-nosed man and the second, a tall, thin, scruffy long-haired man. The third,

Snake Eyes, stood leaning against the Firebird. He straightened up, kicking the front bumper below the radiator grill.

"They're all made of plastic these days," he said shaking his head matter-of-factly at Harjit. "Whatever happened to good ol' steel?" he said in a disgusted voice, implying that somehow it was Harjit's fault.

"This your wheels man?" he asked Harjit, who nodded silently. Suddenly, the lower bumper gave way against his 260 pounds of pressure through his boot, cracking it into two pieces.

"Oops. Didn't mean to do that. I guess they shouldn't have used plastic," he said to laughter from his two mates sitting astride their bikes.

"Why don't you get outta here and run back home kid; there's man's business I have to discuss with your pal," Snake Eyes growled at Aziz.

"I work here and I brought him here and you can say what-ever you have to say to him, in front of me!" Aziz found himself saying defiantly.

Baldy dismounted, stealthily approaching Aziz with a club in hand. "I'll take care of this little shit," he said to Snake Eyes.

"Wait!" shouted Harjit. "There's no need to involve the kid, although I can't imagine what business you have to discuss with me either. I'm just a sawmill worker. Besides, my buddies at the sawmill are real tough guys with big power saws that can cut through your bikes like a hot knife through butter. They wouldn't take kindly to you doing 'business' with me."

This was met with loud guffaws. "Oh, I'm so scared," piped in Hippie, shaking in mock terror, still astride his bike.

Harjit put his hand on Aziz's shoulder and said," Look I'll talk to them and sort out any business they have. You go on home; don't worry about anything."

Aziz looked at him miserably.

"Just go on home. I'll see you at college tomorrow; it'll be okay," he smiled and pushed Aziz away towards the exit.

Aziz hurried away, turning just once to see Snake Eyes, arms akimbo, swearing at Harjit. Aziz ran up the street, praying that he'd run into a police cruiser. As he ran into the McDonalds parking lot, Aziz hoped to find a cruiser parked there on a break, as there often was. But he was out of luck and kept on running along Kingsway Avenue towards his home, still hoping to come across a cruiser. He prayed as he ran that Harjit would be okay, telling himself that nothing bad would happen.

The next day at college, Harjit was absent from classes.

Aziz kept telling himself that Harjit was just taking the day off or probably had to work at the sawmill that day—although deep down he didn't believe it.

After college, Aziz headed straight to the pizzeria where Terry rushed up to him. Terry said he'd be working there all night long, and for Aziz to take the night off.

As Terry propelled Aziz toward the exit, his heart skipped a beat as he caught a fleeting glimpse of Bal at the bar, making as if it was business as usual. *Perhaps it's just as well,"* thought Aziz. *"I don't know how I could have worked alongside that evil man tonight.*

Aziz walked over to where Harjit's Firebird had been parked the night before and immediately spotted shards of broken glass laying on the asphalt, although there was no way to be sure they belonged to Harjit's car. Then he saw something a little more concerning, a dark reddish-black splash on the concrete bumper stop and surrounding asphalt. He kneeled down to rub it with his finger. It was thicker than paint and looked and felt like coagulated blood. Aziz felt a sudden chill run down his spine.

The next day, Harjit had still not showed up to classes. Now Aziz was getting quite panicky, but didn't know what to do. He didn't have

Harjit's home phone number, and didn't know whether to approach the college administration for his phone number. And besides, Aziz didn't have a dime in change for making the phone call either!

Harjit had once driven Aziz past his own home, pointing it out. Aziz could have taken a bus to Third Street, and walked from there. But it might take a couple of hours to get to Harjit's home and he had a 4:00 p.m. to 5:00 p.m. English class with that insufferable Miss Proven that he dare not miss! And after class he had to report to the pizzeria for work at 6:00 p.m.

In the end, Aziz, by default due to his inaction, found himself walking into the Pizzeria at 5:55 p.m. Jimbo looked surprised seeing Aziz and barely returned Aziz's greeting, avoiding small talk for the entire evening.

As they were wrapping up after a busy Friday night, Ryan the owner-manager came by and asked to see Aziz in his office.

"Aziz you are a good employee," he said, "but I'm afraid your conduct outside of work hours is very troubling"

Aziz kept silent.

"I understand you came by a couple of nights ago with a friend and created a ruckus in here, finally chasing a customer out into the parking lot and getting into a fight with him."

"No, that's a downright lie. Who told you that? I'll bet it was that snake Bal who said that!" Aziz retorted.

"Yes, Bal who I trust implicitly told me. And he was backed up by Terry who was also here working in the office and was outside having a smoke when he saw the fight."

"That's an outrageous lie. That's not what happened," shouted Aziz.

"No, Aziz, you're the one that's outrageous!" retuned Ryan. "You are terminated immediately effective now!"

"But... but... that's not how it happened. Will you please let me explain, Ryan?"

"Nothing more needs to be said. Wait outside while I total up your hours for the last two weeks and prepare your final pay envelope! That will be all; please wait outside!"

"But, Ryan. You don't understand. These guys are doing drug deals in your restaurant and we saw it all. That's why they are framing me and have beat up and possibly kidnapped my friend who's gone missing. Don't you see?"

"For the last and final time, wait outside or I will have you forcibly thrown out. NOW!"

Jimbo gave Aziz an apologetic look as he walked past him, his eyes pleading to let Aziz know that he lacked control of the situation and was sorry.

Aziz turned to Jimbo and smiled, saying, "That's okay, Jimbo. I know it's not your fault. Goodbye, my friend."

Aziz sweated over Harjit's disappearance all weekend long, unable to study, unable to do anything, tossing and turning in bed all three nights, unable to sleep.

It was a dreary, rainy Monday morning as Aziz stepped off his bus outside the college. Across the street, another bus coming from the opposite direction stopped, dropping off passengers. All were college students, it appeared. One of them limped up to him in the misty rain. Aziz gasped, for it was Harjit! He was bandaged around the head, had a plaster cast on his left arm held up in a sling, and had cuts and bruises all over his face.

As they walked slowly side by side to their physics class, Harjit said in a broken voice, his mouth revealing a few missing teeth, "I spent two nights in the hospital. They smashed the front of my car as soon as you left, hitting me on the head with a club. They then dragged me to the side of the building, all the while punching my face and body, breaking a few teeth and some ribs in the process. Once out of sight behind the building, they continued to beat me, breaking my arm with a club." They walked in silence for another minute.

"But why did they pick on you? Is it because we witnessed the drug deal and might possibly rat on Bal?" asked Aziz fearfully.

Harjit replied, "It seems they were informed by Bal, their drug dealmaker and facilitator, that I was a rival gang member who was trying to muscle in on their turf. That I was using my friendship with you, the gullible new immigrant, to gain access to the joint to observe the drug deal. I was supposedly scoping out the biker gang members in order to organize an ambush on their next visit, hijack their dope and then force Bal to sell it for me!"

Aziz, although overcome with fear and anxiety, was extremely thankful they'd both gotten away with their lives.

Just then, he spotted Miss Proven rushing by, walking haughtily across the quadrangle to her class, thinking how tame and lame she now appeared, compared to the nightmare they had just been through in his newly adopted country...

GRANDMA GOES TO JAIL!

This is a story about my mother, who everybody calls "Grandma" and I also refer to her as grandma.

Who would've thought Grandma would have ended her days in jail! She was neither a lawbreaker nor a rule breaker, nor a transgressor in any way at all! She was in fact quite the opposite, being a faithful law abiding citizen over her entire ninety years!

She was a decent, helpful, kindly soul with an adventurous spirit ready for whatever life sent her way. Always ready to lend a helpful hand to whomever needed it or didn't need it! She had a bright, inquisitive, and inquiring mind and was on top of her game.

I mean, anybody who has faithfully read the *Readers Digest* for seventy-five years cover to cover and answers questions by Alex Trebek on *Jeopardy* for thirty-five years couldn't be all that bad!

In 1932, she was born Ayesha Kassam to Indian migrant parents in Uganda. She was the fifth of seven children and grew up in a Walton's Mountain-type loving, co-existing, and busy household. She was as fussy and religious as Grandma Walton, as hard working and generous as Liv, as hands-on and pragmatic as Mary Ellen, as pretty and coquettish as Erin, and as precocious and talkative as little Lisbeth. Especially talkative. Boy, she never lost that trait; she sometimes drove us crazy with her maddening, non-stop yet irrefutably logical verboseness!

Being Type A adventurous, Grandma participated in all activities at school. She took as many extra classes as they would allow her. She participated in each and every sporting activity. She was a key member of the debating society, she acted in *dialok*6, or school plays, she participated in dances, and she organized school events. She even served food in the staff commissary. She was co-head prefect with the school jock.

She confided to us that one big advantage of participating in all sporting events has been to meet and speak with the male captains of all the teams! In those days in Indian culture, it wasn't easy for girls to speak openly with boys. One had to find a legitimate reason such as on sports teams, and to rely on "signal" communication between boy and girl. The signals had to be ambiguous so that a girl or more

---

6   Gujerati word *dialok* meaning play, from the English word "dialogue"

importantly her male relatives could not accuse a boy of outright forwardness or lewdness.

When a girl liked a boy, she would glance in his general direction but not directly at him. She would then slowly and innocently brush back loose hairs (real or imaginary) off her forehead with two fingers signalling *pan bo*, meaning "us two," all the while rewarding him with a sly sideways look. The most physical they ever got was with sly, coy looks and "accidental" brushing of hands.

After graduating high school, since there was no higher education available in Uganda, Grandma went to work in an office where she honed her shorthand and typing skills. At the age of seventeen she became the second Indian woman in Uganda to get a driver's licence and the first female teenager ever!

She passed on her ambitiousness to me – her son, many years later when she taught me to drive at the age of fourteen. I subsequently earned my driver's licence at the age of sixteen!

In 1970's Africa, there were no hard and fast age limitations. And well before my time, one of Grandma's two brothers was a part-time truck driver, making deliveries for their father's business at the ripe old age of twelve!

Fast forwarding, Grandma married at twenty-four, moved to neighbouring Tanzania where my dad lived, had two kids, an illustrious career, and an amazing life. While raising my sister and I, Grandma went to classes and learned to speak Swahili properly (and not pigeon Swahili many Indians happily settled for). She took French classes too, and joined several charities and social service organizations.

As my sister and I got older, Grandma's thirst for learning unabated, she convinced my father to allow her to go to England for half a year, enrolling in the Pitman Secretarial School in London. Upon her triumphant return home, laden with gifts for all of us, including for our entire extended family, she took up a posting as executive assistant to a British CEO of a large coffee cooperative. And she simultaneously continued on with her charity work. The corporate exposure ultimately prepared her for coping with my father's untimely death at the age of forty-three. She single-handedly wound up and negotiated the sale of all our family businesses and then moved us to England—all achieved amid the country's socialist government upheavals. We eventually moved to Canada, first to Vancouver and later, one by one, to Toronto.

Grandma's first priority was to find us suitable rental housing in Vancouver. It wasn't an easy thing, for as soon as a landlord determined we were new immigrants or met us and saw our brown skins, the vacancy suddenly and mysteriously evaporated! We eventually got lucky and a Mr. Papadopoulos agreed to rent us his little bungalow on Royal Oak Avenue.

He imparted a pep talk to me once saying, "When I came to Canada seven years ago, I didn't speak English and couldn't even hold a screwdriver, OKAY! I went to night classes to become an electrician and to learn English while working as an apprentice in the daytime and moonlighting on evenings and weekends, OKAY!

"Now, after just seven years of hard work, I am a qualified master electrician and run my own business, OKAY! *Fok,* I own two homes now: my house and your house, OKAY!" he said, flashing his gold front tooth. "But don't worry; you have come here with education and you speak good English and you are *jung,* OKAY! *Fok,* now all you have to do is apply yourself and work hard and the rest will come to you, as it did to me in this beautiful land of opportunity, Canada, OKAY!"

In time, Grandma got back into her groove and was soon working nights and weekends helping others. She was very active in our community helping the less fortunate. She even joined the matrimonial committee, where she matched up singles in need of a spouse! She also joined the Vancouver Ladies Lions Club in Shaughnessy and was the first Asian woman once again, eventually getting elected as president of the club. All of these services of course were performed on a voluntary basis without pay or compensation. It was just her spirit of adventure and service to all!

Fast forward many years later again and we are all now settled in Toronto. My sister with her family, me with mine, and Grandma with her new husband. Grandma's thirst for knowledge and service for humanity, however, continued on. Her newest self-learning was the science of nutrition, which she self-taught and applied to healthy alternatives in Indian and everyday cooking. She gave lectures to community groups, mainly seniors and new immigrants, on how to prepare healthy Indian meals as well as wholesome Canadian lunches.

One such community group head nominated Grandma for the city of Scarborough healthy living award for her selfless service and difference she had made to the lives of immigrant women and their families.

"Why only to women?" she was smilingly asked by the mayor as he pinned the medal on her, to which she replied, "The Aga Khan Development Network has an adage: Educate a boy and you educate one person. Educate a girl, however, and you educate an entire family!"

Nonetheless, there were always male participants in her free nutrition classes and food tastings, including doctors and other medical professionals!

Grandma was also an accomplished politician, navigating relationships with my father's family as well as with her new husband's family, doing her best to please everybody. She did this with sensitivity and genuine concern for all. She was also very forgiving and accepting of human foibles.

I remember when she lost a substantial amount of jewellery. She discovered the loss a day after her Asian house cleaner's visit. She immediately called her cleaner and spoke to her in a very non-accusatory manner, saying that she had misplaced some of her jewellery and was hoping she might have come across it and put it somewhere safe.

The cleaner laughed and replied insensitively, "No. Why would I have come across it? I have no idea where it is, you misplaced it; that's on you!"

On cleaning day the following week, Grandma asked her cleaner again very nicely to help her look for her jewellery, promising her a reward for helping find it. The cleaner performed a perfunctory look around saying, "No, I don't see it anywhere. You must've left it somewhere else outside of your house!"

Grandma was driven to tears explaining that among the gold and diamonds she had a sentimental gift from her first husband, my father, a large blue green Tanzanite ring. This didn't sway the cleaner who maintained her deadpan expression. We counselled Grandma to immediately file a police report and to try and get a search warrant for a police search of the cleaner's premises.

Grandma replied, "She's here on a work visa and is in the process of bringing her teenage son over to live with her. I even helped her fill out the application form! If she's found guilty, I don't want to risk ruining her reunification with her son and ruin his chances at a new life in Canada. And if she's innocent, I would hate to put her through this."

"Grandma, but if she's guilty," I said, "you'll get your jewellery back and she'll rightfully pay for it!"

Grandma sighed. "Turn the other cheek, my son. If she did take it, she obviously needs it much more than I do. Let's leave her alone. God will be her judge."

Here's another adage: " Friendship is like a China vase; once broken can be mended but the crack is always there." Obviously after that, Grandma stopped using the cleaner's services until some years later, when Grandma was in a bind for a cleaner and in desperation called the lady.

She dutifully came in to work as though nothing had happened in the intervening years. Upon arriving she said, "I have to leave early today as I'm preparing for my son's engagement party. He is getting married to a beautiful European girl. I need to dress up, do my hair, and wear my jewelry including my beautiful Tanzanite ring.

Grandma looked at her in shock!

She smiled back cattily at Grandma saying, "Yes I have a Tanzanite ring; do you think that you are the only person that can own one?"

We didn't know what to make of this when Grandma narrated it later. Was the cleaner just being mean and hurtful, or did she take the ring and other jewelry knowing there was nothing we could possibly do about it now, years later?

Grandma is a nonagenarian now. She turned ninety this year!

Her husband has passed away, her knees hurt, she is a little wobbly, and has finally agreed to using a walker. She has failing eyesight and unable to read newsprint and letters anymore, her hearing is not so good, and she tires quickly. And in this Covid-19 pandemic environment her social activities are now very curtailed.

She lives by herself, fiercely independent in her large and tasteful condominium. Grandma and her seventy-year-young bridge partner were their twin-condo bridge champions a few Christmases ago, but now there is no more bridge. Her daily evening prayer and social trips to the nearby Mosque are now also pre-Covid history.

Kids, spouses, and grandkids all try and pitch in to keep her company, do her shopping, take her meals, take her on walks and drives and outings. My daughter punctiliously calls Grandma each morning for her daily wake-up call and to make sure all is well with her. My sister and I get her groceries and speak with her every night to ease her loneliness.

I now have power of attorney over her financial and tax matters, to navigate her through the unseeing documents and related issues, but one item slipped by us recently, involving the Canada Revenue Agency (CRA). They sent her a demand letter for a rebate for a $104.00 HST payout made to her, typically paid to low-income earners like Grandma.

She missed passing the letter on to us. She just plain forgot at her age. CRA was not sympathetic.

Accordingly, a sheriff was dispatched and promptly arrested her, taking ninety-year-old Grandma to jail while we were unfortunately away! Imagine that—Canadians in Canada don't have to put up with former KGB thugs or Putin's totalitarian Russia or Communist China's human rights abuses or Trump's narcissist and egotistical presidency—no this is a democratic, fair, reasonable, ethical, law abiding and compassionate Canada! So how did this come to pass?

Well, that fateful day there was a loud insistent banging on the front door of her apartment. Grandma finally heard the knocking when she turned the TV down during the commercial break on the *Jeopardy* rerun. She shuffled over to the door and asked in a small voice, "Yaar, who's there? Why are you banging on my door, eh?"

"Ma'am, will you please open the door," answered a muffled voice.

She opened it a crack with the chain still on and peered at a large masked, uniformed man in a wide-brimmed hat and a metal star pinned to his tunic.

"I'm Sheriff Dan Lawson, ma'am. I need to talk to you about your GST bill owing; will you please open the door?"

Now, Grandma was old but she was no fool. She'd heard about fake callers purporting to be with government agencies, who were fraudsters trying to bilk old folks and new immigrants out of their money.

"I'm sorry I can't let you in, but I can call security if you'd like them to come up and talk to you," she said politely.

The man's face darkened, but he said, "Go ahead. I'll wait out here then."

Grandma shuffled back to her phone while lamenting missing her precious *Jeopardy* show, which had resumed, but taking comfort from Alex Trabek's kindly, familiar voice. She spoke with Carl at the security desk and he immediately came upstairs to her unit. After speaking with the stranger and inspecting his ID, Carl assured Grandma of his authenticity and she let them both inside, wanting Carl there, just in case.

Sheriff Lawson stood just inside the doorway while he tried to explain to Grandma the issue of the missing $104.

"You're not speaking clearly," she said. "Please slow down and don't slur your words. Please face me properly and pull your mask down when talking. I'm hard of hearing, and I need to see your lips mouthing your words to hear you better"

She moved back several feet as he complied with his mask removal, worn of course to observe "social distancing." regulations.

Although Grandma did have hearing aids, she normally didn't wear them while alone in her apartment. He explained his mission again to which Grandma nodded and replied, "My son looks after my tax and banking matters, and I'm afraid he is away for a few days. Can I have him call you as soon as he is back?"

"Well, why don't we call your son right now since I am here?" he said a little peevishly.

"The problem is, he is away up north in an area where they do not have cellphone coverage," she replied, "but he will be back in two or three days. Can't it wait?"

"Hold on let me check with the collections office," he answered.

Grandma kept glancing back at the TV wondering if she should make a dash to watch the *Final Jeopardy* round while he was yakking on the phone but thought better of it. The sheriff's telephone conversation was quite long and animated and he finally holstered his phone saying, "There is another matter that has just come up regarding tax evasion on your tax return, Ma'am. Do you know what I am referring to?"

Grandma stared at him in shock at such a preposterous accusation! "I told you, young man, you need to speak to my son about all this. I can give you his cell number and you are welcome to call and leave him a message."

By now, Carl had had enough of this assault on the sweet old lady and tried to politely steer the sheriff out, but he barked, "Stop, or I will arrest you for handling an officer of the law!" Carl reared back as though struck by a black mamba, while the sheriff called his office again.

"I'm sorry, Ma'am" he finally said. "The office cannot accept your excuses and has asked me to take you in where they can question you properly about the two charges they have made. Please get your stuff and come with me; we shan't be too long, I hope."

"But there is nothing more I can tell you. Why won't they wait to speak with my son?" Grandma wailed.

"Ma'am, I cannot speak for them. I have been instructed to take you in to our office for questioning. Please collect your coat and anything else you wish to bring. I will wait outside."

In her shock and disorientation at this terrifying turn of events, Grandma totally forgot either her walker or cane, her hearing aids, her prayer rosary and her medication—a selection of twenty-two pills in various shapes, sizes, textures, and colours to be taken at various times and at prescribed intervals each day. Poor Grandma also clean forgot to go to the bathroom!

So, they questioned grandma at the sheriff's jailhouse, where she basically got tongue-tied and stone deaf in the state she was in. They determined they would have to hold her until her son returned to sort this out and pay the delinquent amounts plus interest on her tax issues. Furthermore, if her son was also found to be culpable, he too would have to pay a fine or go to jail!

Sheriff Lawson reluctantly led Grandma to her cell, making sure to give her the larger and more comfortable of the two empty cells. He unlocked the door and gently led her in as she wept silently at the indignity and shame of it and out of fear for being locked up for no apparent reason. The cot was large enough for her tiny frame and the mattress, although hard, was not thick enough for Grandma. She soon recovered her composure and got the sheriff to bring her the mattress from the other cell to add to hers.

She surveyed her cell, critically asking, "What's that tin bucket doing there?"

He replied, "Oh that's a night washroom in case you need to throw up or go in the middle of the night."

"Take it out of here; it stinks. Just give me the key before you go to sleep," she said scrunching up her nose, "so that I can go to the washroom at the end of the hallway. At my age, I need to go two or three times at night."

Sheriff Lawson nodded. He wasn't going to argue anymore if he was to get any sleep he thought. Besides, he couldn't imagine a ninety-year-old grandma escaping and becoming a fugitive on the lam!

Her knees were now beginning to give and he loaned her an unloaded rifle to use as a crutch. She told him that without her pills, she'd most likely start howling at night but a large bag of Cheezies usually prevented that, as she'd stuff her mouth with them each time she felt a howl coming on. The obliging sheriff got her a large bag of Cheezies, a thermos of warm water, another thermos of green tea, a packet of her favourite digestive biscuits, some Tylenol, and a string of beads to use as a rosary—all purchased from the 7-11 across the road.

Well, as luck would have it, the following evening I happened to be driving in a spot where there was brief cellphone coverage, picked up the sheriff's message, turned the car around, and high-tailed it straight back to Toronto, leaving my family in camp. I tried calling the sheriff's office on my way down that night but there was no answer.

I got to Toronto soon after midnight but didn't know where my mother was being held, so exhausted from the long night's drive, I went home to bed. I was up again at seven and made calls to the sheriff's office and to my local police station. I finally got connected and headed down to the jailhouse in Scarborough to spring grandma out of jail!

Walking into the jailhouse that morning wasn't what I was expecting at all. I had visions of a western movie jailhouse with dirty cells and miserable prisoners, watched over by a dozing sheriff leaning back in his chair, legs outstretched on the desk, rifle on his chest. Instead, there was a normal office reception area with a welcoming receptionist smiling up at me. I stated my business as she smilingly pressed a buzzer.

Sheriff Lawson walked out of his modern glass-walled office and greeted me heartily. "You must be Ayesha's kid. I've been trying to get a hold of you for the last couple of days," he went on as he pumped my hand in a friendly greeting. He looked fiftyish and I smiled at being called a kid seeing that I was a little older than him myself!

I explained how I had been northeast of Algonquin Park and how I had frantically driven down, leaving my family there as soon as I got his message.

"You might have made a wasted trip," he smiled back with a twinkle in his eye. "I don't think she's ready to leave yet. But let's first meet our accountant to sort this issue out."

Mr. Ronald Brimble was a short stocky man with round glasses and a double chin framing a sweaty surly face. Any dealings with him didn't appear to portend well. He immediately cut to the chase. "Mrs. Ayesha Allawi, who I believe is your mother, is charged with two counts of defrauding CRA, which I shall elaborate on in a minute," he glowered.

"Bail is set at five thousand dollars should you wish to post it, failing which we shall hold her in this jail for a maximum of twenty-eight days, after which she will be transferred to a federal penitentiary," he said smugly. "Furthermore, any days after tonight spent in this jail will be charged out at the rate of $245.50 plus $50 feeding cost, plus HST, per day."

I looked on, silently seething but didn't dare interrupt.

"She is charged as follows. One, for receiving a GST/HST rebate from CRA and failing to refund the sum of $104.00 that was obtained under false pretences. Two, she failed to report income on the sale of securities in a publicly listed corporation named Trans Canada Bank for net proceeds amounting to $612.15.

"If convicted, in addition to the amounts owing plus interest, she could be liable to a fine of up to ten thousand dollars for a first offence and/or a prison term of six months. However, given her advanced age, it is unlikely she will be sent to a federal penitentiary unless the circumstances are so extenuating as to deem her a public threat," he ended with a flourish and a look of infinite mercy on his pudgy face.

"Well," I said, "I'd like to see my mother right away and have my lawyer come down to sort this out before we pay any monies to the Crown."

"By all means, Sir," he said. Turning to the sheriff, he said, "Dan why don't you take the gentleman in back to see his mother and lawyer?"

I followed the sheriff down a long corridor to the back of house area and we entered a large common room. I wasn't at all surprised at the sight that unfolded before us: two men and a woman were playing cards at a table and a large beefy man in just a pair of gym shorts was lying on his stomach on a wooden table. You could just see the top of the crack above the waistband of his shorts amid the thick black curly hairs and overlapping tattoos, and there she was: Grandma!

Standing over him, kneading his exposed back and softly purring, "Now, just relax and enjoy the effleurage as I massage you in concentric circles... And don't worry about your kids. I'm sure they are just fine and doing well at school." Grandma suddenly slapped his backside, instructing him to turnover. He complied, his wobbly hairy stomach jiggling its ample folds.

"I've been telling you, Ernie, you really need to watch your calories and cut down from five thousand to two thousand a day, while cutting down mostly on eating carbs. Remind me to send you a carb counter disc after I'm out of this hellhole!" she smiled. "And Donna, you need to pay attention to what I'm saying too." Grandma raised her voice glancing at the card playing lady who in addition to facial tattoos, had a number of rings clipped through her ears, nose, and lips.

"Yes, Ma'am, Grandma, I'll be sure to do that," replied Donna in a mannish and gravelly voice, expertly spitting a wad of tobacco into a spittoon on the floor, brown tobacco juice running down the sides of her mouth and onto her chin. She wiped the back of her bandaged hand over her chin and in turn wiped her hand on the side of her baggy canvas pants.

Grandma turned as we approached, exclaiming with surprise, "Why, Sonny, what are you doing here?"

"Hi ma. How are you? Are you okay? Are you taking your pills?" the words anxiously spilled out as I gave my mother a hug.

Tattoo glared at me for interrupting his massage. Grandma made the introductions all around and neither Ernie, aka Tattoo, nor I were particularly impressed with one another. She didn't seem to notice as she continued massaging his sagging breasts saying brightly, "I'm glad you've come to get me, Son. I have a Zoom meeting at 2:00 this afternoon. I'll just be another ten minutes here before collecting my stuff."

"Sure ma, take your time with Ernie. See you in a bit," I replied as I turned away, reassured that she was okay. I called Cynthia, my lawyer, who arrived at the jailhouse within the hour.

As it turned out, the first charge of HST fraud was all about my failing to file Grandma's latest tax return, thereby failing to report her low income, leading CRA to assume she was not entitled to the $104.00 HST rebate she'd received. The remedy was to sign a statement agreeing to file her tax return within twenty-eight days after which CRA would re-assess her. Provided her income was below a threshold amount, she wouldn't have to refund the deemed overpayment.

The second charge pertained to some very old and forgotten shares she had owned in Trans Canada Bank, which I had recently discovered and which she had generously gifted in kind to a charity for orphans. We had assumed since the amount was relatively small and had been donated to a charity there was no tax reporting required. After all, Grandma had not benefited in any way from the stock's disposition. Again, the undertaking was made to report the charitable donation and disposition on her tax return within twenty-eight days and all would be good. Any capital gains would likely be offset by the charitable donation tax credit she would receive.

Leaving the jailhouse, Grandma held on to my hand for support in the absence of her makeshift rifle crutch. Turning to Sheriff Lawson at the door, she promised to get back to him real soon about "that thing" they'd discussed. As we drove away, I asked what the heck that was all about.

Grandma replied, "Danny has been single since his wife passed several years ago and is now ready to meet another woman. Luckily, I just happen to know that Camila at our bridge club, who is about Dan's age, is also looking to remarry! So, I plan to hook 'em up. I think they'll make a great couple; don't you? You remember Camila, don't you? She's the lady who drives the Jeep that you so admire."

REVELBUSH!

———

The rhythmic hypnotic sounds of the train rocking sideways and clacking its way northeast from Vancouver were easy to fall asleep to, as Aziz lay comfortably in his sleeper bunk, in his own little first-class compartment. The train's whistle emitted a long haunting sound to warn off animals or interlopers that might be asleep on the tracks—drunken or otherwise—as they passed through a small unnamed town, rumbling over a railway crossing in the middle of the night!

This somehow reminded Aziz of the army trains crisscrossing Siberia across a frozen wintery whiteness in the movie *Dr. Zhivago*, and he couldn't help wondering if the good doctor's sultry Lara might show up at any moment! Or perhaps Tatiana Romanova, the elegantly coiffed Bond girl in *From Russia with Love* might make an appearance in his compartment... With those pleasant thoughts, the clickety-clack, clickety-clack sounds, and side-to-side rocking of the train, he fell asleep.

Aziz woke at sunrise, his window shade up, letting in the sun's welcoming morning rays of light. He lay on his bunk reflecting on the incredible series of coincidences and plain old luck, that had brought him here on this new adventure. They say that good things, luck and coincidences come in threes... to wit...

First coincidence: Having injured his ankle in a workplace accident at his summer job at a fabrication plant in Vancouver, to avoid putting him on workers' compensation, they reassigned Aziz to odd job pick-ups and deliveries for the company.

Second coincidence: While driving past a Canada Manpower Centre office on the outskirts of Vancouver on light delivery duties, Aziz decided on a whim to take the empty parking spot in front. Ignoring the meter as he had no change, Aziz hobbled up the stairs on his injured ankle to the Manpower office, spotting the job card posted on the notice board right away—which seemed to be meant just for him!

The job card read:

Inspector REQUIRED IMMEDIATELY for Earthworks Wing Dam construction—construction inspection experience required and/or must be third year geology student with good understanding of geotechnical concepts.

Location: Revelstoke Dam Project, Revelstoke, BC. Term: 12-months. Pay: $10.48 per hour; must be member of TechWork union local 999 or be willing to join.

Aziz thought to himself, *Heck I have taken two geology elective courses at McBride College in my first year. That should qualify... no harm in asking about it... right?*

First stroke of luck: Aziz somehow managed to convince the bored Manpower counsellor that he was qualified for the job, especially since the job had been posted over a week ago and nobody had been brave enough to apply for it yet. The counsellor made the call to the employer, who asked to speak with Aziz. After vetting Aziz's dubious credentials, the gravelly voice said, "You better get downtown right away to see me, be here by 4:30 or 4:45 latest as we close at 5:00."

This was, of course, impossible... it was now 4:13 p.m. and downtown Vancouver was at least a forty-minute drive away during normal hours, but it was now almost rush hour! The voice at the other end, a Mr. Meyer, sensed Aziz's hesitation and asked what the problem was.

After Aziz explained the logistics, he responded, "Well, if you can't get down here today, the job will likely be gone by tomorrow morning. Tell you what: I'll wait for you until ten to five, five to five at latest, and if you're not here by then, you can forget about it. There'll be no tomorrow. Understood?"

Second stroke of luck: Aziz wrote down the address, thanked the man, thanked the CMC counsellor, and flew down the stairs, risking further injury to his slow healing ankle. Going outside there was no parking ticket issued yet by "Ticket Uncle"—thank God!

The race was on! Aziz raced all the way downtown, dodging in between cars, honking, running amber lights, driving like his life was at stake. By ten to five, Aziz was parking illegally in prime rush hour on a side street behind the building. He limped into the offices, his ankle now throbbing, and was ushered by the receptionist into Mr. Meyer's office.

"Take a seat. Why are you limping?" asked the man seated across the desk, without preamble.

Aziz explained it was a temporary thing, a workplace accident, and that he would be fully recovered by next week. After some perfunctory questions, mostly a repetition of what had been discussed over the phone, the man opened a ledger and grunted, "How would you like to travel to Revelstoke, by bus or train?"

Aziz started; not sure he was hearing correctly. "But… but… do you mean I have the job?" Aziz stammered incredulously.

Mr. Meyer smiled back. "Sure, why not? That's what you're here for isn't it?"

"But are you sure I can do the job?" blurted Aziz, now full of self-doubt.

"Sure, you can; it's only an inspector's job!"

"Yes, but I've never been an inspector before" Aziz explained, his voice raised in alarm, almost willing the man to change his mind.

"Don't worry; you can do it. You have the right college education, determination, and willingness to work. From what I've seen, all a Hydro inspector ever does is stand around all day long with his finger up his arse and try to look important!" He smiled again.

"The job pays $10.48 an hour, plus room and board. You'll stay in a camp and all travel expenses will be paid. Any overtime required of you will be paid at double time, but you'll have to join the union first. Will that be a problem?"

Aziz shook his head in disbelief.

"So how do you want to travel—by bus or by train? You don't have to pay for it; we will," he went on, reading Aziz's mind, just as Aziz was wondering which might be the cheaper way to travel.

"By train, if that's okay" replied Aziz.

"Good. It's an overnight trip and takes about eighteen hours. Do you want a second-class seat or a first-class sleeper cabin?"

Aziz hesitated, thinking it might be a trick question, then tentatively replied, "By sleeper?"

"Good answer," he said. "I would have chosen that too! Right then, I'm booking you for tomorrow, Thursday evening's train. That work for you?"

Aziz raised his eyebrows in alarm. "No, sir, that's too soon for me. I need to give one weeks' notice at work and make some arrangements for my family before I can leave. But I should be able to leave in a week's time, say by next Thursday?" he asked, well knowing that he also had to give his ankle enough time to heal properly. "Or a little sooner maybe," Aziz hastily added, seeing the look on Mr. Meyer's face.

"Sorry; they require this job filled in Revelstoke right away. We can't wait until next week. The best I can do is to send you there on Friday evening's train he said firmly. You'll get there on Saturday around lunchtime, get yourself oriented, and settled in camp to start work first thing Monday morning.

Aziz hesitated.

"Make up your mind. If you're going, I have to fill in your application for joining the union and fax it out before 5:30 p.m. today and also apply for approval for your train ticket," he said, pointedly looking at his watch, which read 5:17 p.m.

Aziz managed to negotiate an additional day, departing on Saturday evening, while desperately wondering how he was going to manage winding up all his affairs, so soon, so fast!

"You'll be paid one day's pay for travel time. That's seven and a half hours pay, maximum travel pay, union rules. And I don't want you to file for overtime pay either, seeing that you'll be travelling on Saturday—understood?" He went on. "You'll need to take your own steel-toed work boots, which I noticed you're wearing, so that shouldn't be a problem."

Third stroke of luck: Aziz nodded vigorously, thinking, *This is insane. First they are hiring and paying me, a first-year college student, $10.48/hour—more than four times the minimum wage! Then they are paying me to travel first class by train and on top of that, they're also paying me a day's pay for travel only, without doing any work! Of course, I wouldn't charge overtime for that; how could he think that of me!*

After preparing and signing a whole bunch of papers by hand (no computers in those days) and after calling the railway station for a train booking, Mr. Meyer instructed Aziz to go directly to the CN Rail station on Main Street that Saturday by 6:00 p.m. to pick up his ticket, for his departure time at 7:30 p.m. He handed Aziz his work papers to hand in to the site office administrator as well as papers for the union rep upon arrival. Finally, he reverently handed Aziz his very own union card and union hard hat stickers!

Mr. Meyer stood up to shake hands with Aziz and to walk him out…

Third coincidence: it was then that Aziz realized Mr. Meyer also walked with a limp, except his was pronounced and permanent. His right leg appeared a couple of inches shorter than the left leg! Aziz couldn't help but wonder if his own limp had endeared him and been instrumental in winning him this fabulously paid job!

The next day was a mad rush to quit, wrap up his job at the fab plant (they were not pleased) and reorganize his personal affairs in double quick time.

And this is how Aziz found himself in a private compartment looking out the train window somewhere in the wilderness of beautiful British Columbia, watching a glorious rising sun and what promised to be a fantastic adventure!

After breakfasting in the restaurant car, Aziz walked back to his compartment, swaying to the sideways movement of the coach in the narrow corridor. His thoughts once again returned to *From Russia with Love* wondering this time if Malik the brutish KGB agent was lying in wait to pounce on him in his cabin.

Around 1:00 p.m., Aziz breathed in the fresh bracing mountain air with Mt. Revelstoke as a backdrop, as he stood waiting for a taxi outside the railway station. They soon drove onto a wide gravel road through freshly cleared land, cutting a swathe through the tall trees. The glinting and sparkling mica dust and chips on the road and in the rocks all around him took some getting used to as Aziz squinted to protect his eyes from the glare.

They drove through the gatehouse and the guard radioed ahead. Aziz had a short wait at the check-in hut where he was met by the TechWork site union rep. He was a short skinny fellow dressed in cowboy hat, fancy leather boots, studded black jeans, sequined shirt with metal-tipped collars, and a bolo tie around his neck. He walked with a strut and talked hurriedly in short spurts in between cigarette puffs and hollow coughs.

"Welcome to Revelbush," he wheezed with a snide grin. "You can call me Clint," he said, lighting a fresh cheroot. "You are officially now in bush country, heh, heh, heh." After signing Aziz in and issuing him a green laminated camp cafeteria card, he remarked, "What's that fat orange roll you have there with your luggage?"

"I brought my sleeping bag along just in case," replied Aziz sheepishly, now realizing that he would be housed in those incredibly long rows of trailers in the trailer city seen in the distance.

Clint let out a loud chesty laugh. "You didn't think being in camp meant you'd be sleeping out in the open around a campfire, toasting marshmallows, singing 'Kumbaya' and huddling in a sleeping bag, did you, heh, heh heh?!" He bent over in a bout of coughing.

Aziz just smiled in answer as Clint radioed for a teamster driver to take Aziz into camp.

"Oh, you don't need to call a driver for me," said Aziz hastily. "Can't I just ride back with you in your pick-up if you're going that way? Or I can just walk over?" Aziz added noting the disapproving look on Clint's face.

"You've obviously never been near a union project before, kid. It doesn't work that way. I am not allowed to carry passengers—only teamster drivers are allowed to drive workers around the site. I'd get my union into big trouble if I drove you, as I'd be taking work away from the Teamsters Union members. Savvy?"

"Well… it's good they work on Sundays too then, which is handy for me otherwise I'd have to walk," nodded Aziz.

"Oh, no. Nobody's working today," grinned Clint. We get paid a four-hour call-out to check you in. That's four hours at double time pay, i.e., a full day's pay for disturbing us on our day of rest. Standard union agreement rules on Hydro projects. Me, the teamster driver, the camp manager for issuing you a room key—all of us!"

"But that's like less than a half hour of work each!" exclaimed Aziz.

"Yes, and this prevents the employer from exploiting the workers in camp by calling them back to work whenever and however often they feel like it," Clint quipped back before coughing again and spitting onto the ground.

Aziz felt guilty and awful for costing his employer so much money just to check him into camp, which the employer was also paying for. Thinking about it further, he reasoned that he himself had no idea arriving on a Sunday would entail such horrific expense. Mr. Meyer ought to have known and should have asked him to travel on Sunday evening, arriving Monday versus travelling and arriving on the weekend!

Aziz checked in to his tiny room in Bunkhouse B. It wasn't large or lavish by any means, an eight-foot square space crammed with a tiny bed and thin mattress, a bedside table with a tiny lamp, a rough wood desk and chair, and a wardrobe. No Bible in the desk drawer. The tiny window looked out onto a window of another bunkhouse several feet away.

Aziz spent the rest of the afternoon walking around camp, nodding, and smiling back at the few workers who had not left camp for the weekend. There was water, coffee, and cookies to be had on long tables just inside the cafeteria entrance, which was a relief. He wished that he could at least start reading through the project drawings and specifications to get a jump on his work, but there was nobody in the offices on a Sunday afternoon.

Later that evening, Aziz now quite hungry, walked over to the large sprawling dining room at the sound of the first bell, rung fifteen minutes before the final bell when the inner doors would be thrown open to hungry diners. By now, most camp residents were back from their weekend, in time for a free slap-up dinner. A trio of middle-aged guys waiting outside the doors with Aziz struck up a conversation.

"Hey, young fellow. You mast be a-new, I haven't a-sin you a-round a-before," smiled one of them, speaking in a very old country Italian accent.

"Yes, I just arrived this afternoon from Vancouver," Aziz smiled back.

After introducing themselves and their jobs, one of them, a short stocky man with a thick German accent asked, "*Ja* so how much they paying you for your inspector's job?"

"Well, I work for Hydro, not for the contractor," replied Aziz, trying to deflect the question, sensing this conversation was not leading anyplace useful.

"*Jawohl*, but you inspector's work for a union *hein*? Otherwise, you wouldn't be living in camp, *ja*?"

The others looked at Aziz smiling expectantly." Well… I guess they're going to pay me around $10 an hour," replied Aziz reluctantly.

"*Got im Himmel!*" (God in Heaven) exclaimed the German. "How old are you and how long you been in Canada?" he demanded.

With a sense of increasing foreboding, Aziz replied, "About twenty-five years old and about four years in Canada." Aziz was cagey and stretching the truth by five years in the first instance and two years in the second instance.

"Fockh! I'm fifty and I been in Canada ten years now and I'm only making $7.37 an hour!" he exploded. "I work my ass off as a driller's assistant, getting dirty and muddy and getting broken fingernails all day long, and I even lost half a finger one time. See here!"

He held up his left hand. The little finger had been sliced in half, having gotten pinched between steel drill casings in his haste to get them connected.

Aziz reared back, a little shocked, not knowing how to respond. He thought to himself, *I mean how can I tell the guy politely that it's education, brains, a good command of English and luck, not brawn and broken English, that pays better?*

The two Italians smiled at Aziz reassuringly, silently willing him not to worry about their pal's rude outburst.

Suddenly a harsh voice yelled out: "What the fuck are you doing here?"

They all turned to the tall, lanky, ugly brute who had walked up to them and was glaring at Aziz. Aziz swiftly swivelled his head to his left and to his right, thinking the brute was talking to someone beside him.

"Yes, you fucker, what the fuck are you doing here?" he repeated angrily, pointing a massive gnarled index finger in Aziz's face. It seemed like he was looking down the barrel of a smoking gun. Yet it almost sounded as if the brute knew Aziz from somewhere…

Aziz gulped, processing this verbal, almost physical assault before replying in a tiny voice, "I work here"

"Who for?" he demanded.

"Hydro; I'm an inspector for the new Earthfill wing dam," Aziz clarified.

"Pah!" the brute threw up his hands and stalked off grumbling under his breath.

The old Italians once again smiled consolingly at Aziz, "Donta warry about a-him," they said. "He a-drilla, and he like to acta taff, he dinta min no-thin by it."

Later, after a slap-up Sunday roast beef dinner with all the trimmings, Aziz returned to his tiny room. He stayed up late to read a gripping novel titled *The Last Canadian*, which he had purloined from the camp library. He eventually fell asleep, having temporarily pushed back the memory of the evening's unpleasant encounters with the brutish driller and the pissed-off driller's assistant.

Aziz slept fitfully through the night, constantly disturbed by the nocturnal sounds coming through the paper-thin wall partitions in-between the tiny rooms. A coughing fit followed by hawking and spitting, the sound of harsh guttural voices arguing, the long, loud continuous farts—sometimes rude, sometimes musical, the sounds of a door opening and slamming… Not to mention the pervading pungent smell of lit cigarettes.

In his sleep-deprived state, Aziz slept through the first breakfast bell at 6:15 a.m., and again through the second bell at 6:30. Aziz finally got up with a jolt at 7:25, realizing he had to catch the last bus to the office trailers, departing from behind the dining room at 7:50.

Aziz quickly ran to the bathroom a little further up and across the hallway. It was a long narrow room, with two banks of ten wash-basins across from each other. The toilets and showers were further down, but he had no time for such luxuries that morning. He quickly brushed, shaved, and washed himself. There was another late-riser wearing just pyjama bottoms at the far end, face in basin, splashing his face like a whale.

They both finished their ablutions at the same time, glancing up at each other…

"OH FUCK!!! NOT YOU AGAIN!" exclaimed the brutish driller from the previous evening, throwing up his hands in consternation, as he angrily stalked away.

This encounter forced Aziz into peeing before rushing to get dressed and then running out to the dining room to pick up a coffee to go. But he was too late. All the coffee was gone and he couldn't wait ten minutes for a fresh urn. He only had seven minutes to catch the last bus, so he rushed back to his room to make his bed and put on his work boots.

As Aziz was making his bed with the door open, a passerby stopped in the corridor and asked why he was making his bed. Aziz looked at him blankly, and the man explained, "We don't make our beds or clean our rooms. The bullcooks do that."

"What's a bullcook?"

"That's the guy who comes in every day to make the beds and dust and wipe and wash the floors. And clean out the garbage bin and ashtray if you use it," said the man.

"Thank God, and thank you," said Aziz as he locked his room door and scrambled out to the buses. He just avoided colliding with the brute driller who uttered more F-words and grumbled under his breath some more, but thankfully he rushed off to a different bus headed for the river diversion tunnel below.

Aziz reported to the Hydro office at exactly 8:05 a.m. They asked him to take a seat and wait while they searched for someone to deal with him. Finally, about a half hour later, an authoritative-looking man with red hair and beard approached Aziz and questioned him about what he was doing there.

"I've been sent by the union to fill the urgent job posting for an Earthfill dam inspector," Aziz said, a little surprised, handing him his papers. "I came up on the train from Vancouver yesterday."

"Oh," said the man, also surprised. "Wait a few minutes while I call Vancouver, and I'll be right back."

A little later, the man returned wearing a worried look. "It seems that the union office in Vancouver failed to receive our cancellation notice for the job posting! The start of the Earthfill dam project has been delayed by six months. I'm afraid you've come up all the way here for nothing. I'm really sorry for the mix-up," said Redbeard in a kind voice.

Aziz was crestfallen and didn't know how to respond.

"But while you're here, tell me what experience you have in geology and construction."

Aziz explained about his last job reading and measuring from drawings and the extent of his two geology elective courses, his field trips, and whatever else he had studied at college.

"Are you able to recognize the various rock types and formations?" asked Redbeard?

"Yes, I think so," replied Aziz. "Igneous, metamorphic, and sandstone," he elaborated.

"And what about changes in stratigraphy? Can you spot those?"

Aziz thought for a moment. "I'm not exactly sure what you mean, but you only have to show me once and I will know," he said hopefully.

"Wait here," Redbeard said with a smile, "while I check with our project director, Dr. Schaffhausen."

Aziz could see Redbeard speaking with an older white-haired kindly looking gentleman through the glass wall of the large corner office. The man glanced over at Aziz, giving him a slight smile.

Redbeard returned, smiling broadly. "Aziz, we can offer you some temporary work for a week or so in my Geology Department, while the union tries to sort this out to see if they can find you a different job on this project—but no promises."

Aziz beamed back at Redbeard who extended his hand saying, "I'm Rory McMurdo, the chief geologist on the project. Welcome to my team, albeit temporarily, on the Revelbush project! The union will continue to pay you hourly, which will be to your advantage," said Rory. "As a geologist, the intern's pay is much lower, by the way!

"Well, then, let's get to work and I'll introduce you to the team at the end of the day when they come back in from the site. The first thing we'll get you to do today is to help our draftsman with printing out and distributing drawings to all the departments and contractors. He has a very big print order to do today and could use your help!

This was in the days when technology and mindsets were slow to change and health, safety, and the environment weren't high on anybody's lists. The pungent smell of ammonia used in the blueprinting machine was overpowering as Aziz breathed it in, burning his nasal passages and lungs while assisting the draftsman who didn't seem to mind the smell at all. A high-extraction ventilation system wasn't an option of course, nor was any type of ventilation other than an open back door.

Aziz's hands and fingers tingled with absorbed ammonia as he folded hundreds of soggy blueprints the way he had been shown, which was quite neat, actually: folding the forty-eight-inch by thirty-six-inch sheets in a clever prescribed manner into a twelve-inch by nine-inch booklet displaying the title block on the front, like a book cover.

He was relieved as 4:30 p.m. approached, heralding the end of his workday and where he briefly met the other geologists—all young smiling men, all with obligatory beards and khaki uniforms of course—before being bussed back into camp.

Thankfully that night in the dining hall, common room, and washrooms after, Aziz didn't see or hear the brutish driller who he had resolved to keep a sharp lookout for and avoid at all costs.

The next morning, Rory gave Aziz his assignment for the day and the tools he'd need for it. "Here's a hand inclinometer and a safety harness that you'll need," he said. "Have you used either of them before?"

"No," admitted Aziz.

"Okay, no worries. Let me show you then. The inclinometer as you can see looks like a tape measure with a levelling bubble on it. You need to measure the angle of dip of the rock face that I will take you out to momentarily, like so," he said, showing Aziz how to use it. "Get yourself a metal clipboard like mine, a writing pad, and some pencils." He proceeded to show Aziz how to draw an inverted U for the rock face, pencil in angled lines across it, and write in the measured angle of dip from the vertical.

"Keep doing this along the entire vertical rock face to measure the dips in the stratified rock formations as you work your way down the rock face. This information will help us extrapolate the direction of the formations below the rock face. In turn, this allows us to determine the strength and location of explosive charges to drill and set into the rock as we continue to drill and blast the face down to the river below."

Wow, thought Aziz, *this is the real deal!* "And what is this harness thingy for?" asked Aziz.

"Oh, that's for you to wear so that you can be safely tied off to the large crane sitting on top of the rock formation," Rory replied nonchalantly.

He proceeded to show Aziz how to pull it on over each leg, saying "You can figure out the rest, and the crane operator will show you anything else you need to know. Now, let's hurry as I have an 8:30 meeting to get back for."

With tools in hand and a little apprehensive now, Aziz was driven to the rock face below and deposited with the crane operator. "I'll pick you up at 4:00-ish. You can eat your lunch here when they blow the lunch whistle. Did you bring your lunch by the way? They provide takeout sandwiches in the camp dining room, I believe."

"No, I didn't know they had take-out and that I was supposed to bring a packed lunch nor that I wouldn't have access to the dining room at lunchtime," said Aziz.

"Well… I'm sure they have buses to take you back and forth to camp for lunch. You'll be okay. Right. Gotta run now. Here's a walkie-talkie to clip to your belt. Call me if you run into any problems." And with that Rory's truck disappeared in a cloud of dust.

Thankfully the crane operator tightly secured the harness straps around Aziz, also showing him how to make adjustments to it as he moved along the rock face. He then showed Aziz the hand signals required to communicate with him above, as there was no way to use a walkie talkie while dangling from a sheer cliff face (unless you were Sylvester Stallone!).

With a leap of faith and a prayer, Aziz gulped and launched himself into thin air, dangling by his only lifeline—a thin cord from the crane above, clipped to his harness. His life was literally in the hands of the crane operator. Thankfully, the operator didn't appear to have the attitude of the brutish driller.

Aziz looked down at the sparkling green waters of the fast-flowing Columbia River, and at the hive of activity where dozens of men and equipment were labouring to drill and grout anchors for a steel coffer dam. Aziz quickly looked back up, his eyes level with the vertical rock face. He remembered Rory's advice not to look down and understood why now. The twin sensations of vertigo and fear of a horrible death were quite overpowering.

Using his left hand and toes of his boots to dig into crevices in the cliff face as his only means of anchoring himself from swaying, Aziz dangled below the cord. He did his best to utilize his right hand to measure the angle of dip, pocket the inclinometer, then pull out his clipboard tucked in his waistband, and letting go his left hand from a crevice, use both hands to hold the clipboard and draw and write in the information on the rock face. On and on he went with this careful and painful process requiring utmost concentration, in between hand signals for the crane boom to shift him along right, left and lower down from his position. Then rinse and repeat… rinse and repeat…

At exactly 10:00 a.m., a loud booming horn broke his concentration. Aziz looked around and saw a coffee truck pull up on the roadway a little further down and to his left. In the sudden quietness as all drilling equipment and hammering shut down, the crane operator yelled down to him that he was taking a coffee break and for Aziz to remain dangling there, as there was no time to haul him back up. Aziz didn't mind as he also didn't want to go through the rigmarole for a ten-minute break. Instead, he busied himself with tidying up his sketch sheets. At 10:10 a.m. on the dot the horn sounded again and everybody returned to work.

By 11:00 a.m., the July sun was beating down mercilessly on Aziz in his exposed position. His lips and tongue were dry and parched, his mouth and eyes gritty with sharp mica dust, and he longed for a drink of water. But of course, he did not have a water canteen slung on him, as most other men working on *terra firma* appeared to have. The booming horn sounded out again. Aziz glanced at his watch; it was only 11:10. *Another coffee break so soon, jeez,* thought Aziz. The crane operator yelled out something, waving his arms at Aziz as he ran off to join the others. Well, he was stuck here now, as the crane operator had left in a hurry. Nobody to haul him up.

Then Aziz heard somebody yelling at him from below. He looked down at a long rock ledge to his left where a man who he'd never seen before was insistently yelling at him to unhitch himself and get down from there immediately!

Aziz at first ignored him, but as the yelling grew more insistent and urgent, Aziz cursed nervously, unhitched the carabiner clip, letting go of his lifeline. He hugged the rock face tight, the toes of his boots supported on a fortuitous rock outcropping—nothing more than a protruding vein—and shuffled sideways like a crab to position himself above the ledge a metre below him. With heart in mouth, he slid down the rock face, arms outstretched, fingertips and nails scraping the rock as he lowered himself onto the ledge where the man's splayed hands steadied Aziz to prevent him from toppling over the edge.

"Whata you think you doing up there, eh?" the man yelled as they jumped off onto solid ground and he led Aziz running to a long row of massive rock boulders a little way off. "Nobody eva tell you when the special siren sounds you gotta stoppa work and runna like-a-ell for cover, eh?"

Aziz followed the man's lead, crouching down behind the rocks, joining over a dozen men including the crane operator. The man blew a whistle and moments later another siren sounded. The men covered their ears tightly and Aziz followed suit. Then KA-BOOM as a muffled explosion sounded somewhere below where Aziz had been hanging from.

They waited a few minutes for the dust clouds to settle and it was explained to Aziz that there was a special siren sound (as distinct to the breaktime horn) when explosive charges were being set off! At that, all men were required to drop everything and run for cover!

Being young and adventurous, Aziz took all of this in stride, taking a couple of long swigs of cold water from a nearby cooler and washing the grime off his face before being lowered back down onto his perch to continue his work.

And so it went for two more days and Aziz was getting quite used to the work. The crane operator was quite friendly now and perhaps a little abashed at running and abandoning Aziz hanging in mid-air. Especially when Aziz had no idea what was going on, having not received any safety indoctrination and training before tackling this dangerous work.[7]

On Friday morning, Aziz was asked to wait outside the offices. An hour later, Rory called Aziz into his office and informed him the rock mapping work was over for now and that he had no more work

---

7 *Such flagrant offences of ignoring safety regulations, lack of safety training, and indoctrination of workers, especially in high-risk work involving hanging off cliffs, working directly above a blast zone, etc. would be unthinkable today. And they would undoubtedly result in stiff fines, job closures, and severe penalties to the employer and company officers were it to occur in the 2020's*

to farm out to Aziz. The union officer in Vancouver had not got back to them about an alternative position.

There were however, two options for Aziz. Either a salaried position as an intern geologist paying a pittance or a union job position that had just come up that morning – at a remote site connected to the Revelstoke Dam project, about forty-five miles upstream in an area called the Downie Slide.

It was a clerical position and perhaps below Aziz's expectations, but still paying $9.37 and hour which although below an Inspector's pay grade, was still great pay for a first-year summer student. Was he willing to go there and take up the work? It was his to take for the summer or for the next eighteen months if he wanted. Because of its remote location, however, travel in and out for the ninety-man camp would be quite restrictive unless one had a car.

Aziz didn't hesitate for a second and immediately accepted the job.

"Great, laddie" said Rory, rolling his "R". Cowboy Clint will give you the paperwork to fill out and you can take it over to our Chief Clerk Bobbie who will explain your duties to you. After which I suggest you collect your things from camp.

"How long do I have before they come for me?" Aziz asked.

"Well, they've just fired the site clerk there and are bringing him down here for his walking papers from the Cowboy. I expect it'll be a couple of hours at least. And then the driver and you may as well have lunch here in camp before departing for Downie Slide.

Aziz thanked Rory and walked towards the Cowboy's office to get his transfer papers, ready for his next adventure in the wilderness.

Author's note: Aziz's adventures at the Downie Slide satellite campsite to be continued in my next book.

THE INFINITY BRIDGE

Fireworks, jubilation and non-stop partying filled the streets of Macarenhas, the capital city of Tembo, a small African state in East Central Africa. A former Portuguese, then British colony after World War I, Tembo gained its independence following the march for Independence and overthrow of the British colonialists by General Bamako, back in 1989.

Bordering on the republics of Congo to the northwest and Nyani to the northeast, Tembo shared in the mineral-rich geologic formations of those two countries. Tembo was also blessed with lush farmland to the east along the delta of the great Mto-wa-Mbu (Mosquito River). The river wound its course from the north, somewhat parallel to the River Nile, emptying into the Indian Ocean to the southeast. To assist the country with its ambitious goals of self-sufficiency and economic independence, and no doubt to share in its mineral wealth, the World Bank, other international aid agencies, and western countries established fast-track priorities for financial aid, funding massive projects.

Unfortunately, good intentions and unlimited external funding alone do not always work in developing countries. The other essential ingredients needed are honesty, integrity, and patriotism by the senior custodians of the country, which sadly is often lacking. Power, greed, and corruption are the three ugly sisters of the indigenous ruling classes. They tend to usurp and then simply replace and expand on the excesses of the colonial rulers.

The reason for celebrations now was that the self-proclaimed "President for Life," His Excellency Sir General Bamako, OBE, had finally bowed to intense international pressure tied to foreign aid and economic sanctions. The world powers mandated that Tembo hold democratic general elections, the good General Bamako having been in continuous power since independence thirty-three years ago. This, after ruining and destroying the economy of his country, which was now ranked as one of the poorest nations on the planet, despite its mineral wealth. A far cry from pre-independence when it was economically ranked on even par with the economy of South Korea. In contrast, South Korea had moved in the opposite direction and was now ranked among the top world economies.

Sadly, the general citizenship of Tembo had not enjoyed any of the benefits of foreign aid dollars. Instead, billions of dollars had been siphoned off by the general and his cohorts, into fat Swiss bank accounts. In the general's case, he had accumulated more money than any human being could ever hope to spend in a thousand lifetimes.

The democratic election results had just been announced!

Tujenge Taifa, a young, vital social worker and legal aid lawyer, only thirty-two years old, had come out of nowhere to challenge the reigning president general who had ruled the country since before Mr. Taifa's birth! He had garnered voter support from the peasant masses and the younger educated millennials in the cities. Additionally, Tujenge received financial backing from the foreign mining companies that were being fleeced with crippling taxes and trumped-up environmental fines. The mining companies employed and housed some twelve thousand local workers and their one hundred thousand or so dependents. Those of voting age, all voted for change and the hopes of prosperity. These factors led to Mr. Taifa's overwhelmingly decisive win, winning him an astounding eighty per cent of the popular vote!

There was of course a futile challenge to Mr. Taifa's win lodged with the courts by the president and his supporters who cried foul, saying that the elections had been rigged by the foreign mining companies and other outsiders! (Incredibly much like a certain former president of a powerful western democratic nation had cried foul after losing an election). It took just six months for the courts to overthrow the President-for-Life's challenge. No doubt assisted by various United Nations' agencies who had monitored and policed the voting process. In the end, General Bamako had to accept defeat, thankfully without much violence and bloodshed, and retired grace-fully with his harem and collection of antique cars to his Caribbean island heaven and his Swiss bank accounts.

In due course, all major world powers' heads of state including the prime minister of Canada, Prince Charles representing the British Crown and most other African heads of state, were invited to President Taifa's inauguration ceremony. Following the inauguration, the new and young inexperienced president granted requests for one-on-one meetings with several neighbouring African heads of state.

The seasoned African presidents pledged their assistance and support to the fledgling president, inviting him to visit their countries. They pledged to tour and tutor President Taifa on the fine points of governing a mineral-rich country and on how to share his country's wealth with all its citizenry. This was music to President Taifa's socialist ears and he immediately accepted their generous offers.

Some months later, the first batch of African state visits were organized, a whirlwind tour of three countries in seven days. Two days of power-packed visit per country and the seventh day allocated for intra-country travel. It was deemed too risky to be out of the country for much longer, because as history has shown, army coups are successfully carried out when a head of state is away for extended periods.

Although President Taifa had not yet had time to disenfranchise his citizens and make new enemies, there were factions within the army still loyal to retired General Bamako who might well attempt such a coup. Notwithstanding, it might have proved rather difficult to entice the seventy-two-year-old retired billionaire back to Tembo from his ever-growing harem and palatial estate in the Caribbean.

General Bamako was in fact at that very moment in the process of firing a couple of nubile young female employees who had rejected his amorous advances. Crestfallen, he hurried empty handed to greet his hero and business partner, a former president of a western nation with very similar tendencies.

President Tujenge Taifa's first visit was to Nyani City, the capital of the Democratic Republic of Nyani. After a state luncheon (no time for lengthy banquets and nightly pleasures) he flew with his host,

President Paka Jimmy, to the mining area of Chokozi. En route, he was coached on many aspects of diplomacy and governance.

Upon landing in Chokozi, they drove through wide boulevards crowded with brightly dressed people milling about and chatting in their sing-song language. Above them, the trees were teeming with monkeys playfully swinging through the branches, sometimes venturing down to steal a fruit or vegetable or brightly coloured object from the street hawkers' stalls or from a small child.

Their first stop was at a massive new molybdenum extraction project next to an existing copper mining operation. The site was fenced in and a construction trailer park and camp complex were set up to one side, with the contractor's name prominently displayed: Lyons Construction Ltee.

Looking out over the site, the host, President Jimmy, said, "See all that, Tujenge?" sweeping his arm grandly across the entire site… That is our new molybdenum project. This metal is very valuable and extremely expensive to extract, as determined and reported by one of the largest mining engineering consultants in the world, who is on our payroll. The real cost of extraction on our site is in fact very, very low because we are piggy backing onto pre-existing infrastructure and capital equipment already installed in the adjacent copper mine. And because we do not require expensive sequential excavation mining methods and equipment, as stated in our report.

"This is essentially an open-pit mine utilizing existing excavation equipment as I mentioned. So, the World Bank advances us $500 million to build and operate the mine. But the real cost, including all *facility payments,* will be $300 million. And the balance of $200 million goes into my Swiss bank account!

"The citizens also benefit because we are creating thousands of new jobs for the miners and support industries. And the mining companies who will extract and market the molybdenum will pay us royalties which we will use in small part for our citizens' benefit in perpetuity.

"And so that's forty per cent of the World Bank's money in my pocket up front! This is the smart way to conduct business with the western nations - so that everybody in my country wins: yourself, your friends, and all your citizens!"

From there they flew back to Nyani City to visit the state casino hotel that same night. After a scrumptious steak and lobster dinner washed down with Dom Perignon, upon leaving the restaurant, the host swept his arm across the main gambling floor and said, "See all this, Tujenge? We obtained an economic development grant of $200 million to build the casino and fit it out, but it actually cost us $150 million. After all *facility payments*, I pocketed $40 million or twenty per cent into my Swiss Bank account. And from the ongoing casino revenue, twenty per cent is distributed to the citizens of our country and twenty per cent is siphoned off to my Swiss account—some $10 million each annually, so again a win-win for all!

And finally, of course the soft benefits…" he smiled as a bunch of gorgeous casino showgirls laughingly appeared, taking them by the arm towards the hotel elevators, trailed by their bodyguards.

The entire next day was spent at the president's offices, in back-to-back meetings with various ministers and economic advisors, where Tujenge learned and absorbed matters in two days that would have taken him a couple of years at least if he were left to his own devices—presuming he could survive two years.

Tujenge's next stop was Shasha, the capital of the Democratic Republic of Bongo. Here, he learned about an ambitious railway project to get copper ore to the seaboard as well as a passenger express railway system, financed by the Chinese Development Bank and built by the People's Republic of China.

The amount of the loan in the form of a long-term repayable grant was $900 million. The host president swept his arm grandly across the railway station saying, "The real cost to build this railway system with conscript labour from China and war displaced African orphans was $600 million, meaning approximately thirty per cent or $270 million after deducting *facility payments* were diverted to the president's Swiss Bank account!

"And don't forget we have created thousands more jobs as the Chinese taught our children lifelong work skills, which they are now applying to earn a good living on other endeavours. Not to mention the ongoing rail carrier revenues, for everybody's benefit including my own!"

After hearing about a couple more aid projects benefiting the citizenry as well as yielding twenty-five to thirty per cent in siphoned payments to the president, Tujenge was once more tutored to a full day at the ministry offices, culminating in another night of exotic pleasures before departing.

President Taifa's presidential Boeing 707 taxied in to its gate at the Jomo Kenyatta International Airport terminal in Nairobi, Kenya, the last leg of his whirlwind journey. He was greeted by a military band in Scottish attire, complete with bagpipes and a military honour guard, as he alighted onto the concrete apron. The interim president was indisposed but had sent his first vice president instead.

Tujenge was subjected to pretty much the same pattern as before. He viewed two large projects financed by the World Bank and US Aid respectively, where the first VP boasted that hundreds of millions of dollars or thirty to forty per cent had been siphoned off, and the citizens had somehow also benefited, although unclear on the details.

After a dinner at the interim president's private residence on the eve of his departure, Tujenge was versed in the many ways to "work" with various international aid agencies and tutored on how to siphon hundreds of millions of dollars in unconditional foreign aid.

A final word from the interim president, "As you know, East Africa and South Africa share an ethnic and linguistic commonality of the Nilotic Bantu tribes. In our local language of Kiswahili, your name Tujenge Taifa is very auspicious because it means, 'We build our Nation.' May God go with you, young man!"

On his northward flight home, Tujenge summarized the main takeaways from his incredible week of learning.

1. How to ask for and obtain maximum foreign aid dollars, how to leverage aid money and play the donors against each other.

2. How to package cost proposals for aid projects, utilizing "independent" international experts to corroborate his asks.

3. How to utilize alternate resources, procurement strategies, and labour pools to build the project for the least amount of cost, thereby pocketing the difference while providing lifelong work skills to local workers.

4. How to share a small portion of the bonanza with his dedicated and downtrodden fellow citizens, to whom he owed a great debt.

5. How to generate ongoing income in perpetuity from grandiose projects built with other people's money, both for his citizens and for himself.

The humble legal aid lawyer-cum-social worker from a few months ago had in one power packed week undergone a life altering education about the virtue of selfishness, with added measures for benefitting others less fortunate. President Tujenge Taifa rubbed his hands in gleeful anticipation as his plane descended toward the adoring masses waiting to greet their chosen saviour.

Three long years went by and the indefatigable but not-so-young anymore president had garnered billions of dollars in foreign aid. This resulted in an impressive amount of economic growth and prosperity for his people. By all accounts, he was indeed the chosen saviour of his people! However, Tujenge had been too occupied with implementing the lessons learned from his three mentors to even contemplate additional learning trips to other well-meaning heads of state. In fact, he had not even taken a day off in three years and had no personal life, nor time to search for a suitable wife and soulmate!

Around that time, the Pan African Summit meetings (held every four years) were approaching, to be held this time in Arusha, Tanzania, located to the south of Tembo. Tujenge had no plans to take a week off to attend this important event. However, after much insistence from his mentors, he agreed to host them in Macarenhas on a short stopover on their return trip to their home countries.

The big day came, and the three mentor presidents were greeted by a rousing police band and senior government officials at Macarenhas International Airport. They were brought to State House in a grand procession of limousines, in time for a private dinner with their host. The visiting presidents were duly impressed at the change in their young charge and at what he had achieved for his country.

President Taifa had been the talk of the summit they told him, and had won several awards, including those for "Leader in Economic Improvement," "Social Uplift and Betterment," "Most popular African Head of State," "Top Entrepreneur under 40," "Most Eligible African Bachelor!" and a couple more minor awards.

"Now regarding your handling of the foreign aid projects in your country, tomorrow you must show us what you have learned" they insisted over a nightcap.

"Certainly, I would love to showcase my humble achievements to you my mentors," he replied, smiling. "However, I must excuse

myself now, as I have at least another four hours of work before retiring to bed. The limos will take you to your hotel, and I shall see you
early in the morning. Goodnight, gentlemen!"

Disappointed at their early dismissal, for it was only 9:00 p.m., his
three mentors were driven back to their hotel. But…upon entering
their rooms, they were each greeted by a pair of local beauties gift-
wrapped in silver foil and golden bows, supplied for their nocturnal entertainment!

It should be noted for the record that while President Paka Jimmy
of Nyani gladly partook of the proffered entertainment, it was
unclear whether the other two presidents who were older statesmen,
accepted or politely declined their host's gifts.

After an early breakfast, the four presidents set off in a cavalcade
of limos, police motorcycles, and armoured personnel carriers (for
effect only) back to the airport. The visitors couldn't help but notice
long billboards spaced out at intervals along the route. The billboards
displayed a grandiose and impressive looking multi-span bridge
spanning across a river and seemingly disappearing into the distant
horizon, with no apparent end to its length. It was billed as the "New
Infinity Bridge for the People of Tembo—built by President Tujenge
Taifa," his smiling young face prominently displayed at both ends of
each billboard.

The cavalcade drove directly onto the apron through a guarded
gatepost and halted outside the air traffic control or ATC tower.
They were met by a troupe of national dancers and musicians and
stood on the apron watching them, while attendants held large shady
umbrellas over their heads. They beamed at the dancers, thoroughly
enjoying themselves while sipping gin and tonics.

The presidents were then escorted into the building, taking an
elevator to the control centre at the top of the tower where they
were afforded a panoramic view of the airport runway, buildings

and distant snow-capped mountains. The air traffic controllers were instructed by their president to halt all takeoffs and landings and divert incoming flights away if necessary for the next twenty minutes, after which he commanded that they exit the control tower and wait downstairs.

In total privacy now, Tujenge swept his hand across the control tower saying, "My first foreign aid project that I cut my teeth on was to build this new control tower and equip it with state-of-the-art air traffic control equipment inside this control room. Also, navigational aids (N/A) equipment on top of the tower and outside along the runways. We officially tendered the equipment supply and installation to four foreign contractors—one Canadian, one American and two European—as these countries dominate the world market for ATC and N/A equipment.

"Unofficially, though, we secretly invited one Chinese contractor and one Russian contractor to also bid on it. We chose the highest official bidder's price, a European company, to obtain a grant from the European Development Bank (EDB) in the bid amount plus ten per cent for escalation and contingencies. But once we received the funding commitment from the EDB, we found political means to cancel our Letter of Commitment to the selected European company. We then awarded the contract to a lesser-known Russian company, but technically still a European company, thereby still meeting the EDB's lending criteria! The second-place Russians agreed to match the price of the low Chinese bidder of course.

"In the end, we also got the Russians to build the ATC tower for almost nothing by supplying local conscript labour through our Ministry of Prisons, free of charge. The Russians agreed to this in order to showcase their lesser-known ATC and N/A equipment, so far unproven anywhere outside Russia and the former Soviet states. Their equipment too was supplied at bare cost, and we only paid for cheap flights in cargo planes and room and board for the Russian technicians.

"Therefore the $50 million total funding we received ended up costing us around $10 million, and the entire $40 million savings or eighty per cent of EDB monies went directly into my Panamanian Bank Account! For reasons I won't get into yet, I prefer Panama to a Swiss bank account."

President Tujenge's three fellow presidents applauded their approval of this intricate but brilliant coup netting Tujenge a much higher percentage than they were used to themselves, albeit on a relatively smaller dollar amount than they normally embezzled.

Tujenge led them next to the back-sloped windows of the control tower overlooking the airport. "What do you see there in the distance, gentlemen?" he asked pointing at a distant column of dust.

They shook their heads, not able to discern it.

"That gentlemen is the new international terminal building under construction. An additional runway and remote stand aprons are also to be built under the same contract. A similar process was followed, and we awarded the work to the Chinese contractor this time, who agreed to undercut the Russian contractor's price which we showed him.

"The cost of the highest bid from an American contractor was $200 million, and we obtained a grant of $220 million for it from US Aid, eventually awarding the work to the Chinese contractor for $90 million, netting me a $130 million or sixty per cent profit!

"And, of course, many hundreds of local jobs are being created. Also, revenues that will accrue from wealthy international passengers will be shared with the citizenry. I don't wish any recurring payments for myself."

Upon learning all this, the presidents broke out in a loud cheer, hugging and thumping their protégé on the back as they took the elevator back down. Meanwhile, the skies were filled with circling aircraft waiting to be allowed to land and the single runway and aprons choked with aircraft waiting to take off!

Tujenge led his mentors to two more foreign aid projects within easy driving distance where he demonstrated generous benefits accruing to his citizens. As well as fifty per cent to sixty per cent upfront profits generated for himself worth another $130 million. Tujenge had altogether netted $300 million for himself on the three relatively small projects. Tujenge, however, refrained from taking any recurring payments for himself, allocating all net revenues to his citizenry instead.

"Now back to the airport for lunch gentlemen, and then we're going for a joyride to our great river delta, Mto-wa-Mbu (Mosquito River) to view my greatest and most ambitious project: The Infinity Bridge! Tujenge wouldn't discuss anything more about the project during lunch much to the suspense of his mentors.

The forty-year-old Presidential Boeing 707 jetliner, with rebuilt engines and a newly rebuilt luxury cabin interior, afforded each of the four passengers an expansive bird's-eye view from their first-class seats facing each other on the right-hand side of the aircraft. They sipped champagne, snacked on canapes and chatted until pretty soon the majestic river and its wide green cultivated delta came into view.

"That's beautiful, Tujenge, but what exactly are we supposed to be looking for amongst the apples and oranges, pray tell?" asked one of the presidents peevishly.

"Please be patient and you will soon be rewarded with a great revelation," Tujenge answered with an enigmatic smile.

The aircraft descended to five thousand feet and the river delta came into full view in all its majesty. It was much wider than it first appeared as a thin ribbon from twenty-five thousand feet cruising altitude and they could now see the fast-flowing water coursing over miles and miles of large and dangerous rapids.

"Gentlemen, thank you for your great patience, now let me please explain," Tujenge began. "Just coming up ahead of us is the narrowest part of the river. On this side we are flying over Tembo territory. On the other side of the river, we can see our friendly eastern neighbour, the Republic of Nyani," he said, and lightly punched President Paka Jimmy of Nyani on his shoulder.

"As you know, we have a much more developed agricultural industry in the flatter, wider delta on Tembo's side of the river, versus the narrower, rockier delta on the Nyani side. Because the river is so fast-flowing and filled with large dangerous rapids, river navigation and transportation is difficult, if not impossible. We have no economical means of getting our produce, beef, and milk products to market in Nyani," he sighed.

"Accordingly based on my recent successes, we have convinced the World Bank to fund a US$ 2.1 billion project to construct a triple long span cable stayed bridge connecting the two countries. The total length of the bridge will be approximately 2.5 kilometres!"

I am very pleased to announce that the construction milestone for the bridge towers embedded in the river bedrock has been reached, and the tall steel towers that are anchored in place are now ready for pulling cables across next month. This was the most difficult and dangerous part of the operation, working off large river barges in rough water and high winds. We utilized giant barge mounted cranes and teams of professional divers to construct the towers. Accordingly, per our contract terms, we have just last week received full advance payments for the entire bridge project, but discounted to the World Bank by $100 million for advance payment. In this way, everybody wins!

The cabin erupted with loud applause and cheering. President Jimmy jumped up, grabbing a bottle of Dom Perignon in one hand and just as she happened to walk by, grabbed the pretty flight attendant's pert behind with his other hand! She squealed as he led her towards the presidential suite, but Tujenge nixed that. "Please, Jimmy, come back and sit down until you've heard the entire story. There will be time enough for that later, I promise," he said, nodding at the pretty flight attendant.

When everybody was seated again, and after the plane had banked in a large circle to once again approach the narrowest part of the river, Tujenge swept his hand across the window pointing at the river below…

"All of that, including the four bridge towers, the giant barges to help support the cable and bridge deck construction, the vast built-up jetties at the river's edges to assemble all bridge deck and infrastructure materials etc.—that's all worth \$1.2 billion, which has been previously billed and paid for, plus the remaining \$0.8 billion advance that we just received for financing the remainder of construction!"

President Jimmy was by this time happily working on his second bottle of Dom Perignon, distracted by Marina, the pretty flight attendant when the airplane banked sharply. She found herself falling onto his lap (no doubt aided by his strong pulling arm). Marina was now well and truly trapped, held down by his strong embrace, and too scared to make a scene.

I mean, who gets to be at close quarters with four presidents all at one time? Marina rationalized to herself and her protests were less vocal now. The other two presidents were busy squinting down at the bridge in silent puzzlement. Something didn't seem to add up….

Although distracted, Jimmy had been keenly listening to Tujenge's monologue about his bridge, as it greatly affected trade with his country. Just then, he decided to look for himself. "Where is it? I can't see anything!" he exclaimed in frustration, twisting his head around in every direction against the airplane window, searching below for all that Tujenge had described.

"There! Look to your right and you'll just see the last tower disappearing from view!" exclaimed Tujenge, pointing below. "Oh, we're past it now! But you two gentlemen have seen it I presume, so let's turn back; it's getting late." Tujenge glanced at the other two for confirmation.

One of them began to nod assent, too embarrassed to admit his poor eyesight, but the other spoke up: "I'm afraid I can't focus very well from up here looking down through the small water-streaked window, can we take one more fly-by from a little further down?"

"But of course," smiled Tujenge." Tell you what; let's play a little game! The first person to spot the bridge structures gets a tumble in the presidential suite with Marina our lovely flight attendant!"

Jimmy was now one hundred per cent focused on the river below, determined to be the first man to spot the bridge!

On their third and final fly-by, despite craning their necks and squinting their eyes until they hurt, searching desperately for the bridge structures and barges, nobody was able to claim first sighting! They looked at their host, perplexed and frustrated!

"Let me explain further gentlemen. I have been paid $1.2 billion for work done progressively over the last two and a half years, and just received my final payment of $800 million (discounted by $100 million) to complete the bridge construction over the next twelve months. Can anybody guess how much of the $2 billion will go into my bank account?"

"For a mega-project of this magnitude and level of risk involved, I'd say fifteen per cent or $300 million," offered one of them pompously.

"No!" exclaimed another. "Knowing how smart you have become, Tujenge, I think you'll be skimming up to twenty-five per cent or $500 million!" said he judiciously.

"Crap!" said the third. "You'll be lucky to net $100 million due to construction costs always spiralling out of control. You are obviously counting on a long-term return from bridge tolls which you'll split with your country's citizens! This should set you up for life and beyond, provided you can find a way to transfer the tolling income to your children and to their children in perpetuity!"

Tujenge raised himself to his full height, just avoiding hitting his head on the luggage compartment above. "How about I make approximately... $2 billion from this deal... all into my bank account in Panama?!" he shouted.

They looked at him incredulously, not knowing if they'd heard right.

Marina, who through no fault of her own, was still pinned down on Paka Jimmy's lap. She had listened to their entire conversation while cringing at his drunken kisses but managing to ward off his roving hands. She looked out the window with sharp young eyes quickly scanning the river and immediately understood. It was "The emperor with the invisible bespoke suit" moment, where the little boy was the only person brave enough to shout, "Look, the emperor is naked. He isn't wearing any clothes!"

With an effort, she broke free of Jimmy and yelled, "There is no bridge out there; it's all a sham! That's why you'll be keeping all the money from the non-existent construction, Mr. President Sir!"

"You called it, lady. You're one smart dame, in addition to being a very pretty one," Tujenge smilingly replied.

The older statemen were totally flabbergasted, their mouths hanging open at this scintillatingly brilliant and unparalleled scam their young protégé had pulled off. It was the scam of scams, unequalled anywhere on this planet! Their shocked silence was palpable above the dull hum of the jet engines.

Tujenge turned to Marina, saying, "I promised anyone who spotted my bridge a reward, a tumble with you in there," inclining his head towards his suite. "But you're the one who spotted the scam instead! So, you are entitled to the reward. Tell me what your reward should be."

She immediately answered, "With all due respect, Your Excellency, you have already promised me as the prize and I think that you should keep your promise. But as I am the victor of this contest, and since I cannot tumble with myself, I should be allowed to pick who gets to tumble with me, no?"

"Fair enough; your logic is immutable and makes perfect sense!" laughed Tujenge.

Jimmy rose, breaking into a dreamy smile, patting his hair down and puffing his chest out. He hitched his pants up at the waist while simultaneously strangling the bulge in the front of his pants. Paka Jimmy swaggered towards Marina, now very ambitious and ready for action!

"I don't mean to be presumptuous, Your Excellency, but… I pick you! …if you please, sir?" Marina said demurely, batting her eyelids at Tujenge. Jimmy's mouth fell wide open once again, and the other two elderly statemen guffawed aloud!

"Well, I suppose I can't go back on my word to a lady. You've somehow managed to outfox me, that's for sure" Tujenge said. "We don't have too much time before we land, so let's move it!" Tujenge took her hand.

As they walked to the bedroom suite, Tujenge stopped and turning to the other presidents said, "The entire two billion from this bridge scam has already been deposited into a trust account in the Bahamas for all the below-poverty level citizens of my country. There are about two million people affected, netting about $1,000 for every man, woman, and child below the poverty line. Forty dollars per month covers the basic necessities of life in my country. So, one thousand dollars is quite enough for everybody to live comfortably on for two years and for many to get back on their feet during that time. And as most of our citizens have large families, the forty-dollar monthly income per person goes much further when pooled between a family of eight to ten people.

"I have accumulated more than enough money for myself, about $300 million in my Panama account where I will be flying to. Which will be just as soon as we land and refuel after dropping you off to catch your flights back home. I expect it won't be very long before the World Bank sends somebody of their own after my departure and discovers that there is no bridge, that the aerial photos, engineering reports and certified progress reports are all fake, and that they've been well and truly scammed!"

The loud applause and shouts of "Well done" and "Hear! Hear!" were deafening in the pressurized cabin.

"You'll need a flight attendant on your way to Panama, sir, might you be taking me along with you then?" Marina asked demurely, giving him a sly hungry look. "You'll also require a Spanish-speaking assistant in Panama who you can trust, as Spanish is the country's official language. I am of mixed heritage as you can see. My father is native African, and my mother is of mixed English-Spanish heritage, so I learned to speak all their languages!"

Tujenge pondered for a moment. *There is no end to her smart, forward-looking thinking and a little bit—no, a great deal—of sassiness,* he thought. *She is exactly the kind of girl I should have by my side, and she is, after all, from my country. Yes I will make a go with her!*

Tujenge replied, "I speak Portuguese, so Spanish is not a big stretch for me, but here's what we'll do. Let me think about it and hopefully decide by the time we reach Macarenhas Airport in about an hour's time. You're certainly very attractive and sexy. You're also smart and razor sharp, but you'll need to convince me of your skills in the other department first…"

They smiled at each other, clasping hands tightly as they hurried into the presidential suite. Marina had a lot of convincing to do in the next hour, but was fully confident of success and she was going to thoroughly enjoy herself too!

LA COLORADA

——

A strong gust of wind shook the site office building along its entire length, rattling over the corrugated metal roof, momentarily dimming the lights inside. For a brief moment, Aziz thought he heard a haunting female voice calling plaintively in the wind as it swept across the night. *It's funny how your ears and senses play tricks on you when in a foreign and unfamiliar environment,* mused Aziz.

Aziz had only recently arrived at the project site located on the outskirts of Cusco, Peru, for the construction of a new airport. His Canadian employer, Batiment Quebec Limite of Quebec City, Canada, was joint ventured with a local builder, Fernandez y Fernandez Constructores S.A. The joint venture was known locally as Batiment-Fernandez Constructores, S.A or BFC for short. The acronym was the butt of jokes and hilarity with the Canadian expats, their clients, vendors, and subcontractors. The most popular versions of what BFC stood for were Big F'ing Contractor and Burgers, Fries and Coke!

Cusco, a city of about 450,000 souls had the distinction of being sited at a very high elevation of 3,400 metres or 11,200 feet above sea level. Although the month was August, daytime highs were around 20 Celsius and nighttime temperatures fell to near zero because of its high altitude in the Andes Mountains. Aziz shivered as he rose from his desk, deciding to call it a night, unsure if he had shivered because of the cold, despite the *calefactor,* or portable electric heater in his office, or because of the plaintive haunting voice he thought he had heard, or both.

The next morning at the coffee station, Aziz mentioned the previous night's disconcerting incident to Ray, BFC's French Canadian Jack-of-all-trades. Ray's reaction belied his usual cheerfulness, replying with a grim expression, "*Sacrement.* This is not a good thing, we must go speak with our camp manager, Fernando Chinataxi. Over the last few months, Fernando's men living in camp have reported similar experiences at night and in some cases, they have fallen and injured themselves because of it!"

I looked at Ray with raised eyebrows. He went on. "Apparently the men believe that the camp is haunted by an apparition or ghost of a beautiful redheaded woman who they call 'La Colorada,' meaning, 'The Redhead.'"

Intrigued, Aziz followed Ray to Fernando's office. He was a large rotund man in his forties with a buzz cut framing his square head and a mouthful of gleaming gold teeth. He was partial to wearing a Stetson and cowboy boots. Fernando wasn't referred to as "El Gordo" for nothing by his coworkers, albeit behind his back. It meant "The Fat One." Ray narrated Aziz's experience to Fernando in Spanish. Fernando's face lit up and he asked the time of night and direction of wind travel and whether any words were distinguishable.

"About 8 p.m." said Aziz," travelling longitudinally above my office headed towards the camp buildings. I thought I heard a haunting female voice, as though it were calling out to somebody but no words were distinguishable… And even if it had been, it would've been in Spanish, I guess, which I don't understand."

Fernando nodded, explaining that this phenomenon was scaring his men who were very superstitious. "My men have had similar experiences as yours last night and a couple of men even claim to have encountered a ghost! It has the form of a beautiful, tall redheaded woman wearing a long red dress who supposedly was calling for her husband and children. The men have aptly named her 'La Colorada,' 'The Redhead.' She is usually sighted on full moon nights, and last night, as you know, we had a full moon!"

Aziz didn't believe in ghosts and wasn't convinced. "Perhaps it was really just the wind howling over the corrugated metal roofs that made it sound like a wailing woman!" he reasoned with Fernando through Ray translating for him. "And perhaps the men were high on coca and hallucinating all alone at night about a beautiful red-headed woman!" Aziz smiled.

Fernando didn't reply immediately. He took a big bite out of a massive pork hock on his desk, his teeth and fat jowls working hard to tear it down. A trickle of pig grease escaped the corner of his mouth as he looked at the gringos through slitted eyes while he pondered. Then, wiping the grease off his face with the back of his hand and then licking it, he said, "We *Quechua* people believe in spirits. When spirits can clearly be seen and heard by people it is because they make themselves visible and audible for a reason, and that is what is bothering my men very much. In the case of La Colorada, she is searching for her family. Apparently, her husband and two children, and she is very agitated. She won't stop bothering my men who are on the verge of quitting, unless I can send her away. That's why I need you Canadians to call me immediately the next time you hear or see anything because you are always here working late at night!"

"But how would you send her away?" I asked playing along as though I believed she were real.

"I have a shaman assisting me with this. It does not concern you gringos. You understand nothing of our culture!"

With that, the meeting was over. *Fair comment,* I thought as we walked away.

"Don't worry. I'm as intrigued as you are," Ray piped into my thoughts." I'll do some hard digging and let you know what I find."

In the ensuing days, I made a point of leaving work before darkness fell. Although I didn't believe in ghosts, Cusco was a very ancient and spiritual place with a turbulent history. I felt uneasy in my new surroundings, which were beyond the limitations of logical western thinking and understanding.

Two weeks later, all staff were summoned to a far corner of the site, where a hubbub of excitement was brewing. We were about to witness an unusual and unique event. The government archeologists overseeing the work of our excavation crews had spotted what appeared to be large rusting iron crosses in the dig. The D-8 excavator machines were halted and idling in a long straight row. Their military precision, uniform yellow colour, and brute power reminding me of communist army tanks on parade, as seen on TV. A team of labourers were hand excavating in areas as directed by the archaeologists, under the watchful eye of Bruno, our construction superintendent.

They had already uncovered two bodies from the same ancient grave and were working on retrieving a third body. While it was not so unusual to find ancient graves in what had been arable farmland for centuries, the method of burial was what was unusual. The bodies were wrapped in thick cotton burlap, now crumbling, and placed vertically into hand-augured holes. They were shallow graves with perhaps one foot of cover. Even though we were at high altitude, the ground frost in the short winter season between July and October did not penetrate below one foot, and frost heave was never an issue as it is in Canadian climates.

Even more intriguing were the rusted iron crosses, which signified a Christian burial despite it being a traditional Quechua vertical burial method. It was a known fact that the ancient Quechua were short in stature, generally about five feet tall, whereas one of the three bodies had been at least six feet tall! The other two bodies were much smaller, indicating they were likely children.

I rode with Ray the two kilometres back to the site office, having formed a friendship since that fateful night. As I alighted his pickup truck, he said tapping the side of his nose. "I have a strong feeling about this, Aziz. I'll follow up on it and get back to you. *Sacrement;* there's definitely more to it than meets the eye."

The following week, Ray walked into my office, shut the door, and sat down with a conspiratorial smile lighting up his angular Van Dyke face with trim pointed goatee. "You know, Aziz, I had an instinct about the bodies and followed up with the chief archeologist. She owes me some favours. She thinks the bodies were buried more than a hundred years ago. The larger one was a man of European extraction who was at least six feet tall. He was a wealthy man, judging by the gold jewellery buried with him. He wore a gold crucifix and chain and a gold ring inscribed with the markings of the King of Spain. This type of ring was usually awarded to high-ranking individuals or soldiers who had distinguished themselves in the King's service."

"And the other two?" I asked expectantly. "They were a boy and a girl both aged under ten and were likely the men's children.

His smile broadened. "*Voila!* Do we know anyone looking for her husband and two children?"

I felt a chill run down my spine. *Could all this cockamamie stuff about a ghost really be true?*

"My archeologist friend is awaiting lab test results and will be filing her report by end of this week. She has kindly agreed to lend me three of the bone fragments, one from each body, which I must return to her by this Friday morning."

I looked at him blankly shaking my head.

Ray explained. "I've arranged with Chaska our office cleaner to take us to a local witch or shaman, called a *"Bruja."* She is believed to have special powers to enable her to look into the past and future. Hopefully she will be able to divine the story of these bodies and more from their bones."

Ray went on. "It will cost us US $30 for the Bruja and US $10 for Chaska to take us to her and to translate for us. Or if you're not interested, we can turn this over to El Gordo, who I am sure will be delighted to run with it himself."

I mulled it over, not sure if I should get involved. El Gordo had rightly pointed out that this was none of our business. It was his country and his spirits and his people, so why couldn't we just hand it over and be done with it? I mused. But I held back. I sensed something was not quite right about El Gordo. I shared my thoughts with Ray who nodded vigorously.

"Yes, just between us two, apart from running a couple of scams with the locals on the project there is something dark and ominous about El Gordo, and I wish we could get rid of him!"

What sort of scams?" I enquired.

"Well for one he's getting kickbacks from local suppliers of materials and consumables for the camp's needs. And the kickbacks of course get built into the suppliers' pricing to us, which we the joint venture ultimately pay for. Secondly, he's exacting tolls on wages paid to local workers. They have to pay him and his cronies ongoing commissions to be allowed to continue to work. And in cases where the worker is a pretty girl… Well, she has to pay them in a different way, if you get my meaning."

In an incredulous voice, I asked him how he knew all that.

"We found about a quarter of the local ladies hired on the project either quit or are fired within the first month. A couple of ladies have indirectly admitted this to us but will not sign their names to it, as they say they have been threatened with retribution against them and their families if they talk. As for the other ladies here, those who are attractive we regularly see staying behind in camp after work and then being dropped off at their homes late at night. Some to join their impoverished parents; others their unemployed husbands and small children. Now what do you suppose they would be doing in a men-only camp at night? As the main or only bread winners in their homes, they really have no other choice but to comply."

My blood boiled at these suggestions of atrocities. "So why do we put up with it, why can't we fire the ring leaders and make an example of them?" I naively implored?

"Because my friend we are a joint venture in South America... Our local partner allows us to control the finances, selected procurement, and government relations. In turn, we allow them to run the camp and local subcontractors, suppliers, and labour including local staff. This is our agreed-to division of work and project control. We stay out of our local partners' way and they stay out of ours!"

Ray changed the subject. "Anyway, Chaska our office cleaner tells me there are certain people able to control the spirits and make them do bad and evil things, and I'm concerned that El Gordo is one of them!"

"All right, Ray. I'm in. Let's do it!" I sighed knowing now we had to keep El Gordo out of it.

We left the project site a little earlier the next day, Chaska riding with Ray in his pickup truck and me following behind in my pickup.

I was still not used to the spectacular mountain views and stomach-turning drops off the edges of the steep mountain roads. We took a turnoff onto a long and winding road towards the ancient Inca citadel of *Sacsawayman*. My wife and I had toured the amazing stone structure and site earlier and our guide had taught us an easy way to remember the difficult-to-pronounce Inca name. He asked the men in the group to look at their female partners and think "sexy woman." Close enough—easy peasy!

Sacsawayman then was a truly incredible archeological site. Aside from the spirituality one feels immediately upon entering the sacred grounds, the long and tall zigzag stone walls commanding the site are a structural engineering marvel and are said to be one of the seven wonders of the world.

The wall is constructed of smooth stone boulders, up to sixty feet high and weighing between twenty-five and two hundred tons each!

How the Incas cut and moved the boulders into place is a mystery! The edges of each boulder have been hand-hewn in such a way that adjacent boulders along the top, bottom, and sides interlock into one another, with mortarless joints but fitting perfectly. The stone blocks are also shaped to slope inward. This form of construction allows the massive blocks to move against each other in an earthquake, but not fall down! The wall is fully seismic resistant and has remained standing and withstood numerous earthquakes in this highly seismic zone over the roughly five hundred years of their existence.

By contrast, many of the Spanish buildings that followed the Inca civilization as well as modern concrete and steel structures of the 20th century have either suffered damage or fallen down, unable to withstand earthquakes. Engineers of today have a lot to learn from the ancient Incas.

The wall is also an architectural delight to behold! The positioning of the unevenly shaped boulders stacked atop each other, relative to the movement of the sun, casts shadows onto the ground that resemble the surrounding mountain ranges.

We ascended the steep terrain above the citadel of Sacsawayman, arriving at a plateau overlooking it. Hidden in a copse were a grouping of huts in a shanty, accessible only by a small and narrow dirt road. We pulled up our vehicles against a large smooth shaped boulder, dismounted and took a twisting littered footpath into the shanty.

"Mama coco, mama coco," called Chaska in a shrill voice. A small colourfully dressed elderly woman of indeterminate age suddenly emerged seemingly out of nowhere. One moment there was nothing; the next moment she was there! Eerie.

She wore traditional Quechua garb, the *pollera*, or white wool skirt trimmed with colourful bands and a highly embroidered loose blouse. Over that she had a *jobona*, or patterned wool jacket with colourful buttons, and a *manta,* or cape, also brightly coloured. Sitting atop her oiled jet-black hair, which was braided into two short pigtails, was a floppy cloth cap fastened with colourfully beaded straps called a *nonterra.* She also wore cheap beaded jewellery, but surprisingly her feet were bare.

After a brief exchange with Chaska in Quechua, she bowed to each of us and led us behind the huts into a small clearing. Shooing away a group of small children and their goats, she motioned for us to sit on the hard-pack littered ground. She began delicately arranging some intensely black rocks in a tight circle, stuffing brushwood in the core. Then expertly lighting a fire, she piled on larger logs to stoke it. Soon, the fire was blazing and sitting down in front of it she motioned for us to move in closer.

I was able to observe her face more clearly in the firelight. It was uncommonly lined and weathered, and I noticed she had two missing upper front teeth. Chaska beside us also had her upper front teeth missing, as did Maria, our tea lady. I wondered if this was a local native custom or affectation to have the front teeth removed for added beauty, perhaps?

I was well aware that in various cultures on various continents, performing physical disfigurements on women are common. For example, some women have their earlobes pierced and then elongated to allow logs several inches in diameter to be poked through the extended opening. Or having their two front teeth forced apart in childhood to create a wide gap between the growing front teeth, thereby enhancing their beauty in the eyes of the beholder. Then there is the practice of "scarification," which involves steel blade cuts, etchings, and braiding designs to create artistic swellings onto the face, neck, breasts, and upper body as a permanent beauty feature. And of course, body ink tattoos common in both ancient and modern cultures.

We got down to business and Chaska handed over the bones from a cloth bag she had brought along. They were a man's skeletal hand with all the finger bones intact, a child's rib bone, and what looked like a child's big toe bone.

Mama Coco, the witch, or bruja, ran her fingers over the proffered bones one by one, feeling them, squeezing them, then tasting and sucking the bones, getting to know them. She emptied out a small leather pouch, sprinkling coloured crystals into the fire, causing the flames to dance in brightly coloured ribbons. She chanted in an anguished guttural voice, holding tightly onto the bones, staring into the dancing fire just inches from her face. She rocked backwards, forwards, and sideways, eyes turned inward giving her a demonic look. She then emitted throaty grunts and clicking sounds between her teeth. This went on for a few minutes until the flames subsided.

The bruja stood up, bent forward arms akimbo, legs splayed wide and spewed out a long arcing stream of vomit into the fire, dousing it completely. This was a show worth paying for by itself!

Still clutching the bones tightly, she motioned the group to follow her, leading us to a large square polished rock with smaller square rock stools facing it. As we sat on the stools, she pulled out a rosary and recited what appeared to be some sort of short prayer. She then proceeded to tell us her story, translated from Quechua into Spanish into English. I briefly wondered if anything might be lost in the double translation, nonetheless, this is what the bruja said.

"I see a man dismounting a magnificent black stallion in front of an elegant hacienda. The man is tall, handsome, strong, and in his prime. His name is Alejandro Cortez Hernandez, a former soldier in the Spanish army and decorated by the King of Spain himself. With gold gifted him by his king and with his middle-class family money he remained in South America after the wars, buying land outside Cusco. After several years of industrious hard work carving out his farming estate, he returned briefly to Sevilla to marry his childhood sweetheart and to bring her back to the New World.

"Isabela Alvarez del Toro took her new role seriously as wife and mistress of the vast estate and got involved with all aspects of running it. She also produced two beautiful children from her marriage with Alejandro. Susanna, a mature and intelligent seven-year-old girl and Juanito, a precocious four-year-old boy, as I see them in my mind's eye.

The bruja's eyes bugged out and she made a throaty gargling sound. I got ready to leap out of the way and was much relieved when she did not vomit again nor rotate her head 360 degrees like Linda Blair in *The Exorcist*. She continued with her story...

"Isabela is a stunningly beautiful woman, a tall redhead with long red tresses cascading over her shapely bosom, her red dress gathered at her slim waist. She is standing on the balcony of the hacienda smiling happily and waving at her husband as he dismounts. The heavy wood door swings open and the children run out, shouting with joy into their father's open arms. They are followed at a discreet distance by their watchful nanny, Rosita."

I felt the bruja was dragging her story out a little and wished she would hurry it up! She stopped mid-sentence, turned to look at me admonishingly, and pursed her lips. We stared at each other until I shifted my gaze downward. This was really weird; could she read my thoughts, and in English too? As I looked up, she gave me a knowing smile and went on.

"Later that day, Siete Condorpaxi bowed and thanked his patron Señor Alejandro Cortez, respectfully exiting the office, which was an add-on building at the rear of the hacienda. *Siete*, which means "seven" in Spanish, was the seventh of ten children to a Quechua family. His wise parents, not wanting any extended family conflicts over choosing names and because it was just easier to keep track, named their children numerically according to their order of birth. So, for example his sister born two years before him was named *Seis* or "six," and his brother born immediately after him, was named *Ocho* or "eight." Siete was the lead hand and right-hand man, he liked to think, to Señor Alejandro Cortez. He was in charge of all farm workers on the estate as well as overseer of certain operations. Alejandro had spotted the potential of the young, smart, and ambitious Siete from the very beginning and had taught, mentored, and promoted him to his present position in just five short years.

"Siete walked past the stables in the gathering dusk detouring around the far stall, hoping to catch a glimpse of her. He had not seen her at all today, despite doing his best to catch a covetous glimpse. Ah there she was, brushing down her white mare, speaking softly to it. Each time he got near her, Siete's mouth went dry and his throat constricted at her breathtaking beauty and her perfumed scent!

"Isabela presented a perfect picture in her form fitting cream-coloured riding pants and high leather boots, beautiful red hair tied in a long ponytail swept forward down her front. Her open neck black silk blouse exposing the tops of her creamy white breasts still heaving, following her long gallop back from the weaving sheds. She had been attending to the needs of her female staff. They were the weavers who manufactured Isabela's high quality woollen clothing for the local high-end market. Isabela had promised to speak with her husband to provide added benefits requested, and was in no doubt she would convince Alejandro.

"She looked up suddenly, hearing Siete's light-footed approach, rewarding him with a bright engaging smile as he quickly shuffled past on his short stocky legs. He nodded at her with eyes cast down, touching the brim of his cowboy hat respectfully, too scared to look her in the eye, lest he expose his burning desire."

The bruja paused, searching her clothing, pulling out a different leather pouch this time. Grabbing a handful of coca leaves, she offered it to the group. Only Chaska accepted and they each chewed on a large mouthful. Coca leaves contain concentrations of cocaine metabolites, which is an illegal drug in western countries and easily detectible in a urine drug test. Since drug testing was not a requirement on the project, it amused Aziz that Chaska would get away with it. After a few minutes of relative silence, other than the masticating sounds of the two ladies, the distant cries of children playing and dogs barking, the bruja spoke again.

"I can jump to the final scene or continue on with what transpired after the stables scene. As you appear to be in a hurry *caballeros* (gentlemen), which do you prefer?"

Ray and I looked at each other and he confirmed through Chaska that we wanted to hear the long version.

"All right then; let me continue. The next scene is about Isabela and her lovely family…"

"Isabela stared at Siete's disappearing figure thoughtfully as he swept by and she shuddered with a sense of chill. She shook it off putting it down to the cool evening air and walked briskly back to the hacienda, rang the bell and was immediately let inside by Concha, her maid. It was just past 6:00 p.m. when she entered the cozy warmth of the hacienda and she knew the children would be having their bath.

"Isabela sat down on a stool and held on to the edges while Concha pulled off her riding boots, before sponging her face and hands from a bowl of warm scented water. Then slipping into her flats, Isabela ran up the stairs to the children's bedroom and into their bathroom. Susana and Juanito jumped up in their tub, squealing with joy on seeing their mother, both talking nineteen-to-the-dozen about their day's activities. Rosita their nanny hastily towelled them down as they ran naked into their mother's arms.

"After much hugging and kissing, Isabela took her leave promising, 'Papi and I will come after supper to read you your favourite bedtime stories, my dearest Juanito and Susana. Now, let Rosita finish dressing you and giving you supper, then brush your teeth and get into your beds and wait up for us my loves!'

"Isabela reluctantly left her children, going to her quarters down the hall where Concha had already drawn her bath sprinkled with her favourite salts. She quickly undressed and let herself sink into the warm sweet-smelling soapy bathwater.

"'Thank you, Concha. You may leave now and please let the *patron* know that I am back in my room and waiting for him.' Isabela smiled dreamily, relishing her bath and the thought of what might follow.

"*Si senora*," replied her faithful maid as she hastily departed, smiling shyly on her way to deliver the message to her patron.

"Isabela closed her eyes, sinking into the warm water, allowing herself to get drowsy, long red tendrils of hair floating above her body, covering her firm creamy white breasts and flat tummy. She sat up straight with a squeal when he burst in through the connecting bedroom door.

"'My dearest, Bella,' came a familiar strong masculine voice. 'How I have missed you. Why, we have both been so busy that we have hardly seen each other all day!' Alexandro exclaimed, sitting himself on the edge of the bathtub. She smiled lovingly and sighed happily as he raised her long red hair with one arm, then gently sponged first her firm breasts, then her neck and shoulders and around and down her sculpted long back. She lay back again, face turned upward to receive his long lingering kiss.

"Alejandro encircled his strong arms around her, lifting her straight up. Isabela gave a short scream, laughing and splashing soapy water onto Alejandro and over the floorboards. He swiftly strode out carrying her still wet into their bedroom. Some forty minutes later, they disentangled, quickly dressed for supper, and agreeing to sup later, they made their way to the children's bedroom first. After reading the children a few stories each, tucking them in and kissing them goodnight, they went down to supper.

"Later, as they undressed for bed, she asked, 'How is Siete doing these days? Do you find him different and changed in any way?'

"Alejandro gave Isabela a puzzled look. 'Why this interest in Siete all of a sudden, my love?' She went on to tell him about their brief encounter at the stables that evening, ending with, 'I sensed rather than saw him staring at me in a way that made me very uneasy and uncomfortable.'

"Alejandro shrugged it off, reminding her what an excellent lead hand Siete had turned out to be, and that it was in his culture to be shy and respectful of the *Senora del casa,* lady of the house, and not look at her directly."

"'Don't worry your pretty red head about it my love,' and with a twinkle in his eye went on. 'Your pretty red head should be worrying about what might happen to you next!' He gently but firmly pulled her down onto him, fending off her mock blows and protests with a laugh."

Meanwhile, back in present-day Cusco, the mountain air was chilling rapidly although it was still only late afternoon and Aziz could feel the beginnings of a headache coming on. The bruja stood up and led them back to the fire pit, which she expertly re-lit in no time. They held out their hands to the crackling fire, much appreciating the warmth. The bruja called out in the direction of the huts beyond, and a female voice answered her with alacrity.

She ruminated for a couple of minutes before saying, "The final chapter will be very disturbing to you gringos…" but then stopped. "Ah, here it is." She turned her attention towards the smiling lady approaching them. The lady was dressed in similar bright multi-coloured clothing as the bruja, bringing with her a small black steaming cauldron and a tiny child of indeterminate sex in tow. The child had a tangled mass of black hair over a coal-streaked face and wore a straight rough jute cassock, carrying a ladle and some metal cups in tiny hands. As quickly as they had arrived, they were gone

The bruja ladled out the steaming black brew into cups, handing one to each person. "Drink up," she commanded. "You need to prepare your senses for what you are about to hear and see in your minds."

"What is in this drink?" asked Ray.

"*Maté de coca*" she replied. "Black tea made from coca leaves with just a touch of a hallucinogen added to assist you in visualizing my story." As though reading my mind again, turning to me she went on. "In addition, it will also warm you up and will help you get rid of the *soroche,* which you are beginning to feel…"

I looked at Ray quizzically. "Don't worry; drink up," he said taking a sip himself. "*Maté de coca* is a diluted version of raw coca leaves and really helps with the soroche. Judging by your knitted brows, I presume you have a high-altitude headache coming on. Soroche is the Quechua word by the way, for altitude sickness. We are at over eleven thousand feet altitude as you know, and prolonged exposure in the outdoors brings on the headache. My wife Cecile and I take it quite regularly."

"But what about the hallucinogen she mentioned?" I asked, still not sure.

"Never had the mind-blowing stuff before," Ray replied. "I'm game to try it; might be fun," he smiled, taking another sip.

Given the cold mountain air, my oncoming headache, and the situation I found myself in, I nodded and took a sip myself. The tea had a slightly bitter taste but also something else peppery and gritty, whose combined taste made it quite interesting and palatable.

The bruja refilled our drained cups and continued with her story.

"Some weeks later, early one morning, the hacienda courtyard was abuzz with excitement, the groomed horses and wagon looking magnificent, befitting Isabela's status as a noblewoman. Dressed in a smart pant suit and wide-brimmed hat, Isabela hugged and kissed the children goodbye, assuring them she would be back before the weekend with lovely presents for them both. Then giving Alejandro a long lingering kiss, she jumped onto the wagon, sitting down in the plush bench seat next to Nayaraq, her wool expert and head seamstress. Concha sat ahead next to Pablito the wagon driver. Andres Flores, an up-and-coming young man and a crack shot with a rifle, was sitting behind them facing the rear, effectively riding shotgun.

"Alejandro had wanted Siete, his most trusted man, to ride shotgun for Isabela, but he had begged off with a stomach infection at the last minute. Hence young Andres' chance to prove his mettle in guarding his very important charge. Two more utility wagons were positioned, one ahead and one behind Isabela's wagon, with two men riding in each, shotguns at the ready. Each wagon was in turn pulled by a team of four horses and the wagon train was completed by two armed horsemen, riding one on each side of the mistress. All men were of course hand-picked by Alejandro and Siete.

"The wagon train soon disappeared in a cloud of dust on the day long journey into the sacred valley of the Incas and to their destination, the quaint artsy town of Ollyantantambo. They were headed for the two-day annual wool market in the sacred valley. Local sheep farmers would have their various grades of wool on display and on sale. Isabela, being a good negotiator, was expecting to bring back two wagon-loads of premium quality wool for her garment manufacturing business, as per her annual custom for the last few years.

"Nightfall descended over the hacienda Cortez, and paraffin lamps were lit one by one by the house staff who then locked up and took their leave for the night. That is, save for the nanny, Rosita, who would bed down in a small alcove adjoining the children's room. The patron read them bedtime stories and then kissed his children goodnight before going downstairs to his office to catch up on paperwork, as there was no sweet distraction awaiting him in his bedroom that night."

The bruja paused for a minute to refill cups, then continued with a grim expression.

"There was a knock on the office door from the outside entrance. Alejandro bid 'Come!' without pausing to look up from his ledgers. The quick short steps and garlicky breath (tinged with something familiar, alcohol?, he abstractly wondered) told him it was his lead

[194]

hand Siete, who had probably come to apologize for being too sick to be of any use that day. Alejandro finished entering the column of figures before looking up and smilingly joked, 'Siete what are you doing here, have you already got tired of sitting on the crapper all day or what?'

"Although he seemed edgy, Siete laughed dutifully and said, 'Patron I just feel really bad that I was not here to help you with all the work today, especially as the senora is not here. But now I am feeling much better, Patron. Please let me help you with your paperwork or anything else you need.'

"Alejandro considered the offer for a moment then said, 'Okay, why not, Siete? Pull up a chair and I will show you what to do to help me and save me some time tonight.' He turned away, reaching into a cabinet behind him as Siete moved closer.

"Like a viper, Siete lunged forward, plunging a long evil-looking hunting knife with sharp serrated edges into Alejandro's back! Alejandro suddenly impaled gasped with a mind-numbing pain, his spinal nerves screaming as though on fire. He twisted around to face Siete, with a look of total incomprehension and horror. The haft of the long knife embedded between his shoulder blades still reverberated with the force of entry, his muscles and ligaments twitching uncontrollably, vainly trying to escape the sharp knife embedded in him.

"'What... why... why... Siete?' Alejandro whispered. With a loud clatter, his chair fell over and he slid off with a thud, unable to support himself. 'Why? Why?' Alejandro kept mouthing as he lay on the floor, unable to move or speak.

"Siete squatted down beside him. 'I am sorry, Patron, that it had to come to this. I have been your right hand for many years now and can do everything that you do, but everything is yours, only yours, all the time!' he said with a sad expression.

"Alejandro shook his head imperceptibly, and with great effort managed to whisper, 'I have always praised you, brought you forward, rewarded you, and have great plans for you... why Siete?'

"'No! enough!" spat Siete. 'You Spanish Conquistadores have raped and killed our women and children, you have stolen our gold, and sent it back to your Spanish king! You have spilt our blood, massacred our people, and taken our land. This land is not yours to begin with—none of it! Now it is my turn to be the Patron of this magnificent estate that I and my father before me helped build!' Siete was now frothing at the mouth with generations of anger and resentment.

"'No, no, Siete. Please listen to me... you are mistaken. You have been like a younger brother to me,' implored Alejandro, fighting to be allowed to live, even if it meant to live on disabled for life. Isabela and the children needed him... For their sake, he implored Siete again.

"'No, Patron, you listen to me for once!' replied Siete through clenched teeth. 'Your estate is now my estate. Your hacienda is now my hacienda. Your children are now my children, and your beautiful wife is now my wife! This is the way of the Inca who your people destroyed! When a king or chieftain dies, his adult son or kin takes over! And if there are no adult male kin then his next-in-command takes over his kingdom and all his possessions!'"

"'And I am HE—Siete Condorpaxi!' he shouted, barely able to control himself now. 'In fact, I shall have my own children with the beautiful La Colorada! Yes, on second thought I do not need your children to be mine. I alone shall decide what is to become of them,' he smiled evilly.

"Alejandro's brain was pounding and an extreme coldness was enveloping his body. He could feel himself slipping away, but with a supreme effort of will, ignored the coldness and pain, trying to focus. He whispered urgently, 'Siete, please, I beg you in the name of our Lord... Yes take it all, all my land and possessions, but spare my family. Promise me you will provide them safe passage back to Sevilla to our family home.' Tears ran down Alejandro's cheeks, his jaws immobile now and his vision rapidly blurring as he looked imploringly at Siete's unrelenting cold and cruel face.

"'Enough!' shouted Siete. 'You shall not divert me and the Condorpaxi dynasty from our rightful destiny with your useless words and tears!' With that, Siete placed his cold killer hands over Alejandro's throat, squeezing with all his might. Alejandro's long body jerked and twitched for almost a minute, thrashing out, fighting to live, until finally his crushed windpipe had no possible way to breathe oxygen into his lungs, and the great man slowly passed from this world. With a heavy sigh, the patron lay permanently still, a faraway look in his sightless blue eyes.

"Siete too sighed heavily, picked himself up and opening the outside door, stuck his head out, whistling softly. Thankfully, Siete failed to hear the sharp intake of breath and stifled sob coming from the corridor that led from the office into the house, above the sounds of his whistling and the blowing wind outside."

"His henchmen Braulio and Peligroso joined him inside and between them, struggling to carry the large body of the Patron outside, threw him over a horse. One henchman returned inside to mop up the blood and tidy up the furniture while the other two men led the horse and body to the river, about a kilometre away. There, they unceremoniously dumped Alejandro's body into the narrow fast-flowing Rio Chiche, confident it would be swept a couple of kilometres downstream where it would sink in the shallow pools where the river widened considerably. The body would eventually float up and be found by the washerwomen. But by this time, it would have been so badly battered by rocks in the fast-flowing section, that

MAHMOUD HIRJI

the knife wound and crushed windpipe would be indiscernible. He had no doubt however that the Patron could be identified by the remnants of his battered clothing, white skin, blue eyes, and large body frame.

"Folks would presume the Patron's death was accidental, that he had gone for a night swim in calmer waters upstream, but the unpredictable river currents had dragged him downstream into the narrow section where he had tragically met his death. And sadly, nobody had been near the river banks on that dark and windy night to hear his shouts for help. And Siete of course had been sick with a poisoned stomach and suffering in bed while this was all happening.

"Siete's twisted mind reasoned with himself that as the Patron did not have adult male heirs in Peru, he, Siete Condorpaxi, could lay claim as the next in command. And when Isabela returned, she would realize her family's precarious situation and would concede to Siete who would eventually win her over. After all, she would also be getting a younger and more virulent man, especially when hopped up with coca! *It was just a change of leadership at the top, that's all. Everything else would remain the same for her as the mistress of the casa,* he reasoned....

"After Isabela bore him his children, he would find a way to be rid of the Patron's children, he felt confident of this. The key, however, were her children. He had to move quickly to ensure Isabela's children were kept hostage from her unless and until she had bedded down with him! And once this was accomplished she would undoubtably want more and more of him. He grinned evilly, consumed by his nefarious thoughts, his gold teeth glinting in the moonlight. Siete gleefully rubbed his hands together at his brilliant plan."

The bruja paused, ignoring our pained expressions, calling out to the woman for more maté de coca. She stoked the fire until it

[198]

began to spit again and our bellies were warmed. I was feeling light-headed, yet with a sense of serenity.

She continued, "Rosita had been kneeling by her cot in her night-gown, reciting her prayers, and thanking the Lord for the oppor-tunity to serve such a kind and generous family when she heard a muffled crash and clatter downstairs from the direction of the office. Wondering if the Patron had fallen down, she rushed downstairs in her nightgown, picking up a lit candle.

"She entered the corridor to the office and heard Siete's guttural voice shouting. She instinctively blew out the candle and, barefoot, approached the office silently. The door was open a crack, letting out a sliver of flickering light into the corridor. Placing her ear to the wall next to the door she could hear all that Siete was shouting and the Patron appeared to be speaking in a hoarse whisper with words she could not decipher. But she didn't need to understand it to know what was going on. She struggled not to cry out aloud during the act of murder and death struggles of her beloved Patron, petrified and too afraid to say or do anything.

"She heard Siete open the outside door and whistle softly and willed herself to open the interior door a crack further to peek inside. She immediately saw the Patron's blood-stained body splayed on the floor, his noble face wearing a vacant look with eyes wide open. Luckily, Rosita was shielded from Siete's line of sight. Gagging, she immediately drew back as the henchmen entered the office and she swiftly retreated down the corridor. Blinking away her tears, Rosita crossed herself instinctively knowing exactly what to do. They would be a few minutes getting rid of the Patron's body and cleaning up the mess before they came for the children and her… She had ten, perhaps fifteen minutes at most.

"Wiping her tears and crossing herself again, Rosita rushed into the kitchen at the far end of the house. She rapidly filled two large wool bags with water jugs, a jug of milk, a large piece of ham, a left-over half chicken, all the cheese there was, two loaves of bread, fruit, and vegetables. Her shoulders stooped with the weight of the two bags slung over them. Next, she rolled a large cutting knife and tin utensils into a kitchen towel, and clutching them in one hand and the candle in another, she made her way up the rear staircase.

"Rosita had been with the children ever since they were born and entrusted by the Cortez's with a confidential emergency procedure in the event of a mass riot or political uprising in Cusco. With this in mind, Alejandro had constructed two hideouts for their family, close servants and some trusted estate employees. The first was an underground stone and masonry bunker situated below the straw matted floor of the stables, which was quite inaccessible at the moment.

"The second hideout was a secret room inside the hacienda in behind the children's bedroom, which nobody other than the Cortezes, Rosita, Concha, and the cook-Senora Casado, knew about. This room had two access points. The first was from the adjoining library via a sliding section of wall panelling, and the second via a removable section of tiled wall panelling in the children's bathroom. The room itself was long and narrow, approximately eight metres long by three metres wide, and fitted in between adjoining room layouts in such a way that nobody other than a clever architect would have been able to figure out there was a hidden room.

"The wall interiors and wood floor of the secret room were lined with cork to deaden any sound. There were four narrow cots occupying half the length of the room, two on each side, end to end. The other half was furnished with a rug and two armchairs, wall shelving, and a narrow table top with folded legs, leaning against the end wall. The table was for setting up between the cots, which doubled as a dining and kids play and study table. An adequate supply of candles, matches, books, and games as well as necessary bedpans, were stored in boxes beneath the bunk beds. Finally, a round porthole window, roughly thirty centimeters in diameter was framed into the exterior end wall, just beneath the ceiling line."

"The porthole was one of ten operable windows set along the length of the hacienda. They served a dual purpose as ventilation and architectural features. They opened upward and outward, to allow for air circulation as well as direct sunlight into the house. The secret room porthole was an essential feature for survival and had a heavy blackout curtain to be drawn across at night.

"Rosita silently made her way to the children's bathroom and set down her wares. She reached up high to two clothes hooks set about sixty centimeters apart on the removable wall panel, and turned them sideways. She reached under the small shelf seat set in the panel and flipped a hidden lever. Rosita had practised this maneuver at least twice yearly under Isabela's supervision, and so was quite adept at it.

"The panel came out easily in her hands and she slid it against the adjacent wall.

"Stepping inside the secret room, Rosita drew the blackout curtain, lighting a candle. After placing the food bags inside, she silently re-entered the children's room, gently waking Susana first, shushing her as though they were playing a game. Susana obeyed Rosita and allowed herself to be led into the bathroom. Rosita whispered to her to use the toilet, even if she didn't feel like it, and then to wait for her brother.

"Juanito refused to wake, and Rosita gently carried him into the bathroom, setting him down on the toilet. She then turned on the tap, praying the running water could not be heard downstairs. The running water served its purpose right away and little Juanito automatically peed while Rosita held his tiny weenie for him. Once inside the secret room, she whispered to them that their father had told her to hide the children in the room of secrets until their mother came back because he had to go away for a while. She ended by saying their father loved them both very much and would be back soon with lots of gifts for them!

"'Now, go to sleep and we'll speak in the morning.' she whispered, tucking them into their cots.

"Re-entering the bathroom, Rosita could hear the scrunching of boots through the open porthole on the gravel pathway below. She hastily used the toilet herself, then ran into her bedroom to collect a few things—some clothes, her bible and her large silver crucifix, the pride and joy of her possessions gifted to her by Isabela. Running through the children's bedroom, she scooped up some loose clothing, Susana's favourite doll, and Juanito's small wooden horse. Tossing all the items onto the cork floor through the opening, Rosita heard voices coming up the stairs. She stepped deftly inside, pulling and lifting the cork panel over the opening. Turning a duplicate set of levers on the inside of the panel, she secured the panel back into the wall.

"Two minutes later, Rosita heard muffled shouts of alarm as the men realized their quarries were not in their bedrooms! The bathroom door was flung open and Braulio's loud and arrogant voice shouted, 'Nobody in the bedroom nor in the bathroom!'

"Now, Braulio was a piece of work. It was rumoured that he'd had his way with one of the wool shed workers, gotten her pregnant, and then with his cronies threatened her parents to forget the incident and say nothing to anybody, at the risk of "violent accidents" befalling their family members.

"There was also the incident at the staff midnight service one Christmas. Reportedly, as the staff were milling in the foyer of the small chapel on their way out, the candles were blown out by a strong gust of wind. In the momentary darkness and confusion, somebody had pressed his hard body up against Concha from behind and squeezed her breasts violently before letting go and melting into the crowd. The very next day in the staff canteen, Concha noticed Braulio's cronies snickering and smirking at her, while he wore a look of conquest on his evil face. Braulio grinned at her showing off his black rotting teeth. Concha did her best to avoid Braulio after that. She knew better than to complain and risk putting her family in danger. Best to forget, avoid and move on.

"The following two days and nights were an adjustment for Rosita and the children, learning to talk in whispers and not being able to move freely in their cramped quarters. Thankfully, the house servants were confined downstairs and Siete had not yet taken up residence upstairs. Rosita made a schedule for the children and herself for bathroom visits via the wall panel. She also decided to risk locking the bathroom door from the inside leading to the children's bedroom to give them time to escape back into the secret room, should the need ever arise."

"After a short pause for silent rumination and a slight calming of the foreboding evil evident in the others' minds, the bruja continued

"The sun was waning as the wagon rounded a bend in the road, and Isabela sat up with anticipation and excitement! She could just see the red-tiled roof of her family hacienda atop a distant hill. Half-an-hour tops, and they would be home!

"From a business perspective, this had been one of her most successful trips to Ollyantantambo; she had purchased some excellent quality wools. Two packed wagon loads were trailing behind her, and she had made some excellent new contacts at the local market, not only suppliers of wool, but also potential buyers from Europe willing to pay premium prices for her knitted products. She couldn't wait to tell Alejandro all about it, he would be so proud of her, as he always was!

"And most of all, she couldn't wait to be reunited with her beloved husband and back in his strong arms. *And the children! Oh, her beautiful and smart children.* How she yearned to hold them and kiss them! She had managed to find some beautiful and unique hand-made toys and could already imagine and hear the children's shouts and screams of pleasure and Alejandro's delighted laughter!

"Thirty minutes later, they entered the gate to their property. The gatekeeper with a sombre look and downcast eyes let them in and they cantered along the long, straight road to the hacienda. The field workers standing on either side of the road lifted their heads at the passing carriage, but sadly looked away again. Some of the women wore black scarves on their heads.

"'*That's odd*,' thought Isabela. '*I wonder what's gotten into them?*' But she was too distracted with excitement to ponder over their dress and why they were standing there in the first place. Isabela's wagon drew up by the front door, while the other two laden wagons continued on towards the cotton sheds to unload their wares.

"'*Muchas gracias,* Pablito, *muchas gracias,* Andres,' Isabela thanked her driver and guard as she jumped off the carriage and ran to the front door. She would make sure they received a big bonus in their pay packets. The door opened as she arrived, and instead of the children running out to greet her, she was met by Concha and Senora Casado.

"Isabela stopped. They were not smiling nor welcoming. On the contrary, they were crying and dressed in black. Isabela's heart hammered against her ribcage, her throat constricted. and mouth went dry. She was sure it was about one of her children, but which one? She dreaded to find out.

"'*El Patron, Senora. El Patron esta muerto.* - The Patron is dead', they cried in unison, grabbing hold of Isabela as she fainted.

"They gently led Isabela into the house and made her rest on a couch. They kneeled before her holding her hands, while Senora Casado softly told Isabela about how the Patron's broken and drowned body was found by the washerwomen at the river pool downstream from them. They went on to tell her that his body was too broken up and had to be buried right away, and that he was given a proper Christian burial by the Padre.

"Senora Casado went on. 'Siete gave a moving eulogy, and has been with the field workers ever since, to ensure the harvest is not interrupted. As soon as the harvest is completed in the next few days, they will hold a proper service for the Patron and provide a day off in mourning to all the workers.'

"Isabela went deathly white, the blood draining from her face, tears coursing down her face. Finally, in between sobs, Isabela managed to ask, 'Bring me my children, Concha. I want to see them right away.'

"It was now Concha's turn to go pale. 'The children and Rosita have disappeared, Senora Cortez, but don't worry, Siete has search parties out looking for them. I'm sure they will find them very soon, safe and sound,' Concha replied with a tremor in her voice.

"At this further alarming news, Isabela collapsed, and after reviving her, they half-led half-carried her to her bedroom upstairs.

"Braulio, who was posted outside the house as a guard and spy by Siete, witnessed this exchange and slipped away to alert his boss of Isabela's return. Isabela of course did not notice him in her state of agitation and near collapse.

"Isabela slept fitfully that evening and through the night and was awakened the next morning by Concha with a hot cup of coffee and breakfast on a tray. Sitting up in bed, listlessly picking at her food, Concha informed her that Siete needed to speak to her in the office after she had breakfasted, and hoped the senora would agree to it.

'He said he may have some news on the children's whereabouts.' Concha explained. The mention of the children galvanized Isabela into action, telling Concha to inform Siete at once that she would be down shortly, and then to rush back up to draw her bath and help her bathe."

The winds were picking up and the fire had almost died out. Aziz shivered, staring into the dying embers. The bruja stopped talking again and they all took a well-deserved break.

Ray spoke up. "It's okay for you Aziz, you don't have to talk, but I'm getting a sore throat from all this translating, and I'm sure the others are too…"

As though she understood English, the bruja said in Quechua, "It is getting late and dark, my throat is hoarse, and I am tired. I still need to explain to you what happens next, although I am sure you have guessed that La Colorada in your camp is none other than the beautiful and tragic Isabela?"

We nodded in agreement.

"We can end now as you already have a lot of answers… or we can continue tomorrow where you will learn what happened and why Isabela is haunting your camp. But more importantly, I can advise you how you can help Isabela's spirit and in doing so, she will go away and never again return to haunt your workers…" She trailed off for effect.

"Although you brought me three bones of three people to divine today—Alejandro, Susana and Juanito—I have also provided a lot more information on two additional central characters to this story, Isabela and Siete. So, my cost for today will be for five people times ten dollars each or fifty dollars. If you prefer to return tomorrow for the rest of their story, the cost will be another thirty dollars: ten dollars each for Isabela and Siete, plus another ten for both children."

Ray and I looked at each other, nodded, and Ray gave her his agreement. We would return the next day. As we walked back to our trucks, I asked Chasca how old she thought the bruja might be, to which she replied, "She went to school with me, two or three years ahead of me, I think. As I am forty-eight, she must be around fifty." Ray and I were both amazed to learn this, because the bruja looked to us to be around seventy-five!

The next day, yet again our tableau of four were seated around the open fire pit, unlit as yet in the late afternoon. This time, in preparation for the cold evening, we had brought along heavy wool sweaters, gloves, and Andean hats with long ear flaps.

We were dreading to hear what came next, while the bruja looked rejuvenated and raring to get going again. She greeted us like old friends, clapping our shoulders, smiling with camaraderie. But not until we were into our second cup of maté de coca did the bruja resume her spell-binding story.

"Bathed and rejuvenated as best as one can be after losing one's husband in his prime, dressed in a black silk shirt and riding pants, her long red hair tied up and partially covered by a black lace hat, Isabela hurried down to her office. She cut a striking figure as she strode into the office. She fully expected to see Siete standing outside the main door waiting for her to usher him in. Instead, he was seated in her husband's chair and at her husband's desk!

"Siete smiled confidently at Isabela, inviting her to sit in the visitor's chair across the desk. He started out by offering his deepest condolences for her loss, for her children's loss, and indeed for everybody's loss. 'Senora, in addition to everything else, I know how worried you must be for your missing children.' Her crumpled face told him he had hit the mark. 'I assure you that all my men on the estate are searching for them.' Isabela noted he said 'my' men and not 'your' or 'our'.

"'They have searched the river and scoured the river banks from upstream where the Patron went swimming, all the way down to the pool where his body was found, and beyond that too, but have come up with nothing. They were also searching all the workers' homes on the estate, as well as in the little villages in the valley within a ten-kilometre radius of here. I have also posted a reward for the person who finds them first. It is only a matter of time before they are found.'

"Isabela nodded with a faint glimmer of hope in her eyes.

"'We know about the secret hideout in the stables beneath the ground,' he said, 'but they are not hiding out there.' He noticed her flinch at the realization that he knew. Smiling, he went on. 'We also think there might be a second secret hideout on the estate somewhere, possibly beneath the hacienda, and my men are presently searching for it, and we will find it.' His voice rose with determination. 'It would be in everybody's best interest, Senora, if you admitted there is a second hideout and told us where it is—for the sake of your children.'

"Isabela didn't like his presumptuousness and his overall tone. And worse, she didn't like the way he was openly eyeing her up and down, his eyes lingering on her breasts as they heaved beneath her shirt, while she tried desperately to slow down her rapid breathing.

"'There is no other secret hideout that I know of,' she lied, 'but if there is, then Pablito and Andres might know. Why don't we ask them?' she said, hoping in this way to get in touch with her faithful protectors and allies. 'Why don't we call them here and ask them?' she repeated innocently.

"'Oh, I should have told you, Senora, they went out in a boat early this morning to search the river rapids for the children. But unfortunately, their boat capsized and they have both drowned. I'm so sorry; they will be missed.' He hung his head unconvincingly. Siete continued to leer openly at her breasts beneath her thin shirt, which were now heaving again with her rising fear. His account of their accidental deaths on top of Alejandro's accidental death sounded quite improbable and she now feared Siete's involvement in this.

"In spite of Isabela's caring and empathetic nature for her workers, she was a strong-willed and fearless woman and would ordinarily have stood up to this insolent man and fired him on the spot! But the recent tragic events in her life had turned her life upside down. Isabela hid her face in her hands, struggling to control her emotions for a minute or two, before resolving to stop his insolence right there and then!

"'Siete, I don't think you understand that I have suffered a terrible shock upon learning of the death of my husband and finding my children missing. Nevertheless, I am now the Patrona. I command you to get out of my husband's chair immediately! How dare you sit there!' she exclaimed in a steely voice.

"'I want you to gather my entire workforce and have them assembled in front of the stables within the hour. I would like to speak to them about our way forward. Also send a coach and driver immediately to my office. I wish an errand to be run for me.' She would pen a quick letter to her lawyer in Cusco, Manuel Rivera, advising him of Alejandro's suspicious death, requesting him to immediately come to the hacienda with the police.

"'No, Isabela. It is YOU who do not understand!' he spat out while remaining seated. She noted with dismay his insolent familiarity in addressing her by her name, and his disobedience in not vacating the chair, as commanded.

"'Your Spanish king and his armies of conquistadores stole our land and parcelled out pieces of our land to his soldiers who did the stealing and raping and killing of our people.'

"'The lands of this estate are a part of the sacred burial lands of the Inca. Therefore, the laws of the Inca apply to all who live on these lands. When a king or chieftain or landowner dies, such as the Patron, his land and all his possessions must go to his adult male progeny. If none exist, next in line are his adult male relatives. And if none exist, then to his chief advisor and commander, and that man is me, Siete Condorpaxi!'

The blood drained from Isabela's face at this man's insanity!

"'Yes, I shall gather the workers and all others on this estate as you have requested, and I shall stake my claim to everybody, according to the laws of the Inca and their rightful successors, the Quechua! Henceforth the entire Estate Cortez and everything within belongs to me—Siete Condorpaxi—the new Patron. These possessions include the former Patron's wife and children!' he leered.

"'I shall have the padre from the neighbouring village of Aguas Buenas conduct our official union ceremony, which I expect will take a few days to organize. However, to be mindful of your husband's recent death, we will not partake in traditional celebrations following our ceremony. Instead, you shall bed down with me right after our wedding to consummate our union, and henceforth your job will be to give me a succession of male heirs!'

"Isabela reeled with shock and disbelief at what she was hearing! It was too incredulous for words, and she was at a loss to respond.

"'Good, that is settled then,' he smiled victoriously, his gold teeth glinting.

"'Until our union, you shall continue to have free run of the hacienda as the future mistress of this house. However, you or your maids will not be allowed to step outside the hacienda for now. Any disobedience on your part will result in punishment of your children and yourself, and believe me, we will find them! To be doubly sure, my two lieutenants Braulio and Peligroso will be keeping a constant watch on you and your house staff. They will of course, be very discreet and will not bother you, so long as you behave. Is that understood, my dearest Isabela?'

"'Now, go ready yourself for our wedding and we will speak again this evening,' he said with a simper.

"Having nothing further to say, he lifted a generously proportioned buttock, letting rip a loud fart, laughing evilly!

"Isabela reared back in revulsion and fear at the thought of this animal touching her, let alone sexually molesting her. She resolved she would rather die! Braulio who was leaning in the doorway also laughed evilly, unabashedly revealing a mouthful of blackened rotting teeth.

Once again, the bruja paused for everyone to compose themselves before continuing.

"Isabela took her leave, making directly for her bedroom, motioning for Concha to follow her, having a very good idea now where her children were. As they ascended the stairs, hearing heavy footfalls behind them, they turned to see Braulio following them upstairs.

"'And where do you think you're going?' Isabela demanded haughtily.

"Braulio shifted his gaze, saying he was only following orders to keep her in his sight at all times.

"'Upstairs is where I sleep and where I bathe,' she said sternly. 'I don't think your boss would be pleased if I told him that you want to watch me sleep and bathe!'

"'No, no, Senora. That is not my intention!' he shot back hastily, taking a step backward.

"'Good. Make sure you and your companion never come upstairs. Those are my private quarters. Is that understood?' she said sharply.

"'Yes, of course, Senora. I am sorry Senora, I didn't realize...' he mumbled as he withdrew downstairs.

"Once in her bedroom and out of earshot, Isabela instructed Concha to wash the floor in the corridor outside the children's bedroom, making sure the floor between the bedroom and the staircase was too wet and soapy to walk on, thereby slowing down anyone coming upstairs. And should the thugs come upstairs, Concha was to drop her steel bucket with a loud clang to warn Isabela. Isabela locked the children's bedroom door behind her, ran through to the bathroom where the door was locked. Isabela smiled in the knowledge that she had taught Rosita well!

"Using her master key, Isabela entered the bathroom, again locking it behind her and ran to the removable wall panel. Twisting the levers, she pulled the panel aside, exposing the wall opening. It was quiet and dark within, and for an awful moment, Isabela thought she was mistaken. She called out softly, 'Mi cariños Susana y Juanito, it is morning. Are you awake, my darlings?' Isabela stepped inside.

"Two little figures rushed into her arms, crying 'Mommy, mommy, mommy,' and through her tears she saw Rosita soundlessly put down a heavy iron bar, light a candle, and close the wall panel. The three of them hugged and kissed and cried for a full ten minutes, Isabela all the while cooing lovingly to her babies. Finally, Isabela tore herself away from the children and hugged and kissed Rosita, who she drew aside, filling her in on Alejandro's murder and Siete's attempts to hijack her property and her family.

"The hardest part was to leave the children an hour or so later. She explained that their daddy loved them all very much but had to go away to Lima, the capital city, and would be back after a while. In the meantime, some bad people had come to their house and were searching for Rosita and the children, who had to remain hidden until the bad people went away. Isabela also whispered her plan to Rosita to get a message out to her lawyer in Cusco, to alert the police to arrest this madman and his cronies. After this was all over, she let

Rosita know that she would be handsomely rewarded for her brave and selfless act in hiding her children from the monster.

"'Senora, I only want to go back to how things were before, I love your children and that will be reward enough for me,' Rosita protested.

"Promising Juanito and Susana more food, water, fresh clothes, and toys, and that mommy would return soon, Isabela took her leave amidst hugs and tears.

"Back in her rooms, Isabela busied herself gathering toys and clothing including the new toys she had just bought, and writing duplicate letters to Manuel Rivera, her lawyer. She also picked up Alejandro's pistol for Rosita to protect the children with if needed, and a few bits and bobs while being mindful of their cramped quarters.

"Per Isabela's instruction, Concha went down to the kitchen to whisper to Senora Casado what was required of her, then returned upstairs using the kitchen staircase unseen, bringing a bag of food, water, and tea. While Concha stood guard, Isabela delivered all items to Rosita through the wall panel, and with quick hugs and kisses to the children, retreated to her room."

"The mid-afternoon sun was already up high and beating down relentlessly. Peligroso standing on watch outside, yawned yet again, feeling uncharacteristically tired and drowsy. He decided to lie down for a few minutes. Nobody would know. The farm workers were all busy harvesting, and Siete had gone into town. He shooed away the dogs from beneath the shaded porch and settled down in their place amid chewed bones and gristle and feeding insects for a quick nap.

"Meanwhile, Braulio also yawned, standing guard in the hallway, positioned strategically to watch the front entrance, the kitchen exterior door and through the window, he could just see the outside entry into the office. *That Senora Casado sure was a good cook, and not bad looking either, although a little older*, he mused, stifling yet another yawn. He wondered what she'd be like in the sack… but it was the Senora's maid Concha who he was really interested in.

"Perhaps with the new order of things to come, he would scare away her husband Miguel or dispose of him if necessary and claim her for his own. Just like the *jefe*, Siete was doing with Isabela. Tired of standing, he found himself drawn to the comfortable-looking armchair to the side of the front door. *No harm in sitting for a minute*, he thought. Pretty soon Braulio was snoring loudly, dreaming of the two women he would soon conquer…

"Senora Casado sprang into action, congratulating herself for administering in their food just the right amount of *ulluco* root, a mild sedative commonly used to sedate women in labour. She rushed upstairs with a tray containing hot cooked food, honey cake, milk, and more water. Isabela met her at the top, taking the tray from her, while Concha slipped back downstairs to stand watch. Rosita hungrily devoured her first hot meal in what seemed like ages after which she went to fetch more clothes for them all. Isabela simultaneously fed the children while also eating and then gave them a hot bath.

"Downstairs, Concha stuck her head outside the kitchen door, whistling for the gardener, giving him an envelope for 'Senor M. Rivera, Abogado,' bus fare, and extra money for himself. She instructed him to dispatch a trusted person immediately into town to deliver it. The loyal gardener complied, sending his teenage son Teo on this important mission.

"Meanwhile, after their bath, Isabela cuddled up with her children in Susana's bed, letting them nap in a proper bed in their mother's comforting arms, her scent and love enveloping them. She tried not to think of when and how she would have to tell them about their father, sad tears coursing down her cheeks…"

"Siete cursed, uttering obscenities as he stalked out of Lima's main branch of the bank, Banco de Credito del Peru, snarling at the saluting doorman showing him a mouthful of gold teeth. He had a lot to learn about the commercial and legal systems, Siete realized. The bank manager had refused to allow him to withdraw money from the account of Estate Cortez, explaining patiently that Siete was not an authorized officer of the company. Only Senor and Senora Cortez had that authority, no matter that Siete claimed to be their new partner. Besides, the bank manager enquired, 'Where were the legal documents proving that?' He would require signatures from both Senor and Senora Cortez!

"Siete further realized that he must redouble his efforts to find the Cortez children, who were obviously in hiding, most likely still on the estate somewhere with that *puta* Rosita. Siete spat into the dusty street. He vowed to himself that the nanny would meet with a slow and lingering death when he finally located her!

"Once he had Cortez's little bastards, he could control Isabela and have her handle all the legalities of transferring the estate to him. And the first thing he would then do, is have the bank manager Senor Castillo, meet with an "accident." Nobody crossed Siete Condorpaxi and got away with it! Siete grinned evilly at the thought of rearranging the bank manager's condescending face! He climbed into the carriage, instructing the driver to detour via the village of Aguas Buenas, enroute to the hacienda Cortez and Isabela.

"Distant cries from the main gate snapped Isabela out of her pleasant dreams of Alejandro, the children, and herself picnicking in the poppy fields overlooking the river. Rosita and Concha grabbed the sleeping children, making for the safety of the secret room amid the sounds of approaching shouts and galloping horses.

"Torn by Juanito and Susana leaving her so abruptly without even a proper goodbye, Isabela blew them flying kisses while running into her bedroom overlooking the courtyard. She looked down at the commotion below, entrusting Concha to secure the others in the secret room.

"The shouts also woke the two sleeping goons, who, rubbing their eyes, staggered to the front courtyard as two horsemen approached, dragging a body face down on the ground with hands tied to the saddle.

"Braulio the "brave" turned the body over with the point of his cowboy boot, and despite the bloodied and torn clothes, skin, and flesh, he was still recognizable as Teo, the gardener's son.

"The lead horseman handed a crumpled yellow envelope to Braulio, explaining that they had caught the boy scaling the stone wall down from the gate after having been turned back by the gate-keeper. They found the yellow envelope on the boy and nothing else. (They conveniently omitted mentioning the coach fare money, having pocketed it for themselves.) The problem, however, was that the goons were illiterate and unable to read the writing on the envelope.

"While the gardener and his sobbing wife were kept at bay by the two horsemen, Braulio ran inside to fetch the housekeeper, Senora Casado, who could read. Grabbing her around the waist, which was quite unnecessary, Braulio pulled her outside, enjoying the close contact and sense of power.

"Senora Casado drew a sharp intake of breath at the sight of the mangled boy! With a loud sob, she pushed Braulio away from her and as ordered she read out the writing on the envelope:

URGENTE!
Para Senor Manuel Rivera, Abogado
Avenida el Sol, Cusco.
De: Senora Isabela Alejandro Cortez Hernandez.

"There was no point in lying about the letter to Isabela's lawyer, she figured, as Siete was able to read and would soon be back. Thankfully, they permitted the choked-up gardener and his workers to claim the broken boy and take him away. Then, with a sharp smack on her backside, the emboldened Braulio, sent Senora Casado scurrying back into the house.

"Isabela and Concha observed all this from the upstairs window and were heartbroken at the boy's torture and at their renewed plight. Isabela however did have duplicate letters and tried desperately to think of how she could get word to her lawyer now...

"It was late afternoon and the sun had begun to wane when Siete returned to the hacienda. He brought with him the padre from Aguas Buenas, the very same padre who had conducted Alejandro's funeral service. Upon learning that Siete and Isabela were to be married by him, the padre was quite understandably incredulous at this fantastic turn of events! Siete had explained it was good for the estate to have a strong man at the helm and good for the children to have a familiar man as their new father. Isabela, being a pragmatic woman, had seen the advantages of their union. Besides, they had always been physically attracted to one another. To underscore his point, Siete smiled broadly at the padre, displaying his gold teeth which to him were a sign of wealth and beauty.

"Notwithstanding, the padre insisted on seeing Isabela and her children to confirm their willingness to go ahead with the wedding so soon, just mere days after their father and husband had been buried. He felt sure Isabela was still in a state of shock and depression and had to be certain she was mentally fit to marry again. *This wasn't negotiable!* Siete fumed inwardly, but was left with no choice if he wanted to proceed with the wedding as soon as possible.

"Meanwhile, Braulio and Peligroso had demanded Isabela come downstairs to await the jefe to face the music. Isabela, seated in the living room had busied herself going through the company ledger as the business had to keep running.

"Upon entering the hacienda, the padre ran toward Isabela to give her prayers and condolences under the watchful eye of Peligroso. Braulio drew Siete aside and whispering to him handed him the envelope. Siete tore it open, pulling out the letter which read:

'*My dear Senor Rivera,*

I regret very much to inform you that my husband Alejandro Cortez Hernandez has met with an untimely death under suspicious circumstances. I am being held hostage in my own home by my husband's lead hand Siete Condorpaxi. My children are in hiding as he intends to ransom their lives when he finds them, as bargaining chips to force me to legally hand over the Estate Cortez to him… and to force me to marry him!

I appeal to you to come to my rescue and to bring with you the Cusco police force to apprehend the criminals led by Siete Condorpaxi, including Braulio Bruto and Peligroso Rata, among others.

Yours sincerely,

Isabela Dolores Cortez Hernandez'

"Siete was beside himself and could barely contain his rage and urge to strike Isabela for her betrayal and wretched ungratefulness after being offered a golden opportunity to remain mistress of the hacienda and estate!

"The padre seemed not to notice Siete's agitation and seated across from Isabela, he began to gently probe her about her physical and mental state and fitness to marry again so quickly. He urged her to wait a few months for the sake of decency and respect for Alejandro. Isabela sat and listened demurely but did not dare show agreement with the Padre in front of Siete—for all their sakes!

"Siete growled back at the padre. 'As you can see, padre, Isabela is obviously fit and very willing to marry me right away! This is not about your feelings, but about ours! Do I detect a little envy on your part, eh, padre? Well, I don't blame you. You should unfrock yourself, get yourself a nice woman, unfrock her, and settle down.' He flashed his gold teeth, smiling evilly at the embarrassed padre.

"'Perhaps after my wedding, padre, we can set you up with our housekeeper Senora Maria Casado. She is the widow of my predecessor Ignacio Casado.'

"Ignacio had been a foot soldier under his commander Alejandro and had decided to remain in Peru with him, taking a beautiful local woman, Maria, as his wife. Soon after, he was afflicted by the plague and succumbed to it. Alejandro and Isabela created the new position of "housekeeper" and persuaded Maria to stay with them under their care and protection.

"Braulio, who was standing behind his boss, gnashed his teeth as he wanted to sample Senora Casado's affections first, before revealing his intentions for Concha as his woman - and dealing with her unfortunate husband, one way or another.

"The padre shook his head politely. 'No thank you, Senor Siete. I prefer to remain a man of the cloth. Now if I may, please fetch the children who I also need to see and speak to.'

"'Yes, of course, padre,' replied Siete. 'Braulio, run upstairs and ask the nanny to bring the children down.'

"Siete's calm acquiescence to the padre's request unnerved Isabela. *What was he up to? Did he know of the children's secret room and was Braulio going to drag them downstairs?* she wondered anxiously. *No, he must be playing a trick.* She was now quite familiar with his deviousness! They made small talk until Braulio came back down a few minutes later.

"'I am sorry, jefe, but the little girl has a headache and is in bed resting, and the boy is already asleep as they are very tired from staying up all night mourning their father.'

"'Thank you, Braulio. There you have it padre. I am sure that you understand, but no matter, the children will be at our wedding—the sooner the better, so you can meet them!' Siete said with a flourish.

"But Concha who had hidden herself in the hallway upstairs had heard the entire conversation and knew she had to cause a distraction to allow Isabela to get the padre alone for a few minutes. As Siete rose, ushering the padre to do likewise, they heard a little girl's plaintive cry from upstairs.

"'Mommy, mommy, where are you? My head hurts!'

"Siete and his goons looked stunned! Reacting quickly, Siete and Braulio leaped up the hallway staircase, taking the stairs two at a time.

"'Thank you for your concern, padre,' Isabela spoke as she rose. 'I must leave now to be with my daughter,' when suddenly she fell to her knees in front of him. Peligroso, who had remained in the room watching over them, was distracted by the cursing sounds upstairs as the men searched for the child. The padre stooped to help Isabela up. Giving him a pleading look, she slipped an envelope in the folds of his cassock. He nodded his understanding as they went their separate ways.

"Isabela raced upstairs while the padre hurried towards the exit and his waiting carriage, escorted by Peligroso to ensure he left the estate. Once upstairs, Isabela ran towards the shouting in her bedroom, where Braulio had Concha's arms pinned behind her back and Siete was slapping her face and yelling at her.

"'Let go of her this instant!' screamed Isabela. 'What in heaven's name do you think you're doing with my maid? How dare you!'

"Barely able to contain his anger, Siete replied with clenched teeth, 'This puta called out pretending to be your child and I need to beat out of her what she is up to!'

"'I will speak for her because she is too terrified of you to speak for herself,' Isabela replied, pushing Braulio aside and cradling Concha. 'Concha was standing in the hallway listening to us and the padre, who she respects and knows from her village. Even though Braulio told the padre the children were already in bed, the padre continued to insist on meeting them. Concha feared he might come upstairs to see them, so she pretended to be Susana calling for me to convince the padre that Susana was safe and make him willingly leave our house!'

"Siete appeared mollified by this explanation and calmed down for a moment before flaring up at Isabela.

"'And how dare you betray me by writing this trash about me?' he shouted, taking out and waving the yellow envelope, spittle flying out of his mouth.

"For a brief instant, Concha could not resist sneaking a quick glance at the beautiful inlaid writing desk by the window, but it was enough. Siete had seen her furtive glance and strode over to the desk. And there, neatly stacked up, were two more yellow envelopes. Siete tore one open to find an identical letter to the one in his hand! He looked at Isabela with realization and murderous rage.

"'Why, you double-crossing puta. You are worse than Judas who betrayed our Lord! Quick, Braulio, we must stop the padre and search him. She might have given him one of these letters!'

"Running downstairs and outside, they jumped astride their horses, galloping down to the front gate.

"The guard was just clanging the steel gate shut when they got there. Siete snarled at the poor guard, '*Tonto!* Fool! Open it quickly! Which way did the carriage take?'

"The guard pointed in the direction of Aguas Buenas as they galloped after it. They caught up to the carriage within minutes, yelling at the driver to pull over, which he managed to do on the narrow strip of road as it rounded a cliff edge.

"The padre had by now torn open and read the letter and was suitably horrified by its contents.

"Hearing the shouting and galloping horses in pursuit, he knew the game was likely up and he had to somehow get rid of the letter. He had no doubt they would strip search him if it came to it, so with no other option, the padre tore the letter into little strips and ate them as quickly as he could. He gulped down the last shreds, his throat feeling like sandpaper, when they ripped his carriage door open.

"'Give it to me,' demanded Siete springing into the carriage. 'Give me her damn letter!'

"'I am sorry Senor Siete, I am not following you?'

"Siete struck the Padre a hard slap on the face. 'Don't play games with me,' he shouted, 'Give it to me now!'

"'God save you from your own anger, my son. I did not take anything from the Cortez hacienda. I fear you have been misguided,' the padre replied bravely, wiping blood from the corner of his mouth.

"Braulio, who was standing outside the carriage and at lower eye level on the ground, suddenly spotted something yellow poking out from under the padre's bench seat. Reaching inside and beneath the seat, he triumphantly fished out the yellow envelope!

"Siete glared at the padre with raw, unadulterated murder in his eyes. Holding out his hand, palm upward, he said menacingly, 'Give me the letter or you shall draw your last breath on this earth, padre!'

"Sighing, the padre replied, 'I wish that I could, my son, but when we were stopped, I panicked, tore up the letter and ate it!'

"'And did you happen to read it first, padre?'

"'Yes, my son. I implore you to give up this madness and surrender yourself to the Lord, who is your shepherd.'

"'Why, you pompous piece of shit,' snarled Siete. 'Braulio, take him outside!'

"The padre's eyes watered with sudden, sharp pain as Braulio grabbed him by his hair and dragged him outside. They pushed and shoved the unfortunate padre to the edge of the cliff overlooking the village of Aguas Buenas, some two hundred metres below.

"'Well, padre, it is adios to you, I'm sorry to say.' Siete crossed himself.

"The padre, resigned to his fate and content to be going to the Lord, uttered his Hail Marys before being violently pushed over the cliff.

"Siete was consumed with rage as they galloped back to the hacienda. He had to show this woman who was boss and end her acts of sabotage, once and for all! Dismounting, they sprinted inside, running up the stairs. The three of them burst into Isabela's bedroom, kicking in the locked door splintering the door frame. Isabela was seated at her writing desk with her head held high while Concha stood cowering next to her.

"Siete roughly yanked Isabela out of her chair, upending it, dragging and hurling her onto the bed.

"'Take the maid to another bedroom,' he commanded his men, 'and make her talk- find out where this puta's bastard children are hiding! I don't care what you have to do to her—just make her tell you!'

"Grinning like Cheshire cats, the men dragged the sobbing Concha to the bedroom at the far end of the hallway.

"'First, puta, I have some unfinished business to take care of, then you talk!' Siete flashed his mouthful of gold teeth at Isabela, unbuckling his pants.'

The bruja stopped her monologue, sighing. She had lost her cheerfulness now, and appeared as she was – an old woman, tired of the brutality of mankind all around her. She lit the fire and ordered more maté de coca. They donned their woollies while she resumed her story. "I won't get into details, but needless to say, both women were brutally violated by their respective aggressors."

Ray and Aziz glanced at each other, sadly shaking their heads, sorry to learn that Isabela had not managed to somehow escape Siete's evil clutches.

The bruja resumed.

"'Siete was well and truly spent, he had never pushed himself so hard, while poor Isabela was a bloody mess from the blows, bites and pounding he had inflicted. He heaved himself up, kneeling on her chest, crushing her ribs and lungs, while also choking her with his thick fingers clamped around her long slim throat. 'You have less than one minute to tell me where the children are, or you will die right here and now!' he screamed, shaking her violently.

"Oh, it was so tempting to take the easy way out and let him suffocate the life out of her, but she had to stay alive to protect her children. The thought of what he might do to them was unbearable. She must stay alive to find a way out, even if it meant killing Siete and her dying too in the process. Then mercifully, she blacked out.

"Siete was mortified thinking he had killed her already. He needed her to sign over the property deeds and bank account to him. But then he felt a weak pulse in her swollen and reddened neck. It'd be a while before she regained consciousness, he figured, so he jumped off the bed and padded naked into the corridor to the end room.

"*'Perhaps they'd had more luck with getting the children's whereabouts from the maid,'* he hoped fervently.

"He opened the bedroom door and was revulsed at the sight and smells before him. Braulio and Peligroso were laying naked on the floor in a drunken stupor, having managed to find the patron's stock of whiskey somehow.

"Unable to revive the goons, Siete surmised the fools had finished off the maid and then gotten drunk.

He left the room and rushed back to Isabela, hoping that she was not badly injured.' *Perhaps I should fetch her some water to try and revive her,'* he thought as he approached her room. Siete had only been gone a couple of minutes, which was time enough for Isabela, who had been faking unconsciousness, to stagger out of bed to the writer's desk. Unfortunately, she had given Alejandro's gun to Rosita for the children's protection, but there was still… she rummaged in the bottom drawer… '*Ah, found it!'*

"It was the heavy gold letter opener that the king had also gifted to Alejandro! Isabela had just laid back down in bed, the gold letter opener hidden beneath her thigh within easy reach of her right hand, when Siete burst back in.

"It had gotten dark now and Siete lit a candle, taking it to the connecting bathroom with him.

"Isabela could hear him pissing loudly amid other disgusting sounds through the open doorway. She heard water running followed by his heavy footfalls approaching her, bracing herself, eyes shut. The splash of cold water in her face came as a shock but it also felt wonderful! She half opened her eyes and moaned, as he lifted her head up and made her drink from the tall tumbler.

"Siete needed her alive—for now. He had to find another way to make her talk unlike those unthinking animals next door! Siete uncharacteristically felt a twinge of remorse looking down at her once beautiful face. Her nose, teeth, and jaw were broken and bleeding and he wondered if she would ever regain her looks. *'But it was all her fault'*, he decided, *'she should not have struggled so hard and so violently,'* and his ribs still ached from the kicking he had received.

"Isabela gripped the handle of the gold letter opener as she sipped from the tumbler and suddenly plunged it upward into Siete's chest below the ribcage, twisting it this way and that inside him to cause maximum damage—just as he had done when impaling her earlier. *Quid pro quo*, she thought grimly.

"Siete felt sharp, excruciating pain as his lung punctured, and could feel the air expelling his deflated lung, hot blood flowing into the surrounding flesh, followed by a warm gusher of blood up his throat and spilling out his mouth, leaving him with a harsh salty taste.

"Despite the rapid numbness spreading through his chest, Siete gripped Isabela's slim wrist in a pincer-like grip with his thick fingers as she tried to escape. They struggled violently for a minute, knocking the flaming candle off the bedside table. Hitting the carpeted floor, the candle dropped off its holder and rolled beneath the bed. The bed skirting immediately caught fire, which spread up to the bed and around to the floor length curtains. Within seconds the fire had spread through the drapes and wall hangings and along the rug, encircling the room. Isabela groped for the gold weapon embedded in his chest, finding it as he was gouging her eyes, and twisting it lower this time, slicing off the bottom lobe of his lung, causing him even more unbearable pain.

"Siete loosened his grip on her wrist finally and she rolled off the bed onto the floor, but he gripped her again by her ankle this time. She crawled toward the door, dragging him off the bed with strength borne by desperation, his hand still clamped onto her ankle.

"By now the fire had ringed the room leaving the central part of the room relatively unscathed yet, with nothing to burn there other than the wood flooring, which was now also beginning to curl and crackle. Isabela kept crawling to the centre with renewed strength, dragging Siete behind her. The fire quickly spread into the corridor and towards the other rooms.

"Suddenly, a naked figure leaped into the room, blackened by the fire and a mixture of seeping and coagulated blood from numerous cuts and bruises over her entire body. Concha picked up a heavy cast-iron bust of the Spanish king, striking Siete's arm and breaking it in two places, to his sharp yelps of pain. Now freed from his grip, Isabela staggered up, also naked, and just managed to stop Concha from smashing the heavy bust down onto Siete's head.

"'No, Concha! That would be too good a death for the monster! Let him lie there in pain and feel himself burn to death!'

"To make sure he could not stand again and escape a fiery death, Isabela grabbed the bust from Concha and brought it crashing down onto Siete's knee. The audible snapping of his kneecap was truly satisfying to the women. Just then, a tendril of flame ran up his foot and raced up his apish, hairy body in an instant.

"Siete's terrified squeals to smells of burning skin and flesh as he writhed and burned to death still assaulting their senses, they ran through the flames in the crumbling doorway towards the children's room—but the fire was too intense and singed their hair and bodies even more. Thick, black smoke and flames were now everywhere and Isabela collapsed to the floor in a coughing, gagging fit of smoke inhalation. Concha held her breath and half-carried, half-dragged her mistress down the stairs and into the kitchen. She grabbed a few blankets from the heap of laundry, wet them thoroughly in the sink, and wrapped a couple of them around Isabela.

"'Wait here. I'm going upstairs to get the children and Rosita,' she said, wrapping herself in more wet blankets. Concha ran back upstairs.

"'No Concha, it is too late; save yourself!' screamed Isabela, knowing how futile it was to go back upstairs.

"The entire house was now filled with thick black smoke as long licks of flames raced downstairs. The wood ceilings were beginning to buckle and collapse in various places, and burning embers were dropping down upon them. Isabela wrestled desperately with her emotions versus her pragmatism knowing it was indisputably over for her dearest Susana and Juanito. Nobody could survive the inferno upstairs, now collapsing onto her downstairs. With a gut-wrenching effort, she threw herself out the kitchen door, coughing and hacking, and into the arms of Senora Casado and the gardener's wife before collapsing into the safety of their embrace."

Aziz and Ray hung their heads, too shell shocked and depressed to say anything. They were thankful for the calming non-stop drinks administered them by the bruja, which greatly helped them deal with the graphic details they were subjected to in the brutality, rape and killing of innocent women and children.

The bruja continued in a subdued voice,

"A month had elapsed since that fateful day. Isabela awoke in a white antiseptic hospital room one morning, feeling rested for the first time. She had endured painful surgery, morphine-induced nightmares, fitful sleeplessness, and ebbing pains in a non-stop repetitious cycle. Her doctors gathered around her, and after a thorough examination deemed her to be out of danger and strong enough to be told everything.

"Senora Casado was summoned, bringing her famous chicken soup and fresh fruits from the valley for Isabela. She tried unsuccessfully to not show her shock at seeing Isabela, now a small shrunken frame, wrapped in bandages over her head and entire body. She was only recognizable by the fixed, determined look in her beautiful eyes, still emerald green, tinged with flecks of yellow. The eyebrows and lashes that had burned off were now slowly growing back. Her nose was taped up, but her red full lips and mouth seemed intact. Her jaw had been expertly wired back together with just some red dots on her healing skin, revealing the wire entry points.

"Isabela's throat and lungs still ached from smoke inhalation, and she whispered hoarsely, 'Did my children have a proper Christian burial?' Isabela's eyes spoke of her sorrow, although she was unable to cry tears yet, her damaged tear ducts still not healed.

"Senora Casado sadly brought Isabela up to date. They had found the blackened, charred remains of all upstairs inhabitants. The little bodies of the children and their nanny Rosita in the debris of the collapsed secret room, the body of her brave maid Concha, and the bodies of the two thugs Braulio and Peligroso, who incidentally had multiple stab wounds. Concha must have stabbed them at some point as they slept in their sated and drunken stupor.

"And finally, they had come across the almost indistinguishable charred remains of Siete Condorpaxi! He had at first been mistaken for a charred log but then identified by his gold teeth and gold chain. The hacienda itself had been razed almost to the ground, with just a skeletal framework of blackened stone and masonry walls, columns and ground beams remaining. The blackened and twisted iron bust of the King of Spain was found lying next to Siete.

"The padre's broken body had also been recovered on the rocky slopes above Aguas Buenas—hurled over the cliff edge by Siete as confirmed by the coach driver.

"The gardener's brave son Teo was recovering well, his flailed skin healing and expected to make a full recovery over time. He was young, after all. Teo's two tormentors were found hanging by their necks in the gardener's tool shed. Who would do such a thing was a mystery – one that the Cusco Police were unwilling to solve. Their deaths were simply documented as death by misadventure.

"The harvest was all in and gone to market. The knitting women had spun their magic and the pre-ordered clothing had been delivered to their customers. And all monies from net sales had been deposited into Isabela's bank. She had been right; this year had turned out to be a bumper sales year all around.

"In response to the burning question in Isabela's eyes, Senora Casado replied, 'Your lawyer, Senor Manuel Rivera, helped us with the commercial matters regarding collection of monies and properly accounting for and banking it. And I handled the sales and deliveries to your customers, Senora. Isabela smiled her gratitude and closed her eyes to rest.

"The next day, Senor Rivera paid Isabela a visit, bringing with him a beautiful bouquet of flowers. He pledged to her that Senora Casado and he would continue to look after her businesses until she got better and able to take back the reins, no matter how long that took.

"Later that evening, Isabela's doctor updated her on her condition. The good news was that she had only suffered first-degree burns and they were healing well thanks to the brave and selfless Concha. Her cuts and bruises were also healing and she had not sustained any infections. Her beautiful thick red hair had slowly started growing back and in time would grow back to its former magnificence.

"Now, the bad news. Isabela's womb was irreparably damaged by the savage rape and she would never be able to bear children again. Isabela shook her head saying that after what she had been through and being robbed of her beautiful family, she had no desire to start another family ever again. And finally, she was told that her nose had been smashed pretty badly and there was no doctor in Cusco able to restore it.

"However, there was another option. She could see a specialist doctor for facial reconstruction, who might be able to reconstruct her nose, using a bone graft from her hip bone. The doctor recommended a well-known surgeon in Medellin, Colombia, who was renowned for "creating" beautiful women. The doctor urged Isabela to consider it adding there was no hurry to leave the hospital yet and she could take as much time as needed to decide. It took Isabela just a few minutes to come to a decision. She would go to Medellin, although she was not in pursuit of beauty. She just could not bear to live with a smashed nose and inexpertly patched-up face.

The bruja paused again, adding "But before Isabela went away, she had one pressing but sad task to perform. She ordered her husband's and two children's bodies to be exhumed to be wrapped individually and buried together in a single grave, together with their favourite toys and jewelry. Furthermore, in recognition of their Christian faith and respecting the Inca lands that they were buried in, she ordered them buried with iron crosses—but in a combined vertical grave, as per Inca tradition—hence the bodies you dug up on your site and their bones that led us to their story!"

We all looked and felt suitably flabbergasted by this revelation.

"I will not get into Isabela's time spent in Medellin except to say that she returned rejuvenated to Cusco three months later, with a beautifully sculpted new nose and after a long recuperative rest" the bruja added with a happy smile. "Now let me continue."

"Isabela sat astride her horse at the mountain lookout one late afternoon, looking down at the winding river and the town of Aguas Buenas, reflecting on the past six months following her return to

Estate Cortez. The gardener had moved out of his cottage, which had been sumptuously renovated for Isabela under Senora Casado's expert eye while Isabela was in Colombia. The garden, although compact, was adequate for now until Isabela decided what she wanted to do with her broken life. Between Senora Casado, who Isabela now addressed as Maria, and Manuel Rivera, her lawyer, they were expertly managing the estate. No day-to-day input was required from Isabela—only executive decisions when requested.

"In fact, in addition to working well together, Manuel and Maria had become good friends. *Perhaps it was more than that*, thought Isabela, smiling to herself. Manuel had never married, having remained a confirmed bachelor into his late forties, about the same age as the widowed Maria. She wondered if the invitation to Manuel's home that evening would be about something more than dinner. Both Maria and Isabela were scheduled to take the carriage together to Manuel's home in a couple of hours' time.

"The three of them sat on the candle-lit veranda after a plain dinner prepared by Manuel's cook, sipping on brandy and coffee. 'Isabela, are you content with us helping to run the estate, and more importantly, with the direction your life is taking?' began Manuel with a note of genuine concern in his voice.

"'No, Manuel. I don't think I want to continue living on the estate. It has too many sad and painful memories, no matter where I turn. I miss my Alejandro and my darlings Susana and little Juanito very much, and I see them everywhere I turn.'

"After a short silence, Manuel went on. 'Isabela, why don't you consider visiting Spain for a while, to your hometown of Sevilla? I believe your parents are dead, but you must still have some relatives there... and Alejandro must also have relatives living there?'

"'Do you mean that you are both tired of looking after me and want to get rid of me?' she said with a laugh.

"'No, Isabela, on the contrary. We have grown very close to you and we only want and wish the best for you,' replied Maria, squeezing her hand.

"'Isabela, you are what, thirty-two, thirty-three now?' asked Manuel. 'You are still young and vital and beautiful. You might meet and consider re-marriage with a wonderful gentleman in Spain. You never know,' he smiled.

"'Not sure I could or would want to handle something like that ever again,' she said. 'Besides, I can't have children anymore, remember?'

"After another silence, he finally said, 'Why don't you go to Spain for a little while, for a year perhaps, even for six months. It will be a much-needed change of scenery, and once away from here, it will provide you with a different perspective on life and what you really want to do. Maria and I will continue to run the estate while you are away. In fact, I would be prepared to resign my partnership at the law firm and work full time managing the estate, with Maria's help, of course.'

"'Hmm, you two have grown rather close, it seems,' Isabela smiled slyly.

"Manuel cleared his throat and looking at Maria, replied, 'Well Isabela, I must confess. I have proposed to Maria, and she has accepted to give me her hand in marriage—if and only if you approve. Maria lovingly thinks of you and Alejandro as her family.'

"'Well, congratulations to you both. I approve! Of course, I approve!' Isabela said with a squeal of delight.

"They talked about wedding plans for a while until Isabela said 'Let me think it over. Now that you both will be getting married, that changes things for me too. If I have to leave the estate entirely to you both to look after, I will have to make you partners so that you are suitably and rightfully motivated.'

"'That is more than generous of you, Isabela. You don't have to do it, we love you and promise to look after your business as your employees,' he replied. 'Besides, I don't have enough money to invest in the estate,' he smiled, shrugging his shoulders.

"'Well, I think we could work out some sort of a loan arrangement,' she insisted. 'I will speak to our banker, Senor Castillo, about it.' After another short silence, Isabela announced, 'Well, that was a wonderful dinner. Thank you Manuel. But it's quite late now. Please have your maid call my carriage. I just need to stop in the bathroom first,' she said walking out, wanting to give them a few minutes of privacy.

"They stood up, Manuel clicking his heels and giving her a slight bow, as Isabela went inside. On the ride back, Isabela and Maria talked mainly about work matters for the coming week, both of them avoiding the topics raised by Manuel.

"The following week went by rather quickly, and it was extremely busy once again with another harvest season approaching. By week's end, Isabela had made her decision and asked for a meeting with her banker, Senor Castillo, for the coming Monday.

"Isabela also arranged to meet privately with Senor Vargas, Manuel's senior partner at his law firm. She ended up spending the following three business days in meetings in Cusco, going back and forth signing papers as they were drawn up. She also visited the little church in Aguas Buenas where the padre had met his terrible end at the evil hands of Siete. Over the following two days, she breakfasted early, taking packed lunches and riding up and down the large estate until sunset, stopping to talk with each and every employee: the ranch hands, farmworkers, her knitting women, and all their families living on the estate.

"The next day being a Saturday, Isabela sent an invitation to Manuel and Maria for dinner at her cottage. They discussed their wedding plans mostly, and as they were preparing to leave Isabela briefly brought up her own plans. She had decided she would be going away soon and was very pleased to leave the estate in the capable hands of the two of them, 'while I am away only mind you,' she laughed. Senor Vargas, Manuel's boss, had been given instructions to draw up some paperwork and to obtain their signatures. Manuel was surprised that he knew nothing of it, but put it down to conflict-of-interest rules.

"Isabela would not be drawn out yet on her travel plans or time table, only smiling enigmatically.

Maria protested that Isabela must at least stay until the wedding! Isabela shrugged it off, hugging them both warmly and lingering with Maria, kissing her on both cheeks as they parted.

"Early the next morning, Isabela breakfasted on her usual ham and eggs and fresh greens, washed down with lots of excellent high-altitude Cusco coffee. She mounted her mare stopping at the burned-out ruins of her hacienda and crossed herself, lost in thought and prayers for a few minutes. Finally clicking her tongue and digging her heels in hard, Isabela galloped away in the direction of the river.

"She arrived at the bend in the river where Alejandro had supposedly gone in to swim on that fateful day almost a year ago now. She demounted, speaking softly to her horse, allowing the mare to nuzzle her hands. Murmuring a soft farewell, she slapped the mare sending it back in the direction of the stables.

"Taking in one last look around her estate, red head shimmering, Isabela smilingly walked into the river fully clothed heading downstream. She would take the route of her beloved Alejandro... how she longed for her soul to leave her body and merge with Alejandro's soul resting in the soft foam in the pool beyond the rapids..."

Aziz and Ray sat in silence digesting all this information, and Aziz wondered if this was all true or if the bruja had been spinning an elaborate yarn that they could never corroborate, though it had been very gripping and entertaining and well worth the hundred bucks it cost them.

The bruja looked at Aziz quizzically. She stoked the fire with more logs, speaking in a resigned voice, "Tell the young man that I speak the truth and not to doubt my story. I will now explain how you can help Isabela's spirit in its quest for joining her family's spirits if you wish to do this service to her. But before that, and unrelated to the present day, are you interested in knowing what happened after Isabela's death?"

Aziz looked abashed at having been caught out by the mind reading bruja again, for he had forgotten she could read his thoughts.

Ray answered for them both: "Of course, Senora, we want to hear it all. Please tell us."

"The river banks by the pool where the washerwomen and their children played was the site of after church Sunday picnics for the workers and their families. Unfortunately, it was spoiled for them that Sunday upon discovering their mistress Isabela's lifeless body floating in the pool, pounded by the rocks.

"Following Isabela's funeral, a meeting was held between her lawyer Senor Vargas, her banker Senor Castillo, Manuel Rivera and his betrothed Maria, where Isabela's will was read out. The will stated:

'I Isabela Dolores Cortez Hernandez of the district of Cusco, Peru, having no family living in Peru, hereby leave all of my late husband Alejandro's and my lands and possessions to the following beneficiaries and bequest to them the following:

- *To all fifty-two of my workers presently employed on the Estate Cortez I leave the sum of 5,000 pesos each, which should greatly improve their quality of life and that of their children. Half of this amount, 2,500 pesos, will be held in trust to pay for the education of their children. I appoint Senor Manuel Rivera and the future Senora Maria Gloria Rivera as joint trustees for the children's education.*
- *To my gardener's son, Teo Lopez, I leave the sum of 10,000 pesos for his bravery and loyalty towards my family and for the suffering he has endured at the hands of our tormentors and killers. It is my recommendation only that Teo considers using a part of this money to visit a Dr. Francisco Botero in Medellin to help him rebuild the damage to his*

body, and to transition him back into a handsome and confident young person—as I had done so myself.

- *To the Iglesias in Aguas Buenas I leave the sum of 25,000 pesos to be used for the maintenance and upkeep and for engaging a new padre and which hopefully will last for at least ten years. My lawyer, Senor Vargas, shall be trustee of the Church bequest.*

- *To the families of my heroic and brave maids Rosita Samuella and Concha Buenanos, who selflessly helped my children and myself in our time of great need to the extent of giving up their lives for us, I leave the sum of 25,000 pesos each.*

- *Furthermore, I wish their names to live on forever, and the appropriate fees must be paid to the Township of Cusco to rename two streets after my two heroines.*

- *A statue of my husband Alejandro Cortez Hernandez is to be commissioned and situated in the Plaza de Armas, the central square in Cusco, with a brass nameplate naming him, my children, and myself. In this way, we shall remain forever in the hearts and souls of the citizens of Cusco.*

- *The Estate Cortez itself, and any and all residual monies I wish to leave to Senor Manuel Rivera and his bride-to-be Senora Maria Gloria Casado. I am confident that they will make the best possible wards of my husband's and my estate. In time, I would hope that the new couple will themselves construct a new hacienda for themselves on the property.*

- *The lands comprising Estate Cortez shall forever be named as such, and the name "Cortez Hernandez" shall be deeded in perpetuity to transfer over to all future owners as the property's official name.*

- *Finally, I wish the ruins of hacienda Cortez to also be deeded to remain untouched forever, as a reminder to all of the greed and avarice and brutality of mankind.*

Respectfully,

Isabela Dolores Cortez Hernandez'

"Now, here's what you must do to help Isabela's spirit reunite with her family," instructed the bruja.

"It is really very simple… keep your eyes and ears open at night on your project site until you are visited by La Colorada. Take this flute," she said, handing it to Aziz. It was a hand-carved cigar-shaped wood instrument, longer than a whistle but shorter than a standard flute.

"Blow on it when you hear or feel La Colorada passing by. The human ear is not able to hear it but spirits can. Once you see, hear, or feel her presence, go and seek Fernando Chinataxi in camp, blowing short, sharp bursts on the flute as you walk. She will follow you, but do not worry; she will not disturb you in any way. Why seek Fernando, you may wonder?" She smiled broadly, revealing her sharply filed, pointed teeth for the first time.

"You see, after Siete Condorpaxi's death, his parents and entire family had to leave Cusco in a hurry, as they were reviled and ostracized by their local community due to Siete's despicable acts. They dispersed to various towns in Peru, never to be heard of again in Cusco, until one day one of Siete's brothers—Quatro's descendent Fernando Chinataxi—moved to Cusco. But by now, the Condorpaxi family had changed their surname to Chinataxi to avoid detection."

Ray and I looked at each other knowingly, now understanding our innate dislike of Fernando!

"It is said that a wronged spirit of a great person who is wandering in misery unrequited is able to achieve release and bliss by fulfilling the desires of its enemy or their direct descendants."

We looked at her, uncomprehending. Smiling, the bruja explained, "La Colorada must make Fernando believe that he can fulfil his and his ancestor's desires with her, and upon achieving that, her spirit will be transported to join the spirits of her loved ones, who she still seeks. That is the reason she has been heard moaning for Susana and Juanito. Both inside your camp and in the surrounding villages as she searches for their spirits! And once she is also fulfilled, she will be gone forever!"

"But how can a spirit fulfil a human's desires?" Ray asked incredulously.

"A spirit is able to create the illusion and feel of a flesh and blood human form for brief moments only," the bruja answered matter-of-factly.

After a brief exchange between Ray and Aziz, Ray asked for assurance that in this process Aziz would not be harmed by the spirit of La Colorada in any way. The bruja gave her solemn promise that Aziz would only be an intermediary and would suffer no harm during and after this merciful act.

The two Canadian expats hesitantly took the flute, promising nothing to the bruja, saying only that they would think about it before making any decision.

"Whatever you decide, remember the flute is on loan, and you must promise to return it," were the bruja's parting words.

Aziz gratefully paid the bruja the balance of her fee, thanking her deeply for her help, as they made their way to their vehicles in the growing cold and to the safety of their warm homes.

Early one evening almost a month later, Aziz was packing it in at the site office when he heard her again—a sudden gust of wind shook the light-framed prefab building! Rushing to the window, he observed a long reddish light slowly approach, and clearly heard this time a familiar plaintive and haunting cry.

"Susanaaaa… Susanaaaa…" as she swooshed by his window.

Despite his new-found knowledge, Aziz was petrified and couldn't move a muscle, let alone reach for the flute in his desk drawer. And the apparition or spirit or whatever she was, had passed.

Aziz happened to run into Fernando the next morning and asked him if there was any further news on La Colorada? Fernando looked at him strangely, admitting that his men had reported a sighting, but he himself had not been in camp that evening, he said grinning, showing his magnificent gold teeth. For it had been Fernando's night out to visit the Pussycat Club, a local house of ill repute.

Later that day, Aziz informed Ray of his encounter, and Ray valiantly offered to stay late with Aziz that night in the hopes of another sighting. Ray further offered to accompany Aziz to lead La Colorada to Fernando. Aziz gladly and willingly accepted!

Every evening for the following week, at around 6:00 p.m. when almost all the workers and staff had cleared out of the offices, Ray would drop into Aziz's office and work on his laptop, seated at the round meeting table. They would work for a couple hours more before quitting for the night, disappointed at no further sighting of La Colorada.

Ray skipped a couple nights after that to placate his irate wife, which caused considerable anxiety to Aziz! But on the third night, Ray sat again with Aziz, and nothing happened. Then on the fourth night at around 7:30 p.m., just as Ray was packing it in, they both heard and saw her!

This time her features were distinguishable: the long red dress, long red hair, and beautiful glowing face floating by the window in a horizontal position.

"Susanaaaa… Susanaaaa… Susanaaaa…" she cried hauntingly.

Buoyed by Ray's presence, Aziz quickly got out the flute and blew hard soundlessly on it… Nothing at first, then incredibly La Colorada was back, this time at the opposite window! The two of them gingerly stepped outside, and with Aziz blowing short blasts they headed towards Fernando's trailer. La Colorada was no longer visible now, nor could she be heard, but they could sense her strong presence hovering above them.

They found Fernando sitting on the steps of his trailer, smoking a joint.

"Fernando Condorpaxi!" Aziz called out to him.

"My name is Chinataxi," retorted Fernando, visibly rattled at hearing his family's real name, for he was familiar with Siete's story, and was determined to one day somehow avenge his great uncle's death and their family honour!

While they engaged Fernando in conversation, his back to the trailer, they observed La Colorada materialize behind Fernando as she floated through the open doorway into the trailer. Then making their excuses, they quickly left Fernando to finish his joint and to the delight awaiting him inside, praying and wishing that La Colorada would now finally attain her salvation.

The next morning, Fernando was a no-show at breakfast. His assistant, Guido, assumed he was sleeping off another late night of debauchery and thought nothing more of it. By 11:00 a.m. Fernando had still not turned up at the office, so Guido went looking for him.

He found Fernando naked on his bed, frozen in a face down crouching position, his generous butt sticking up in the air. The instant Fernando had attempted to mate with the spirit of La Colorada, he suffered an instant flash frozen death. And sucking the life out of him kick-started her own life, instantly transporting her to a familiar field of poppies.

Isabela looked and felt as she did when her family were all last together on that fateful day when she departed on her trip to Ollyantantambo! Gone were her burn scar tissue, her reconstructed nose, her damaged lungs, and her damaged womb. She felt whole and alive again! Looking yonder, running toward her in the tall field of poppies were Juanito and Susana! Juanito wearing his favourite leather shorts held up by suspenders, and Susana in her favourite pink dress, her soft red hair tied neatly behind with a pretty pink bow. And yes, following closely behind them, a tall handsome man with ruffled hair and stylish beard, laughing a great big laugh, his loose white shirt billowing in the wind, was her very own dearest Alejandro, whole again!

The children squealed with pleasure, jumping into their mother's arms, and they hugged and kissed and hugged each other some more until Alejandro scooped all three of them up in his strong arms, lovingly embracing his wife and children once again.

Three years had elapsed since that fateful day when Fernando had mysteriously died under suspicious but unsolvable circumstances. The sudden disappearance of La Colorada from camp and from the surrounding villages at about the same time as Fernando's bizarre death was very noticeable by the local inhabitants, who just knew— call it their innate spirituality—that this was no coincidence.

Aziz and Ray put their incredible adventure behind them after returning the flute to the bruja and letting her know about the encounter between La Colorada and Siete's descendant, Fernando. This pleased the bruja tremendously as the villagers in the camp's vicinity would no longer be haunted and scared – including some of her family members. The two intrepid expats now applied themselves to their mission, working long uninterrupted hours towards the completion of the airport construction project – however they still made time for a couple of side projects as noted below...

The grand opening of the new airport in Cusco was a splendid affair, with no shortage of food, booze, Mariachi bands, rock groups and cultural dance performers. As expected, the *alcalde* or mayor and other high-ranking politicians took all the credit for this wonderful new airport - conceived, financed, designed, built, and operated by Canadians!

At the end of his long-winded, self congratulatory speech, the mayor finally proclaimed: "It gives me great pleasure to declare open our much-anticipated brand-new airport of Cusco: ALEJANDRO CORTEZ HERNANDEZ INTERNATIONAL AIRPORT!"

It was all thanks to Aziz and Ray's unflagging canvassing of their Canadian employer, the Historic Society of Cusco, government officials, and bureaucrats. For the Cortez's name was after all deeded in perpetuity to the former Estate Hernandez, which the airport lands now occupied. The ruins of a burned-out hacienda could be seen just on the other side of the Rio Chiche, situated next to a small handsome hacienda now turned into a museum called El Museo de Hacienda Rivera, named after the former owners Maria and Manuel Rivera.

Ray and Celeste and Aziz and Serena, partied late into the night at the after-party for VIP guests held in the Isabela Business Lounge. As they made their way to their pickup trucks in the now almost empty parking lot, a sudden gust came out of nowhere blowing over them. Looking up, they all saw a long red streak shimmering above them, slowly taking the form of a beautiful redheaded woman, two little children, and a strong handsome man.

"*Muchas gracias. Muchisimas gracias.*" "Thank you. Thank you very much," she whispered, smiling and waving happily. "Much love from, Susana, Juanito, Alejandro, and me—Isabela." Then, just as suddenly as they had appeared, they were gone!

Eyes watery with happiness, Aziz, Ray and their wives looked at each other, silently holding hands, all of them aware of the significance of this spiritual encounter.

Finally, Aziz spoke with a lump in his throat, "It has been a long and bumpy journey together Ray, with an incredibly happy and satisfying ending that nobody could have imagined! And in doing so, we have forged permanent bonds, something special shared together that none of us shall ever forget for as long as we shall live…"

Ray nodded in agreement, "Sacrement, this has been the most mind-blowing and blessed experience of my life, even the bruja's special mate-de-coca does not compare to it!" he said with a grin. "And yes, we shall be friends forever Aziz, bound by a common life-altering experience I think, no?"

"Yes! And tomorrow we will take Chaska to the bruja and tell her what we saw today, it will make them both happy too" replied Aziz.

"*Certainemaint!*" and we must reward the bruja with an extra hundred dollars each, and Chaska with some cash too, what d'you say *mon cher ami* ?" bubbled Ray.

"Actually Ray, Serena and I have been working… well mostly Serena has, on another side project. I will let her tell you both about it," said Aziz, bowing towards Serena with a flourish.

"Well, it's nothing really" Serena said self-consciously.

"Go on Serena, let's hear it sacrement!" shouted Ray smilingly.

"Well, actually I did some research and presented my findings to Luc Lebiche, your VP Operations, and Hector Picard, the airport concessionaire's Chief Executive, during the last few days leading up to the airport opening. I have demonstrated just how poor and underprivileged the bruja's shanty community as well as our project maids and their families are – particularly the kids" she paused.

"Sooo… I convinced them that it is our corporate responsibility to do something for them, and they both agreed! Tomorrow and for the next few days I will be at the project offices, speaking to every expat and to every professional local staff member, collecting donations from everyone. I am expecting every expat to donate at least one hundred dollars, and every local at least twenty dollars. I hope thereby, to raise approximately five thousand dollars. And don't worry, it will be tax deductible, processed through our company's BFC Charitable Foundation."

"Bravo, bravo!" returned Ray and Celeste.

"Not quite done yet guys! Both BFC and the Airport Concessionaire have each agreed to match whatever we raise, dollar-for-dollar. Which should triple our funds to fifteen thousand! And finally, to top it off, the mayor of Cusco has promised to raise matching funds from his supporters – giving us a total of thirty thousand dollars! squealed Serena.

They stared at Serena in wonderment, then rushed forward and hugged and kissed her!

Serena laughed out "The first thing I will do is to go myself to the bruja's village and burn all the cassocks those kids are wearing! I will clothe and bathe them properly, give them books and toys and nutritious food. And access to music classes, dance classes, sports clubs and equipment! And build showers for them with piped hot water - versus their present ways of washing intermittently in the cold and dangerous Rio Chiche!

Ray's grin widened as Aziz and he threw their arms around each other's shoulders, encircling their wives' waists with their other arms, walking proudly to their trucks...

EPILOGUE

At exactly the same time as the two couples had encountered La Colorada, Paco Jiminez called out sharply to his superior Alex Hernan, a tall and handsome young man. Alex, who was just about to go downstairs on a smoke break, was urged to take a look at Paco's console monitor. Other than the inaugural Iberia Airlines direct commercial flight from Madrid earlier that day, there were no other scheduled flights that night.

They were the only two air traffic controllers on duty up in the control tower pod, duty bound to monitor the air space regardless, per international civil aviation regulations. Their faces appearing green in the light cast by the radar monitor, they observed a hovering red blip above the staff parking lot at a height of just six metres above ground level which signified either an aircraft, which was impossible, or an unidentified flying object. Then seconds later it disappeared.

The two men looked at each other not knowing what to think. Finally, Alex shrugged and headed towards the elevator, getting out his cigarettes. "Unless it reappears on our shift tonight, Paco, don't record the incident. It might be a simple bug with our brand-new ATC equipment, which will work itself out. Or it might just be our imaginations, considering how much alcohol we have consumed tonight," he smiled.

Alex was referring to the food and beer and bottle of whiskey secreted up to them by the shapely, green-eyed, redhead Maria Isabel, one of the servers at the party below, who had her pretty green eyes set squarely on Alex - and one who Alex Hernan definitely had his eye on too… he could just feel the electricity and sense the possibilities between them.

Alex Hernan and Maria Isabel— namesakes and likenesses of Alejandro and Isabela – a future Peruvian power couple to watch out for…

Lightning Source UK Ltd.
Milton Keynes UK
UKHW042134310822
408081UK00003BA/51/J